FEB 25 2019

Also by Frances McNamara

ʗ

Death at the Fair
An Emily Cabot Mystery

DEATH AT HULL HOUSE

Frances McNamara

ALLIUM PRESS OF CHICAGO

WILLARD LIBRARY, BATTLE CREEK, MI

Allium Press of Chicago
www.alliumpress.com

This is a work of fiction. Descriptions and portrayals of real people, events, organizations, or establishments are intended to provide background for the story and are used fictitiously. Other characters and situations are drawn from the author's imagination and are not intended to be real.

© 2009 by Frances McNamara
All rights reserved

Corrected first edition

Book and cover design by E. C. Victorson

Front cover image (bottom) of Hull House
courtesy of University of Illinois at Chicago Library,
Special Collections

ISBN-13: 978-0-9840676-0-4

For Fr. Philip McNamara
the social worker in the family

Death at Hull House

ଓ

ONE

"As I have warned President Harper on many occasions, the weaker sex simply is not able to cope with the stress of rigorous academic activity. The female brain is not designed for such things. This incident is a disgrace. I only hope this will bring the faculty to their senses and result in a change of policy."

He had gone on like this for twenty minutes now. I hated the sheen on his high forehead. The white and gray prickly hairs of his moustache and the full beard that outlined his square jaw were despicable. I gritted my teeth as the full pink lips mouthed the words. I loathed the man. Worst of all was the deep authoritative ring of his impressive voice. I do believe Professor Lukas carried more arguments by the tone of his voice than the strength of his logic.

Through the window behind him I could see figures in black academic gowns flocking to what would be convocation for the second year of the University of Chicago. It was a convocation I would not attend.

"Thank you, Professor Lukas. I think that is sufficient. We must all get along to the ceremony this morning." Professor Albion Small was shorter than the tall, overbearing Lukas who frowned, pursing his lips with displeasure. But the dapper little man with a bald dome and a smudge of dark moustache under his nose was Chairman of the Department of Sociology. As such, he was Lukas's superior. It was the department to which I had belonged the previous year, and the department from which I was being expelled as I was being expelled from the university.

The other participants in this sorry meeting to pronounce my final disgrace were Jonathan Reed and Marion Talbot. The young, ungainly Professor Reed had sponsored my work collecting police statistics the previous year and Dean of Women, Marion Talbot, was a petite little bird of a woman whose presence was equal to anyone, even a Professor Lukas.

"It is unfortunate," she snapped. "Unfortunate for all of us. However, since Miss Cabot must go, I am glad to be able to report she will be joining Miss Jane Addams at Hull House in the city."

This was a calculated and well timed shot across Lukas's bows. His large face turned red. "A settlement, that settlement house," he sputtered. "Oh, yes, that is just the sort of place for someone like this regrettable young woman."

But Professor Small's eyebrows rose. He did not share Lukas's skepticism and disdain when it came to the settlement movement. "Well, well, Miss Cabot, we must all wish you the best in these endeavors."

Lukas looked outraged. He did it so well. Hull House, the settlement that Jane Addams and some others had begun several years earlier was a phenomenon that attracted international attention in the area of sociology. Professor Lukas deeply resented that so much attention was lavished on efforts by those he considered ignorant amateurs. Lukas himself specialized in labor relations and was a consultant to many businessmen in Chicago. He was well known to have a low opinion of the immigrant masses swarming into the cities and filling the lowest paid jobs. The activities of settlements in such communities were to be scoffed at in his often published opinion. "A gaggle of well meaning women with nothing better to do with their time. Ridiculous. Setting up housekeeping in the midst of the tenements. Absurd."

But there was a gleam in Professor Small's eye. "I understand the settlement has compiled a survey of households in the ward. There is some anticipation that they will publish the data from that. It could be most useful." The accumulation of data was an important activity in the opinion of the department chairman. It was already an emphasis of the school of sociologists who had come to Chicago.

I could see the smallest glimmer of a satisfied smile on Marion Talbot's heart shaped face. She was trying hard to suppress it. "Yes, I have suggested to Miss Addams that Emily may be able to help complete the preparation of that study for publication."

"Splendid, Miss Cabot. We will look forward to the publication of that work." Professor Lukas had puffed up his chest as if ready to launch into yet another harangue on the follies of including women in higher education but Professor Small forestalled him. "Now, I'm afraid we must say goodbye and prepare for convocation."

Dean Talbot marched out the door with a signal for me to follow. I nodded goodbye to Professor Reed. I wanted to thank him for his attempts to defend me but this was not the time. As we walked the corridor of Cobb Hall to Dean Talbot's office, I felt a weight drop on to me, bending my shoulders. How could this have happened? Here it was the first day of the new university term and I would be leaving. The fact of it hit me then and took my breath away. Stairs to my right led up to the classrooms, like the one where I had studied the Bible in the Hebrew original under the tutelage of the young President William Rainey Harper. I remembered how proud I had been to be one of the first women fellows at the new university. But

I took myself in hand and turned down the corridor stopping to grit my teeth before following the Dean into her office.

The office was a book-lined room with wooden file cabinets, a large desk for the dean and a smaller writing desk to one side. I glanced at it. As the dean's assistant, it had been mine the year before. Now, I took the straight-backed chair opposite the large desk as she indicated I should. But Marion Talbot did not sit down. The pacing she did, swinging her black academic gown as she turned did not bode well for me. She frowned and the tassel on her mortarboard shook when she came to a stop. "Convocation will begin promptly in thirty minutes, so there is not much time. I am sorry to say your expulsion will stand." She grimaced. "For now, at least. Professor Reed and I did all that we could, but you can see the opposition we met." She paced again, stopping this time to look out the high window behind her desk. She was shaking her head. Then she swung around to face me again, like a little bird perched on a twig. "You will go to Jane Addams at Hull House. The arrangements are made?"

I nodded.

"Good. Emily, I must impress upon you how important it is that you use this opportunity to redeem yourself. Your disgrace and expulsion reflect on all of the women here. You owe it to them to make things right."

"I am very sorry to have caused so much trouble. And I am grateful to you and Professor Reed for your efforts on my behalf."

"That's not enough, you know. You must go to Hull House and demonstrate by your work there that you belong back here doing serious research. Emily, I know you were trying to help someone but the fact that you, a woman scholar at this university, could be found in a gambling tent on the

Midway is just something the university authorities cannot ignore. Your actions make it appear that women enrolled here are so loose and undisciplined as to make this acceptable. Of course it is not. It is against every university regulation. You know that and you should have thought of it before you acted.

"Surely you must understand how important it is that we, the women of the university, remain beyond reproach. You saw all the fuss that was caused last year by the mere suggestion of unchaperoned dances. How could you think you could go to a gambling hall without destroying your reputation as a serious scholar here?" She stamped her foot and I felt a rush of blood turning my face red. I said nothing. We had been over all of this before. Many times.

"Never mind, never mind. What is done is done. What is important now is to repair the damage. You know how unusual it is that this university was organized with the intention to admit women scholars to every level of study."

It was true. Many women, like me, had been educated in colleges like Wellesley only to find on graduation that the only avenues open to them were marriage or teaching. It was considered unsuitable for a woman to pursue study beyond that degree. But when the businessmen of Chicago had approached William Rainey Harper to establish a world class university in their city, he had planned for an institution devoted to advanced research on the model of the German universities. And he had insisted from the very first that women, as well as men, would be enrolled. When he raided the East Coast educational establishment for the best of their professors, he had also convinced Alice Freeman Palmer and Marion Talbot to come from Wellesley College to shepherd the women. And they had recruited other female students, like me, hungry for the opportunity to be part of this plan. Participation of women had not been without opponents, so there was a struggle that first year to ward off criticism. And I had damaged our case by my actions. Of course, I regretted that.

"It is the future you must attend to now," she continued. "Your expulsion will stand. You will go to Hull House. As I have told you, Professor Small has a great admiration for Miss Addams and her co-workers at the settlement. He has often attempted to recruit them to your department but they are too busy with their own activities. The study he mentioned is of particular importance. That survey of the West Side neighborhood is expected to be a landmark document when it is published." She fastened her small dark eyes on me. "You will bring that study to press, Miss Cabot. And in the process you will redeem yourself and the reputation of the women here. Is that clear?"

"Yes, Miss Talbot."

She sighed. "Don't be so downcast, Emily. You will find the inhabitants of Hull House a most interesting and unusual set of companions." The way she said this I could only assume that she herself did not necessarily consider "interesting" or "unusual" to be good qualities. But she had a certain openness of mind not shared by the likes of Professor Lukas. "And Dr. Chapman will be there as well. He, too, has a reputation to live down."

"But he was released, the charges were dropped. He is innocent," I protested. Our friend, the doctor, had been charged with the murder of a man he had known in the past. But when the real murderer was revealed, the doctor was released. During his imprisonment the university had distanced itself from him in a manner I found disappointing.

"Emily, the university abhors any kind of sensationalism. We cannot afford it. Dr. Chapman understands that. This university is dependent on the contributions of the eminent people in Chicago. They are the ones who have matched the generosity of Mr. Rockefeller. It is only through their contributions that this institution can continue to exist. Although the charges are dropped, the scandal persists. Dr. Chapman understands the memory of that must die down before he can be readmitted to the university."

"But he can continue to work in Dr. Jamieson's laboratory while I am completely exiled," I pointed out. It was not fair and, much as I liked the doctor, I had to protest the lack of fairness.

"The doctor was unjustly accused, Emily. You, on the other hand, are guilty of a foolish disregard for university regulations. When you accepted the fellowship that Mrs. Palmer and I obtained for you last year, you agreed to abide by the rules of the university. It is your impulsive disregard for those rules that has damaged not only your own career but that of every other woman here. Men like Professor Lukas are only too willing to point to you, Emily, as an example of why women are not fit for rigorous academic work. They have even proposed a separate course of study for female students. It is not for such an arrangement that we have come here and worked so hard."

She was right, of course, but how many times did I have to say so? Marion Talbot was not one to spare anyone's feelings, especially not a self-confessed miscreant like me. But she was right. I did agree with her totally. "I will go to Hull House tomorrow, Dean Talbot, and I promise you that I will do everything I can to succeed there."

"It will be a good place for you, Emily. You are impatient of rules and regulations. In Miss Addams and her followers you will find people who manage to defy the constraints of society and still maintain the respect of all who know them. If you cannot exhibit the self-discipline necessary to succeed at the university, I hope you will be able to learn from the women of that settlement how to gain the respect of society. Now, I must go. I wish you luck and I expect great achievements from you despite your disgrace."

With that, she shooed me out the door, closing it behind us with a click, and hurried off to join the academic procession. Convocation would be held in Cobb Hall but I would not participate. As I glumly left the building to return to my rented rooms and prepare for my exile, I wondered when I would ever be back.

"Emily. Are you forgiven?" It was my good friend of the previous year, Clara Shea. She was a tall, strikingly beautiful girl, who left behind the life of a belle in Kentucky when she came to the university. In the course of that first year Clara had come to find her place among the beakers of the laboratories and the numerical calculations of the chemistry department. Over the summer the bond of friendship we formed that first year had been sorely tried, but we had managed to mend it again, so it was stronger than ever. Now she was ready to plunge into the round of lectures and experiments while I was leaving. Seeing Clara really rubbed gall into the soreness I felt.

"No. It's Hull House for me."

"Oh, Emily. When do you leave?"

"Tomorrow."

"It seems so unfair. And now we finally have a real home. You should be with us, Emily."

She was talking about the new women's dormitories that had been completed for this fall quarter. We had endured makeshift accommodations and moves that first year, hardships that had only brought us all closer together.

"Dean Talbot thinks I can redeem myself. Perhaps I'll be back next year."

"I hope so. You can come and visit." I think she saw from my face that would only be a punishment. "Oh, I'm so sorry, Emily." She reached out to put a hand on my arm. "Is your family still here with you?"

"My mother has gone home to Boston."

"But your brother remains? Alden, is he still here?"

I stiffened. My younger brother was another problem and I did not wish to discuss him. "He is fine. You'd better go, Clara."

People in academic gowns were sweeping past us on both sides but she held my hands a moment longer. "I'm so sorry, Emily, I must go."

"Yes, go. It's convocation, I know. Goodbye, Clara. Be careful. Don't go spilling those chemicals over a new frock." She smiled at the joke but shook her head with regret as she turned away.

Snow was beginning to fall as I trudged back to the rooms I had shared with my mother and brother during their visit from Boston. There was a brisk wind as I walked across the campus of the University of Chicago that November morning in 1893. The scent of burning leaves was left hanging in the air when the breeze dropped. Under a sky of heavy gray clouds things were stirring. There was a sense of anticipation in the air, the sense of starting on new journeys I had always felt with the start of a new academic year. It was painful and exasperating to realize it would all go on here but without me. I had made such a mistake in getting myself expelled. It made me realize the only thing I really cared for was succeeding here in the academic world where I had always been able to shine.

When I entered our lodgings I realized my brother Alden had packed up all of his things and left without a word—or without an additional word. We had had all too many words to say to each other in an argument at the train station after seeing my mother off.

Alden, four years my junior, was quick witted and lithe. He had a mop of dark brown curls and bright blue eyes, but most importantly he had an engaging manner and an unquenchable curiosity about people. Somehow he always managed to charm his way into any company and he scorned the book study that I had always excelled in. He was fearless in a way I found reckless and he was undependable and irresponsible in the extreme.

After our father's death, Alden accepted a job in a bank managed by my mother's brother. He was given leave from his job to bring my mother to visit me and to see the World's Columbian Exposition this summer. It was only at the end of the trip when my mother was preparing to return that he announced his intention to give up his job and stay in Chicago. Coming on top of my own troubles it had been too much to bear but I waited until my mother's train left to tell him what I thought. I accused him of being irresponsible and he countered that I was worse, as I had deserted them all by coming to Chicago.

As for my own life, I knew my father would have wanted me to continue my studies. In fact, I would have been even more devastated by my expulsion if I had had to face him to explain it. Yet any embarrassment would have been a small price to pay to have him back with us again. Perhaps what was really bothering Alden was that the excursion to the gambling tent that had brought my downfall had been a plan jointly concocted by both of us. It was true that I bitterly regretted it now and, it was true that, although I had never voiced the thought, in my heart I blamed my brother.

TWO

Snow was falling again on the day of my departure for Hull House. There had been a heavy snowfall several days before and now an icy wind from Lake Michigan cut through every open space making exposure of any inch of skin unbearable. The cost of a rented carriage was dear but there was no other way to transport myself and my two trunks, so I counted out my money remaining for the month and set aside what was needed.

When she left the previous week, my mother assured me I was welcome to return to her in Boston if the situation did not meet my expectations. But I knew she thought it would have been my father's wish that I succeed. I dreaded disappointing her. Of Alden I had had no news. Our parting had been so bitter and resentful I felt stung. I was not inclined to heal the breach and thought it best to let time do the healing. I imagined that he continued his association with Mr. Marco, the man who ran the Ferris Wheel on the Midway during the Fair. My brother seemed intent on a life of random dissipation without purpose or intention, though how he proposed to accomplish this without even his meager monthly allowance was unfathomable to me. I resolved not to tell my mother of our final argument. I would omit all mention of my brother in my letters until he contacted me.

I huddled in the carriage as we traveled north on the treacherously ice covered streets. I was numb with cold when I saw we were at Eighteenth Street but I bent forward to look out, hoping to catch a final glimpse of the Glessner house to the east on Prairie Avenue. It was through my association with the university that I had met that wealthy and generous family. I remembered the beauty of the parlor where we listened to Mrs. Glessner at her piano and Mr. Langlois on his violin. I could still picture the pearls and silks of the ladies in the glow of the dining table candles. With regret I acknowledged to myself that there was little hope that I would ever be invited to such an evening again. Not that such activities were the reason for my coming to Chicago. It was the opportunity to study at the university that I most regretted throwing away. It was the opportunity to do something important, to have an impact on the world around me, to participate in that great endeavor that would use the city as a laboratory for experiments in the study of society. The prestige and recognition that participation in that effort gave one was only an incidental advantage. That is what I believed at that time, at least.

That impression that I was leaving all connection with Prairie Avenue behind me became fixed when we turned west on Twelfth Street and entered the crowded area filled with immigrant populations where Miss Addams had established her settlement house. It was heavy going to find a path between the streetcar track and the blackened piles of snow on the curb. At one point we were halted for some time and when I asked the driver the cause I was told a horse had fallen ahead of us. A shot rang out and when we began to move again I saw the poor animal had been dispatched, then deposited on top of the snow bank to make way.

My heart sank as we pushed through streets thronged with men in wide brimmed hats and long beards, the women shrouded in shawls. I recognized Hebrew characters and realized we were traveling through a section of kosher butchers. It seemed strange to see the ancient language I had studied with President Harper the year before displayed on the buildings of such a modern street scene.

Finally we turned north on Halsted and I began peering out nervously, anxious to identify the numbers on the buildings so that I would recognize the settlement when we reached it. Here every other building was a saloon and I began to feel so discouraged that I very nearly called to the driver to turn around and take me back to the station where I could board a train for Boston. But he stopped before my resolve failed me completely and I saw we were in front of a tall old house situated between an undertaking establishment and another saloon.

With great trepidation and revulsion at the surroundings I descended and found my way to the door. When it was opened by a woman holding a gurgling infant on her left arm while she held back a rambunctious toddler with her right hand, I thought I had made a terrible mistake.

"No, Angelica, you must stay until mama returns for you. I'm sorry, you must be Miss Cabot. I am Jane Addams. Welcome. Yes, yes this is Hull House, please come in." She made way for me and stepped to the door to instruct the driver to put the trunks in the hallway and to invite him to partake of a hot beverage and warm himself at the coffee shop in an adjacent settlement building.

"It's a cold day, isn't it? I will be with you in one moment. Angelica's mother has gone to get her sewing work for the day and had nowhere to leave her. Angelica, you must go in to Miss Dow."

Miss Jane Addams was quite a short woman in a high necked dark dress with voluminous sleeves and cinched in tight at the waist. Dark hair was pulled back from her face in a simple style and she kept a pair of reading spectacles pinned to her bodice. I learned later that she often answered the door herself, like this, despite the very real fame she had acquired. It was a primary concern of hers that every visitor feel welcomed.

We were in a high-ceilinged hallway with a steep staircase straight ahead and open doorways on either side. To the right was a large room where at least a dozen toddlers scrabbled around in play while a pretty young woman read to them from an illustrated book. She broke off and came to the door to take charge of Angelica with a smile. Meanwhile, still holding the infant, Miss Addams led me through the doorway on the left while we heard the carriage driver drop a trunk on the floor behind us. She turned back to tell him how to reach the coffee house and I surveyed the surroundings.

This side of the house was cut up into three rooms, a small front parlor with some mahogany pieces and a desk by the front window, a darker back parlor lined with shelves of books and a small sun parlor that extended out of the south side of the house.

"That is the octagon room," she told me seating herself by the desk in the front parlor. "It is the center of our activity."

I could see there was a large case with labeled pigeonholes that must contain the residents' personal mail and two desks and chairs with various volumes, charts and other papers piled around.

"We are happy to have you join us, Miss Cabot. Dean Talbot has spoken so highly of you and we are always in need of another hand to help with our classes and clubs and other activities." She settled the baby in front of her where the child could sit and play with a ruler. Perched on the desk, the infant flailed the wooden baton and it occurred to me that Miss Addams was not accustomed to caring for children. This turned out to be correct. While she demonstrated a huge amount of concern about the well-being of children, she had little practical knowledge of their care. I never did see her personally tend to one again, which was probably all for the best. I barely restrained myself from reaching out and taking the ruler from the child before someone was harmed, but Miss Addams was proceeding to talk to me as if nothing were amiss.

"As you can see, we tend to be very busy. I do hope you will not need a great deal of quiet for your studies." She looked worried. "I'm afraid the last young lady from the university was very disappointed. She insisted she needed complete quiet for a certain amount of time each evening and tried to impose a rule of silence. It was quite impossible, though. You see we have classes and club meetings every evening—quite often there are several going on in different rooms. And during the day we have the kindergarten and the coffeehouse and later there are the clubs and music lessons for the older children. Will you be able to cope, do you think?"

She appeared very worried on this point but I assured her I would not be enrolled at the university this quarter, realizing that Dean Talbot had not informed her of my expulsion. She was relieved.

"That is all right then. And the Dean told me you would be interested in some other duties."

At that moment a tall, businesslike woman passed through the room to the octagon where she consulted some papers and retrieved others from a pigeonhole; then she returned to us.

"Mrs. Florence Kelley, this is Miss Emily Cabot. Mrs. Kelley is the first Chief Inspector of Factories for the state and she is in need of another deputy. Would that suit you?"

Even at first sight Florence Kelley was an impressive person. Taller, sturdier and more vigorous than Miss Addams, she had dark blond hair set in an elegant braid around her head.

A person with little patience for vanity or pretense, she nevertheless had an air of fashion and an innate style that betrayed the fact that she had more experience of the world than most of us at Hull House. That day there was a sense of command and a certain foreignness that impressed me about her.

She regarded me with sharp speculation. "Seven hundred and fifty dollars a year. We can discuss the details later." It seemed she had sensed my need for money by a mere glance. She also clearly saw the potential for catastrophe in the scene before her and, without consulting Miss Addams, she gathered up the baby.

"I am very interested in the position," I told her. "But, can I ask, what are the duties?"

The dark blue eyes held mine. "After a report we did to the state legislature last year concerning the terrible state of the local manufacturing conditions, Governor Altgeld appointed me chief factory inspector and authorized eleven deputy positions. As an assistant inspector you will go to these places of business, survey them as to number of workers, hours of work, pay and working conditions. You will also ensure the proprietors are aware of the regulations that apply to them and report any infractions. We investigate, Miss Cabot, then we educate legislators and the public and then we agitate for reform. All that is required is a sharp eye, a map and a sturdy pair of walking shoes. So, do you think you could do it?"

"Yes. Oh, yes. I would be grateful for the position."

"Good. The office is across Halsted half a block south. You can report tomorrow morning. But there is something else you can work on while you are here." Still carrying the baby she took two strides over to the octagon room and patted a foot high stack of papers. "I understand from the Dean that you can compile the work from our survey last year for publication."

Miss Addams gave me a worried look as if she thought I was being imposed upon. "Oh, yes, Miss Cabot, do you think you could help us with that? We are in very great need of some help to organize it all and get it to press."

"Of course she can, that's why Marion sent her," Mrs. Kelley insisted. She thumbed the first inch of the stack. "When people learn the facts that are contained in this study, it will lead to changes. It is absolutely essential that we get this study published. When people learn the reality of the situation for the workers in this ward there is bound to be a movement to change. What people are really being paid, how they are trying to subsist, the numbers occupying each building. It is all here, and it must be made known."

"Dean Talbot did mention the need to bring your work to publication and she advised me to help with that. I will be very happy to do so." I looked with curiosity at the piles of paper and maps colored with inks on the table. Mrs. Kelley patted the stack.

"Good. Like all of us, you will have to attend to it outside your regular duties, but don't let it fall by the wayside." She turned to the child in her arms, bouncing her on her hip. "Now, as to this little one. Jane, I see you have been letting her run amok." I learned later that Mrs. Kelley was the only resident who always addressed the famous Miss Addams by her first name. Florence Kelley had no patience with formality or most other things. "I'll put her down for a nap, then be off to work." With that, she hurried away.

"Does Mr. Kelley also live here?" I asked when she was gone.

"Oh, no, Mrs. Kelley is divorced. Her husband is in New York. She has two children of her own but they are presently enrolled in a boarding school north of the city."

I tried to conceal my shock. I had never before met a woman who was divorced and living apart from her husband and children. In the Boston society where I had grown up, a woman in such a state would lose all her connections. She would be shunned. This was a new world on the West Side of Chicago. But then it was a place where my own disgrace at being expelled from the university could also be ignored. I told myself to be grateful for that.

THREE

After Mrs. Kelley left like a whirlwind up the front stairs, Miss Addams explained the conditions for residents. This included a very modest fee for room and board and a probationary period of six weeks after which continued residence was dependent on a vote of the others. All of the residents held jobs or followed their own occupations in addition to helping with the house activities.

"We have found that settlement life is not for everyone," she explained. "The settlement is a kind of experimental effort to find solutions to the problems of society in the modern city. I know you have been studying social and economic thought, as we all have. And after study there is the need to find a way to live. So many times I have seen young girls grow sensibly lowered in vitality in the first year after they leave school. I felt it myself. We are taught to think of the improvements needed by society, then we are protected by our situation from the need or even the opportunity to do anything about it. In this way a girl loses something vital out of her life to which she is entitled. It was in reaction to this that we first established Hull House."

I was thinking to myself of criticisms of settlement work that I had often heard voiced by Mr. Lukas and others at the university who dismissed the movement as trivial. She continued as if she had read my thoughts.

"Yet we hope that Hull House is not a mere pretense and travesty of the simple impulse to 'live among the poor.' Critics would dismiss our work as one of those unnatural attempts to undertake life through cooperative living. But it is more than that. I truly believe we can do no good cut off from the more than half of mankind that must struggle to survive. Any good we secure for ourselves is precarious and uncertain. It is floating in midair until it is secured for all and incorporated into the common life."

She seemed troubled as she made this assertion and my eyes followed hers to the portrait of a heavily bearded man wearing a peasant's costume that hung in a place of honor on a wall covered with photographs and paintings.

"Is that Mr. Tolstoy?" I asked.

She smiled and nodded, still looking at it as if the famous Russian author would answer her doubts even now. I saw it was inscribed to her and assumed she must have met the great man.

"I'm afraid he would not admire our work here. He believes one ought to suffer the toil and deprivation of the poor, not just to work among them. But unlike many of our neighbors we keep ourselves well supplied with mutton and coffee."

"I have never supposed that by suffering as much as the poor we should therefore be better able to improve their lot," I protested.

She turned her stare from the portrait to my face. There was the hint of a smile. "It is true. And yet there have been experiments in communal living that might be considered purer than our own. I visited one in a Western state where the circumstances of the group were so constrained the poor who had left a nearby poorhouse to join them eventually abandoned them. They found that even the poorhouse occasionally provided pork or bacon with their grits while the communal group could not." She stared off as if visiting the place again. "It is a curious fact that in the midst of such privations the inhabitants of that community embodied a peace of mind which comes only to him who insists upon the logic of his idea whether it is reasonable or not. I suppose it is the fanatic's joy of seeing his own formula translated into action."

She smiled, yet it seemed to me she was wistful, as if she longed to be part of such a group however ill fated the experiment might turn out to be. "But I must tell you there is no one theory being expounded here, no definite set of rules. The most important quality is flexibility and the ability to adapt quickly to needs as they arise. You will find all kinds of ideas expounded here but you will see that no one is dominant. You will have to make your own decisions concerning the worthiness or otherwise of our work here. Now, let me show you the house and your room."

She had sensed my doubts concerning the enterprise although I had said nothing negative and I had thought to keep my suspicions concerning the goals of the settlement house buried deep in my heart. She had answered them. I knew that Hull House had become quite famous by its work, yet I still had doubts. She seemed such a well-meaning sort of person, yet so exasperatingly vague in her plans. I had spent a year doing rigorous thinking about social problems and it seemed a disappointment to be placed in a practical situation where thought about the larger context of the problems of society was subsumed in day-to-day tasks. I was sure the real work was being done at the university, not here.

I followed her on a tour of the kitchen in an extension at the back of the house where the mother of the infant was busy cooking. Miss Addams explained that residents and visitors alike were invited to help with preparations and washing up. In the basement, there were rooms used for classes in wood and metal working, and three baths open to the community in the summer. On the second floor were more bedrooms, including mine, a small but adequate space. In an adjacent building were a communal dining room and more bedrooms

"I hope privacy is not a very great concern," she said with a crease between her eyebrows. "I am afraid we are sometimes forced to commandeer the bedrooms in the afternoons. We have found a number of children locked from their houses while their mothers work and for now, at least, we feel we must try to take them in during the day." She gently shut the door of one room where two children were napping and saw me glance at a pitcher full of water that sat on narrow steps leading upwards. She laughed self-consciously. "Oh, dear. We have our little superstitions. You see, the attics are rumored to be haunted and I am not sure where the idea came from but I think someone suggested ghosts cannot pass across water or some such." She stopped for a moment in thought. "I am not sure who keeps the pitcher filled."

On the way downstairs we stopped at a window where she pointed to a building that housed the male residents of the settlement and another that contained the art collection and a coffee shop where, as she described enthusiastically, the scientific tenets of the Rumford Kitchen were being put into effect in an attempt to provide nourishing meals at low cost to the working people of the area. She regretted to admit that it was thus far more of a success as a social gathering place than as a source for proper nutrition. Local residents tended to find the food too bland for their taste.

"When I returned from the trip abroad that included my visit to Count Tolstoy, I was determined to spend two hours a day baking bread with my own hands in order to experience that unity with working people that he insists upon. But it was impossible." She shook her head and began to lead me down the front stairs. "Invariably after breakfast there are half a dozen people waiting to see me, letters to be opened and answered and other pressing demands of human wants awaiting my attention. How could I push these all aside while I saved my soul by two hours work at baking bread? My pretty plan had to be abandoned."

As we returned to the front parlor she asked, "Are you by any chance an early riser, Miss Cabot?"

When I told her I was, she looked pleased.

"I wonder if you would be able to accompany me tomorrow morning. You see, the state of garbage collection in the neighborhood is a serious threat to health conditions. When Hull House failed to procure the contract for collections, the city appointed me as local inspector of the process. Miss Gyles, who has been accompanying me, has developed a serious cold so I would be very grateful if you could take her place temporarily."

When I made a disparaging remark concerning the corruption of a city government that would require such monitoring, Miss Addams expressed a sentiment which was clearly a basic premise for the work of Hull House. It was a sort of rebuke to me.

"We believe whatever of good the settlement has to offer should be put into positive terms. We seek to live with opposition to no man, with the recognition of the good in every man, even the most wretched. We sometimes depart from this principle but it is always a confession of weakness when we do so. For we have always found, Miss Cabot, that antagonism is a foolish and unwarrantable expenditure of energy."

It was a speech that explained much about Miss Addams and how she managed to keep such a crowd of people with such a hodgepodge of beliefs always around her. It also went far to explain the air of serenity that she maintained even in the most trying circumstances. For those of us not so willing to tolerate situations we judged clearly wrong, this attitude could be exasperating. Yet for all her lack of rigidity and her tendency to bend under pressure, she had remarkable endurance and, in the end, she could outlast us all. It would be some time before I came to realize that, however.

I agreed to the early morning ride to follow the garbage carts and she accepted my offer gratefully. I could not help feeling I had come down in the world quite far to take on such duties, but I readily agreed to other assignments such as helping with English language classes and with the working people's clubs and organizing invitations to speakers. Dean Talbot had spoken highly of my organizational abilities as her assistant and Miss Addams seemed relieved at the prospect of my help. I spent the rest of the day organizing files and attending to mountains of correspondence. I did not have a chance to start on the mounds of papers that were to be part of the published study, but I promised myself I would start on them the next day.

The dining room was on the second floor of an adjacent building. Six plain refectory tables in two rows were set on a floor of broad wooden planks. The chairs were hard wood with rungs in their rounded backs. We took turns setting the tables and bringing up dishes from the kitchen. Residents and guests alike helped with the clearing away and were assigned to weekly washing up duties.

At dinner I found myself opposite a talkative young man named Mr. Milton Bierly who wore workingman's Levis and addressed everyone as "comrade." He was plump, with a round face and earnest brown eyes peering out at you through cheap wire rimmed glasses. His hair was cut very short and he affected a wispy goatee. Learning that I was a newcomer he was quick to explain the customs of the house and to name the residents. There were about twenty women and a dozen men who lived in the house or adjacent buildings and another dozen or so people who came regularly to help.

"Miss Faraday helps Miss Addams to raise monies," Mr. Bierly was telling me when I felt a tap on my shoulder. "Ah, Comrade Dr. Chapman, here is Miss Cabot, Comrade Cabot, who is our most recent addition. She comes from the university. The doctor is also connected to the university, Comrade Cabot, perhaps you …"

"Yes, Milton, Miss Cabot and I are acquainted." I had not seen the doctor since immediately after his release from jail. It was a relief to see his square face and kind brown eyes. A dozen years my senior and a medical doctor who was expected to be a brilliant researcher, he had sometimes chided me during that first year of acquaintance. But I had been sorely distressed when it seemed he would hang and we would never see him again. I had seen him once or twice since his release but it was reassuring to have him beside me now, anything but dead.

"If you will allow me," he pulled up a chair on my left, forcing Miss Gyles and Miss Lewis to scrape their chairs along to make room. Single-minded in his intentions, the doctor was often oblivious to his own rudeness in such situations. He ignored their sniffs of disapproval and frowned, concentrating his attention on me. "Miss Cabot, I have attempted to speak to the university authorities on your behalf …"

"Doctor, I am grateful but …"

"No, no. It is not right that you should be expelled. However, I have been unable to find a way to convince them to retract their verdict. I have spoken to Dean Talbot and she assures me everything possible has been done. She believes that work here at Hull House is the only way for you to eventually regain your position."

"Yes, I am trying to live up to the Dean's expectations," I told him, feeling a need to grit my teeth coming on again.

"I wanted to advise you, Miss Cabot, to listen to Miss Addams and to follow her example." He looked down the table to where Jane Addams was talking. "I know this is not where you want to be. I know how much you enjoyed your position at the university. That is where you should be. Not here. I am so very sorry."

"It is all right, Dr. Chapman. It is my own fault, as Dean Talbot has told me. But I will be all right here, I assure you. Why, Mrs. Kelley has already offered me a position as an assistant inspector of factories."

He frowned at that. "I'm not sure you should accept such a position, Miss Cabot. This can be a very dangerous neighborhood. For someone like me, or Mrs. Kelley, who has lived in such places before, well, we know how to behave. But for a young woman of your background, it may not be wise. You must be careful of your reputation at this point."

The doctor was chiding me again as if I were a child. I was not in the mood to accept his warnings. "I am sure I am as capable of fulfilling this assignment as any of the others, Doctor. If I were not, Mrs. Kelley and Miss Addams would not have offered it to me."

"I will speak to them about it."

"I beg you to do no such thing, Dr. Chapman. As a matter of fact, you should know that I could dearly use the salary from this position, so please do nothing to prevent me from accepting it."

This stopped him, as I knew it would. He grimaced, unable to think of a response that satisfied him. He always felt his own lack of wealth. In that, he was unlike many of our fellow students at the university. But the doctor came from a poor background and when he had given up his practice for study, he had retained only a very small income to live on.

"Really, Doctor, I am quite well able to take care of myself. I thank you for your concern but I must make my own way here and I will. Dean Talbot, at least, has confidence that I will succeed here." I said this to him as if I had great confidence. It was necessary in dealing with the doctor not to show weakness or he might feel required to interfere. I did not tell him that to succeed was the dean's command to me, come what may.

"I'm sorry if I offended you."

"And I have no wish to quarrel with you. Won't you eat, Doctor? There is meat still on the platters."

He stood up. "You will excuse me. I have to return to the university this evening. I usually go there directly from the clinic but I heard you were arriving today and I wanted to be sure you felt welcome." Miss Addams had told me that Dr. Chapman was training visiting nurses as part of a plan to provide medical attention to the people of the area.

It was kind of the doctor to hurry to welcome me to my new home but, as usual, he spoiled it by insisting on warning me against myself. I felt sorry to start our new enterprise so badly. "I trust your work for Dr. Jamieson goes well?"

"Very well, thank you. We are accumulating some important data. Every day we get closer to understanding the origins of disease and the methods Nature provides to fight against it."

I looked up at him. "Perhaps it is you, Dr. Chapman, who belongs at the university doing research rather than here. At least Dr. Jamieson ignores the strictures of the authorities. Is he not afraid it will reflect badly on him to employ you?"

"Luckily he does not care for such things. He is an older man and he says he has no time to waste on foolishness. He huffs at the supposed scandal and says it is smoke in the air. However thick it may appear to be, one good puff of wind will blow it all away." He looked at me anxiously. "He says they will soon forget your trespass as well. He is sure of it. He even laughed when he heard of it."

"There. You see? Dr. Jamieson as well as Dean Talbot has confidence in me, Doctor. So how can you doubt me?"

He gave me a formal little bow and swiftly left to catch a train to Hyde Park. As I turned back to the astonished Mr. Bierly I only wished I had as much confidence in my future as I claimed.

"He is a recent arrival, like you. He rooms in the men's residence with me and I've been showing him around. He doesn't have a lot of time to spare, however, what with the clinic and the laboratory. I'm trying to educate him in the plight of the masses."

Mr. Bierly was around my own age of twenty-four. Dr. Chapman was more than a decade older and I knew he had worked among the poor of Baltimore before coming to Chicago. I doubted that the younger man was qualified to instruct his more experienced elder but I could see and hear that Mr. Bierly was determined to instruct all of the world, including me, in a socialist theory to which he had been converted. I tried to listen politely but my eyes and thoughts kept straying as Mr. Bierly talked. Finally, I was rounded up by Miss Addams to assist with the evening's activities. No one was ever left idle at Hull House. At least I was left no time to indulge the pang of jealousy I felt knowing the doctor still had access to the life of the university where so many of my hopes and thoughts still dwelt.

I had noticed that Mrs. Kelley flinched at some of Mr. Bierly's remarks. He tended to paraphrase socialist treatises, and Miss Addams told me that while he had pretensions to the label socialist, Mrs. Kelley had experience as an actual member of that party. She had been active in New York until she was "read out" of the Socialist Party. She said it was because the foreign members of the group suspected her fluent English. At least that was her ironic explanation. Mrs. Kelley had a tendency to indulge in sarcasm, unlike Miss Addams and the other residents who were predominantly sincere in all they said. It was one of the things that set her apart, along with her manner of addressing Miss Addams as "Jane", something that none of the rest of us would dare to do.

After dinner it was necessary to clear away in good time for the Working People's Social Science Club to convene. The noise of the heated discussions of that club was interspersed with hammering from the woodworking in the basement and chants from the English class in the drawing room while a committee met in the library. I was delegated to take the minutes for this last group. It was easy to see why the student who needed quiet had not survived.

I was in a state of some exhaustion when the evening drew to an end, leaving only a few diehards deep in discussion around the library fire. As I waved goodnight, Miss Addams reminded me apologetically of our mission in the early morning and it was only then that I remembered I had yet to unpack my trunks.

As I climbed the staircase, my ears still ringing with the sounds of chanting from the English language class and arguments from the political studies group, I remembered climbing the stairs at Snell Hall to work on Hebrew translations or the compilation of my precious cards for our study of criminal statistics. So much of the year before had been consumed by the production of that three hundred-page report. I knew Professor Reed would use it but now I would not be allowed to draw the conclusions or argue for the changes that I had planned. Vexed and annoyed at my present position, I couldn't help wondering if all the paper used in the printing of that report would not have been of better use for feeding a fire.

I longed for the sense of purpose that had spurred me on. Then, I had felt that I was living up to my father's hopes for me. What would he think of me now, exiled to this ramshackle structure filled with the Babel of competing plans and theories? It humbled me to think of riding behind the garbage carts in the morning. The memory of my brother Alden's accusations that I could not see the world beyond my bookshelf rankled like an itchy wound and as I reached the top of the stairs my eye fell on the pitcher of water set out to keep the ghosts away. If this was the world beyond my books I had little hope of reforming it.

My little room was cold as only a room with no fire to cut the piercing chill of a winter night in Chicago can be. I unpacked my trunks as quickly as possible, stowing my few possessions in a weathered wardrobe, leaving the books at the bottom as I shoved and kicked them into a corner. Putting on my nightgown, I rushed to warm myself under the patchwork quilt of the bed. I would spend my time here, as I had promised Dean Talbot. I owed her that. But I had little hope of achieving anything at Hull House.

FOUR

*I*t was easy to become absorbed into the life of Hull House where the constant activity soon filled up all the nooks and crannies of my time. Miss Gyles, a hefty young woman who reigned over the gymnasium, seemed physically well to me. Nonetheless she remained indisposed enough to beg off the early morning outings, so it became my duty to accompany Miss Addams on her forays after the garbage wagons of the neighborhood. At six o'clock I would join her on the seat of a small cart that was used to trail along behind the city wagons. Jane was no horsewoman but she was conscientious and insisted on taking the reins. The condition of the alleys made the trips perilous but we persisted.

During the days I was fully occupied by my duties as a deputy inspector of factories. As chief inspector, Mrs. Kelley would gather the six of us deputies each morning in the tiny office on Halsted Street and hand out lists of factories and sweatshops along with piles of printed regulations. It was our task to troop around distributing the printed material, making sure to find and hand them to the man in charge, and to return with enough information to make a written report of the size and state of the facility, the number and sex of the workers with appropriate ages, and the names of manager and proprietors.

This sounds a simple enough task but in practice it required trudging miles and miles over the snow packed streets trying to locate "factories" that were often poorly lit basements of brick buildings or top stories of rickety wooden tenements. But finding them was only half the battle. In most cases the man in charge had little English and if he did understand what I said as I proffered the printed materials he was sure to feign ignorance. I found myself shouting slow and simple phrases at men who gesticulated and countered with a slew of syllables beyond my comprehension. It was as if we were firing missiles of words that collided in midair. It was one of the most frustrating experiences of my life and I would be hoarse by the time I conceded, slapping the papers on to the nearest desk or table and announcing, "These are the regulations. You have been warned. Eight hours only for the women workers. It is the law."

Inevitably the room would be filled with workers, heads bent over their machines anxious to complete as much as possible, since they were paid by the piece. As I turned on my heel and walked out, head high despite how much it was aching from the screaming session, I would sense some of them stop to look up and wonder what this mad woman was about. I sensed how much they feared these men who had power over them. It was almost like a scent that hung in the close air of the crowded rooms. This had been a year of economic depression with few jobs available and many out of work. Their lives were perched precariously on their earnings, barely enough to keep their heads above water, and the men who employed them knew it. It would risk their jobs, and therefore their lives, to speak out against anything. So they watched me out of the corners of their eyes as I marched out and they said nothing.

It was after one such exasperating experience that I found I had failed to bring enough copies of the printed materials to complete my rounds and had to return to the office for more. Vexed by the sure knowledge that I would never complete my tasks in time for dinner, I blamed myself as I pictured the cold and hurried meal of leftovers I would have to partake of in the kitchen. And I had planned to spend time on the publication project as well. It irked me that the all important task of getting the papers organized and sent to the publisher kept getting pushed aside for other duties.

So I was not in a friendly frame of mind when I opened the door to the office and saw Milton Bierly in conversation with Mrs. Kelley. I had hoped she would be out so I would not have to admit my mistake to the chief inspector and I found Mr. Bierly's enthusiasm more than I could bear at the moment. He was not officially connected to the factory inspector's office but he insisted on hanging around offering his services during those frequent times when he was between the workingmen's jobs to which he, like Count Tolstoy, aspired but which he never was able to hold for long.

Mrs. Kelley's sharp blue eyes were upon me while Mr. Bierly continued to try to talk to her.

"I have had to return for more copies of the bills," I admitted.

"Good. You can come with me, Miss Cabot." She rose and began to put on her cloak. "Go ahead, Mr. Bierly, and stay out of sight."

I had no time to ask where we were going as she swept out the door, so I just followed. We marched briskly down Halsted and then through a maze of streets to a tenement where Mrs. Kelley quickly mounted the stairs to a large room on the second floor. There must have been thirty women bent over sewing machines clacking away in the dim light. Piles of clothing materials were on every surface including a table at the front where a slight dark man in shirtsleeves was sifting through pieces and checking against a tablet of paper he held in his hand. Mrs. Kelley descended on him.

"My name is Mrs. Kelley and I am chief factory inspector for the State of Illinois. I come to charge you with violating the eight-hour rule for the women working in this room."

The man looked at her, clutching his tablet to his chest and I saw a small boy unwind himself from where he had been sitting on the floor. At a nod from the man he pushed past me out the door. The man muttered something under his breath, then spoke in a foreign language. Italian, I believe. He splayed his hand and waved it at Mrs. Kelley as if shooing away a fly. But Mrs. Kelley would not be shooed.

"Mr. Lugano, the State of Illinois has decreed that female workers may not toil beyond eight hours in any twenty-four hour period." She stepped to the table where a corner of paper peeked out beneath a pile of cloth. "I see you have been informed." Pushing her shoulder into the pile she managed to retrieve the sheets of paper, which she waved at the man as she advanced on him. "Here. You have been informed. Eight hours. We will have to shut you down for this violation."

At this point the little boy came clambering up the stairs followed by a gray suited man with thinning red hair, a moustache and thick sideburns. Some of the women in the room had stopped working although others clattered on. The man pushed past me.

"Mrs. Kelley. What a surprise to see you."

Mrs. Kelley did not seem surprised. "Mr. Hanrahan. I might have known you would appear." She saw my confusion. Without taking her eyes from the man's face she provided an explanation to the room in general. "Mr. Hanrahan is employed by Franklin Enterprises. Franklin does not actually own this place, you understand, they merely purchase the output of this sweatshop thereby retaining their own immunity from prosecution. This way Mr. Hanrahan and his employer can keep their hands oh so clean, isn't that so? But Mr. Hanrahan is on call to assist these subcontractors so that they can continue to produce the goods that are bought at a pittance to be sold at great profit. He thinks he can keep us from shutting the place down, thereby inconveniencing his employer. Isn't that so, Mr. Hanrahan?"

"Always glad to be of assistance. What can we do for you today? I'm sure Mr. Lugano would be happy to entertain you but, as you can see, he has a very busy enterprise here."

"Mr. Lugano has unfortunately been so busy that he has violated the eight-hour rule for female workers. These women began at seven o'clock this morning and it is now five o'clock."

Hanrahan pulled a watch from his vest coat and examined it. Meanwhile the little boy was clinging to the legs of the man still clutching the tablet. He watched with wide dark eyes sunken in their sockets. I could see he was afraid.

Mrs. Kelley waved a hand full of papers. "He has had notice, Mr. Hanrahan; you cannot plead ignorance this time."

Hanrahan blinked. "Unfortunately Mr. Lugano is not entirely fluent in our language. He had intended to take one of the courses so generously offered by you ladies of Hull House, but the pressures of business ... You understand."

It was an argument that might have actually worked with Miss Addams but Mrs. Kelley was unmoved.

"The eight-hour rule is law, as you know. He will have to close."

Hanrahan shifted, looking at his watch again. "I'm sure you are mistaken, Mrs. Kelley. These women began late today."

"Oh, no, Hanrahan, I have a witness."

At that there were sounds of a scuffle on the stairs and kicking of wooden slats. "Let go of me, let go." Mr. Bierly was yelling as he was thrust into the room by a tall man all in black who held him by the scruff of the neck with one hand while the other hand twisted his arm behind his back painfully.

I recognized Mr. Weaver, a dangerous man who had been involved in highly questionable duties in the past. He worked for wealthy businessmen, doing what they did not want to do themselves. He always wore a wide brimmed black hat with a silver chain around the crown, a long black overcoat, black gloves and embossed leather boots with spurs, a useless accessory in the city. I could see his teeth as his mouth twisted in a smile. Milton Bierly shrieked, trying to kick but Weaver only clutched him more tightly, causing more pain.

Behind the tall man I saw another familiar figure. Red hair and an easy smile made Mr. Sidney Franklin easy to recognize. He was the son of the proprietor Hanrahan worked for. I had known the younger man at the university. He stopped his studies to follow his father into the family business.

I stepped over to Weaver who still held the struggling Milton Bierly. "Let him go."

Weaver just grinned. I could barely see his eyes under the brim of his hat. Mr. Bierly was panting. Hanrahan had turned. "I see. This must be your witness. And this lady is…?"

"Miss Emily Cabot," Sidney Franklin announced. Then he strolled into the room and passed the other men to examine some of the pieces of fabric on the front table.

"Miss Cabot is one of my deputy inspectors. Release Mr. Bierly at once." Mrs. Kelley demanded.

But Weaver just yanked on the man again.

"Stop it," I said as he yelled with pain.

"Miss Cabot?" Hanrahan appeared distracted by my name. "Are you by chance from Boston, Miss Cabot?" I noticed Sidney Franklin turning to look at the man, his eyes narrowed with speculation. I had no use for the former student, however. My attention was on Weaver.

"Let him go," I insisted, turning towards Hanrahan. I glared across his shoulder at Franklin but he shrugged and turned his back on me.

"Let him go," Hanrahan waved at Weaver.

With a final jerk and a push he released Milton Bierly who sprawled on the floor. I bent to assist him but he pushed me away, sitting up rubbing his arm.

"Are you from Boston, Miss Cabot? Was your father Judge Cabot?"

"Yes, he was."

I saw Hanrahan look at Weaver who slouched against the door jam, blocking the way out.

"Mr. Hanrahan, you have no right to manhandle Mr. Bierly. I do not see what your interest is at all. We will close Mr. Lugano for violation of the eight-hour law. You cannot prevent that," Mrs. Kelley told him.

Hanrahan did not look at her. He was still looking at me, with an occasional glance at Weaver. He sighed.

"You know very well, Mrs. Kelley, that you can do no such thing. I represent Mr. Franklin, Mr. Leo Franklin. Mr. Lugano is one of his suppliers." By the glance at Sidney Franklin's back I suspected some animosity existed between the two. Hanrahan worked for the father, Mr. Leo Franklin, not the son. He seemed intent on making that very clear. "While you may try to impose on a poor man like Mr. Lugano who is trying to run his business, Mr. Franklin knows that you have no such power. Like you ladies of Hull House, Mr. Franklin and I endeavor to assist our immigrant friends in understanding the rules of this new country where they find themselves. If you wish to accuse Mr. Lugano of any infraction you will need to convince a county prosecutor to bring charges in a court of law. And, as I think you are aware, there are many other cases which also require their attention."

"On the contrary, Mr. Hanrahan, I am empowered by the powers invested in me to shut down any establishment that on inspection is found not to be in compliance with the law," Mrs. Kelley waved the printed copy of the act in her hand and Hanrahan finally turned towards her.

"On paper, Mrs. Kelley, on paper. But in practice Governor Altgeld and his friends have supplied you only with deputies of the likes of Miss Cabot here to carry out your orders. You know very well that you may try to intimidate the likes of Mr. Lugano but without a court order backed by the police you have nothing but words. You can only lodge a complaint. Return to work, all of you," he motioned to the room at large, and the machines began to clack again. Mrs. Kelley was red in the face.

Hanrahan turned back to me. "Miss Cabot, I don't know what your father would say to your association with known socialists and anarchists such as this." He waved at Mrs. Kelley and Mr. Bierly. "I cannot believe he would approve. Now, I will have to ask you all to leave these people to their work and to let the rule of law prevail." Sidney Franklin had turned to watch his father's business manager. At this speech his eyebrows rose.

There was something ironic in Hanrahan's tone. The rule of law was, of course, what my father had stood for. But had he known my father? Certainly not as a friend. I did not recognize the man and I could not believe my father would have aligned himself with men like Hanrahan and his wealthy employer. Weaver moved into the room, relaxed and ready for more action. Mrs. Kelley stood poised for a minute, bristling with anger, then she swept from the room followed by the bruised Mr. Bierly and then me. For a moment, Sidney Franklin blocked my way. Then, with a smile, he stepped back and offered me a bow. I brushed past him. It was disheartening. It was such a public defeat.

When we came out into the sharp cold of twilight I turned right to head towards Hull House, thinking we were done but Mrs. Kelley was marching to the left. I ran to catch up. "But where are you going?"

"To make a complaint."

"To the courthouse? But it's so late. And it's more than a mile. Besides, what use is it? Didn't he say they wouldn't pay attention anyhow?" I was running to keep up with her long steps but she stopped suddenly and faced me.

"They will not want to take the complaint, Miss Cabot. They will whine about their case load. They will doubt Mr. Bierly's testimony." That young man stood behind her, puffing, with his head hanging down. "They will not want to offend the powerful wealthy men like Mr. Franklin who want their goods finished for the Christmas trade. They will argue. They will delay. They will attempt to avoid the matter. But what do you think we are here for? Do you really believe distributing copies of the law will make them obey it? No, Miss Cabot. Getting the law passed was only half the battle. That was done at great cost by Governor Altgeld and others. But it is up to us to carry it to completion. It is up to us to refuse to cave in to the complaints of overwork and more important matters and political expediency. Hanrahan knows they will probably refuse to press this case but if we do not push back, if we do not insist, if we do not nag, they will never press any case. It is quite true we may not succeed with this one but there will be others tomorrow and next week and sooner or later they will give in. In any case, your presence is not necessary. Return to Hull

House and your meal. Mr. Bierly and I can handle this. Come." She motioned to him and marched away.

I stood there trying to decide whether to try to catch up to them or to accept her dismissal and return to Hull House. In the end I turned back. I had an English class to teach and the garbage cart in the morning. And as she had said there would be plenty more opportunities for frustration in the coming days.

FIVE

I continued to be so busy with my new duties and responsibilities that I made little progress on the Hull House maps and papers until the year was coming to an end. It was difficult to steal time between my days trooping around as an inspector and nights involved in the house activities.

"Is that Mr. Langlois I hear?" Clara Shea, my friend from the university, came to visit me at Hull House one evening the week before Christmas. We were in the study where we could hear a rehearsal of the Christmas pageant going on in the drawing room.

"Oh, yes. Mr. Langlois comes and teaches at the music school. He still plays violin with the Chicago Symphony Orchestra but he comes to help the students here. I am not entirely sure how wise it is to have a professional musician teaching, however. While our students have the benefit of excellent training, the demands he makes put a great strain on them."

"The woman who is singing has a wonderful voice."

"Maria Magliano. She does have a wonderful voice but she works long hours in a sweatshop and, while she loves to study singing, she is quite exhausted by the time she gets here and he is unyielding in his demands as a tutor." It was one of the many concerns that flooded my thoughts these days. Activity at Hull House was so incessant I seldom had time to think of anything else now. Looking at Clara, I suddenly realized how much I had missed her. But now talking to her felt like yelling across a divide, as if we were each on separate cliffs. I could see her over there, which was where I wanted to be, but I could not see how to get there.

"How is the new dormitory?" I asked, struggling to reach her.

"Foster is turning out to be wonderful, Emily, especially after all the moving around last year. Remember when we had to move from the hotel?"

"It seemed like we had just finally settled in when the lease ran out." The hotel the university had used to house the women had been needed to cater to visitors coming for the World's Columbian Exposition and we had been evicted.

"Then Snell Hall, barely finished and some of the men resented it so much," she reminded me. After being forced to leave the hotel, we had been lucky that the dormitory, Snell, was just being finished when we so desperately needed it. It had been intended to house some of the men who were also forced to use temporary quarters, but it had been relinquished to the women for the rest of that first year. "But the two women's buildings are finished now and they are all ours. It hardly seems fair after all you went through with us last year that you should not be there now. It is truly not fair to you, Emily."

I grimaced. She saw that and hurried on. "But there has already been a controversy about the food. You won't miss that, I'm sure. It got so bad more than sixty people signed a petition." I clucked in sympathy. If there was one thing I did not miss from the many duties when I had acted as Dean Talbot's assistant, it was the constant concerns about the sensitivity of the scholar's stomach. I shook my head at the memory, but Clara went on to more important things.

"Miss Talbot has asked me to tell you that Mr. Small is wild to get his hands on the Hull House study. She has advised Miss Addams to insist on full publication before she releases any of it. She said to tell you, you must not settle for anything less."

"The Hull House maps and papers," I told her. "I have been working on them when I get the chance, although that's not often." The truth was I had sorted through the stacks during my first few weeks and never really returned to the project. I found myself making excuses. "It is massive, Clara. They interviewed every household in two wards. It is really amazing. The compilation is underway but there are difficulties about printing the colors on the maps." Editorial work for that tome was certainly on my list of things to be done and I thought guiltily of the piles of papers and surveys shoved aside in a cubbyhole of the octagon room. There was never enough time between the factory inspections and the daily activities to get to it. Yet I knew it was an essential part of Dean Talbot's plan to get me reinstated in the Sociology department. "There will be progress after the holidays," I promised. "But how is your work? How is the chemistry this year?"

"Burners and beakers to my heart's content," she assured me, her Southern drawl becoming more pronounced. "Some of them are grumbling about the facilities promised not being ready yet, but I believe it may be a blessing in disguise. I do fear some of my less competent fellow students may yet blow the place up and should they do so, I feel sure it would be better for it to happen in the old warehouse we are using rather than the nice new building still under construction." I stared at her, never sure how serious she was about that sort of danger but she reached out and patted my hand. "I do miss having you around to become alarmed and to warn me all the time to be careful. I declare, some of the young men who share my laboratory table could use that advice.

"I am taking a course with Mr. Gridman, did I tell you? It is biology. He encourages me to enroll in a summer course of study at the Marine Biological Laboratory at Woods Hole in Massachusetts. That is not far from Boston, is it? Have you heard of it? It's becoming quite famous and it's an honor for him to suggest it to me. Of course my mother will not approve but I've written to Gram and she is all for it." Clara had the great good fortune to have a wealthy grandmother who abetted her in foiling her mother's prejudices against women's education.

"Dr. Chapman has been asked to apply as well," she continued. She seemed to watch my face for a reaction. Clara had hinted before that she thought the doctor had an affection for me but I knew very well it was the affection of an adult for a child. "I see Dr. Chapman in the laboratory. He speaks of you all the time and says you thrive here."

I was surprised to hear this. Of course, I saw the doctor at Hull House dinners and meetings but life here was so busy I had hardly spoken to him. The times I had seen him, he treated me in a way that seemed distant, even paternal. I hated to admit it to myself but I was disappointed in that. Nor would I have said I was thriving. I was busy but not wholeheartedly engaged in the work. I simply had no time to worry about the future and I shrank from thinking about the past. I still thought I had made a great error by getting myself expelled from the university. That was the place where I was meant to be and I was deeply disappointed to be cast out of it. But my pride prevented me from letting even Clara, my good friend, know how bad I felt about that. Deep down I realized my lack of attention to the publication project was a stubborn gesture of annoyance. I also knew I needed to correct myself in that.

Clara was going on, "He says Miss Addams profits enormously from your organizational abilities. But there is another even closer to you whom I have seen, who asks after you. I have been visited by your brother, Alden. I know he worries about you, Emily."

I was astonished. "I haven't seen him for more than a month. I do not even know where he resides or how he lives."

"But don't you wish to, Emily? Especially now, at Christmas?"

"Clara, my brother and I parted in disagreement. I did not approve of his resignation from my uncle's bank to remain here with no purpose other than catering to his own inclinations."

"Is that what you think? Don't you know why he stayed on?"

"I don't know what you mean. Alden's only excuse for remaining was to continue to visit the Midway. And that was even after our friend, Detective Whitbread, warned him against associating with those people. But the Midway is closed down finally. What excuse he offers after even that incentive is gone, I have no idea."

Clara shook her head at my answer. "Emily, he has remained here to search for the man who killed your father." She paused, searching my face. "I see you have no idea. I am sure he did not wish your mother to know. Perhaps that is why he never confided in you. You never guessed? But you must have known there was something important that kept him here? From what he has told me, it was by visiting the Midway that he heard rumors that the man wanted for your father's shooting was in Chicago. He has been tracking down the sources of those rumors and twice came close to locating him."

"The man, Flaherty?" A flood of memories came back then. My father, a judge, had been hearing a case against striking workers who had thrown rocks from rooftops at the South Boston Horse Car Company trolleys. Sitting at home in his study one night while I was away at college, he was shot to death. The brother of one of the accused men was seen leaving the house, but he escaped. It was five years ago. That Alden would take it upon himself to try to track down the man wanted for our father's death was incredibly reckless. I could not imagine how in the world he would ever manage to pursue the man himself. What was he thinking of?

"Yes. That is what has kept him here, Emily. It was not selfishness. It was this quest of his. I do not know how severely you quarreled with him but I think pride prevents him from contacting you." She held out a card. "Here is his present address. I believe it is in this area. He shares rooms with Mr. Marco. I could not return home for the holidays without at least trying to heal the breach between the two of you. Won't you go to see him, Emily? Please?"

I fingered the card recognizing the street address as being in the Bohemian section. "I do not know." Clara was well intentioned but I continued to believe it would be better for my brother to seek me out. After all, he knew where I was. I found it hard to believe what she had told me. How could he have confided such a thing to her and not to me? My brother was intruding himself into my life again but I had no idea how to reach him. I had the address on the card, but that was not nearly enough.

"You will. I know you will." She embraced me in a warm hug and wished me a Merry Christmas, then left for her waiting carriage. Putting the card in my pocket I returned to work undecided about whether to attempt to find my errant brother.

SIX

After Clara's visit, I began to work on the papers again. I forced myself to finish the editing. Meanwhile the thought of Alden might have worried me more if it weren't for the time of year. Christmas was an especially busy time at Hull House.

There was an ongoing struggle between the settlement and the local political machine for the support of district residents. This year the rivalry between the corrupt alderman, Johnny Powers, and Hull House was increased by the effort to promote a candidate against him in the coming elections. Aware of the bribes and patronage that greased the machine, Miss Addams and the others were determined to bring change and so had launched a rival candidate. But everyone thought that Powers was the likely winner. To my surprise I learned it was Mr. Fitzgibbons who was organizing for Powers.

I had met that hearty Irishman during the turmoil of the final days of the Fair. With the assassination of Mayor Carter Harrison, Fitz had lost his position at City Hall. It seemed to be a comedown in the world of politics that he had become the local ward boss charged with running the campaign for Johnny Powers.

It was the custom of that politician to gain support of the voters by a distribution of free turkeys on Christmas Eve. By means of the contribution of a wealthy patron interested in our efforts to reform local government, this year Hull House planned a similar offering. All of the arrangements had been made for delivery of a cartload of birds on the afternoon of

Christmas Eve. We were completing decorations and dressing for the festivities when we heard a frantic cry from the kitchen and ran down to see what the matter was. There we found Mr. Simms, who should have driven the cart, half lying in a chair with a bloody head.

"They shot him," Simms told us with tears.

"Good heavens, Mr. Simms, who has been shot? And Mary, get water and bandages," Miss Addams demanded.

"Swerve, my horse, miss. They shot him dead. I've had him for on to ten years. They shot him." The poor man wept.

"Who did?" she asked as she began to wash his wound. The rest of us piled into the kitchen, including Milton Bierly and Florence Kelley. "Who did this to you?"

"Oh, they knocked me down is all. But they shot old Swerve and they robbed us of all them turkeys. Except them two they pulled apart and threw down and ground them into the dirt with their heels right in front of me. They said to tell Miss Addams the alderman says Merry Christmas. Oh, miss, I'm so sorry. It was that tall man all in black, him what has worked for the owners lately."

"Don't worry, Mr. Simms, we are just relieved you are all right." Jane Addams signaled Mary to take over bandaging the man's head and led me through to the front parlor. "Oh, dear. All those people are going to come and they are counting on us for their Christmas dinner. What are we going to do?"

I couldn't understand how she could be so calm. "You know who's responsible," I said. "It's Powers. It was probably that troublemaker Weaver. They can't get away with this! Let's go to the police."

Milton Bierly, who had trailed along, turned red in the face. I knew he was remembering his humiliation at the hands of the odious Weaver.

"But how would that help the families who won't have a turkey, Emily?" Jane Addams asked.

I looked at her with amazement but I realized she would never become agitated over something like a cartload of turkeys. It would take much more than that to disturb her. It was how she endured the many injustices and contradictions we witnessed every day. She was right, after all. Going to the police would not replace the turkeys, nor would they lift a finger against a man as powerful as Alderman Powers.

Florence Kelley agreed with her. "You won't be able to prove anything against Weaver, or Hanrahan, if he's the one who put him up to it. That man knows how to stay just the right side of the law. You'll get no satisfaction that way."

"Of course, you are right." I had to concede the point. I knew that Mrs. Kelley was not enthusiastic about the type of social gathering and turkey distribution that was planned for the evening, in any case. She thought such efforts frivolous. "Besides, he has pull. They won't dare to do anything. It makes me so angry." I dropped into a chair, at a loss. But Jane Addams grabbed her bag.

"Come with me, Emily. Mr. Bierly, you see that Mr. Simms gets home all right."

We got our coats and I followed her to the druggist across the street where there was a public telephone. She spoke briskly into the phone. As we hurried back she explained the call. "You must go to Louise Bowen, Emily. Here is her address and money for a cab. She has promised to provide us with money to distribute instead of the birds. It is too bad but at least our guests will not leave empty handed."

"But, Miss Addams, we are expecting three hundred people. Mrs. Bowen cannot possibly have that amount of cash on hand and the banks are closed."

She stopped abruptly in front of the door. "She promised. I don't know, Emily. We must trust she will find a way, poor good woman. I called her away from her own preparations for a dinner party. You must go to her and do the best you can. We will arrange some musical entertainment and delay for as long as possible. Just do your best."

I hurried away to find a cab. All of the people expected at Hull House that evening would have passed up an opportunity to receive a free turkey from Alderman Powers in order not to feel obliged to vote for him in the next election. But now they would be disappointed. It was a sorry state of things. It was so typical of Miss Addams that even in such a crisis, she remained comparatively serene. Certainly I did not feel confident that my errand would produce a satisfactory result. I dreaded returning to Hull House to face all of those disappointed people.

Mrs. Bowen was in evening dress when she rushed out to join me in the cab, instructing the driver to take us with all haste to a bank in the Loop. When I protested it would not be open she told me grimly that she had been on the telephone demanding that someone of authority meet us and dispense the cash or she would remove her considerable assets on the next business day. Her holdings were impressive enough that we were met by the manager. He was extremely grumpy but in the end he provided the funds. I took the waiting cab to rush back to Hull House while Mrs. Bowen had the bank manager find her another.

Back at Hull House I was able to hand the heavy bag to Miss Addams, who retreated to the library with some of the others to parcel out the cash while the crowd of neighbors dressed in their Sunday best were mesmerized by Maria Maglione's singing. Mr. Langlois looked on with glowing eyes as he watched his protégé's success.

As I stood in the doorway listening, I glanced across and saw Dr. Chapman looking at me. I thought at last I might have time to talk to him and renew the friendship that we had formed during my first year at the university. But before I could move towards him, I found Mr. Bierly standing in my path.

He had kept his workmen's clothes and added a new kerchief around his neck for the festivities. Whenever I saw him in those clothes I always thought he would be more comfortable in a regular suit and tie and bowler hat. Perhaps it was that those working clothes were always too clean and not at all worn.

"Miss Cabot, I must say something to you." Impatient though I might be, I waited politely. He cleared his throat. "I just wanted to say…"

"Please, Mr. Bierly, speak softly. The music…" I beckoned him out into the hallway.

"Oh, sorry. I just wanted to say, I hope you do not think the worse of me for that scene the other day. That man Weaver, he caught me unawares. He is an evil man, very evil."

"From what I know of him, he is a very dangerous man, Mr. Bierly," I whispered. "I do not think you should have anything to do with him."

The tips of the man's ears burned red. "You must not think I am afraid of him. The next time I see him or that Hanrahan, I'll know what to do. I will be able to protect you. See this." At that he pulled from his belt a large and heavy revolver.

"Mr. Bierly, please," I fended it off, pushing the barrel away from me. "Is that loaded? You should not have it here. Take it away. Please, take it away."

"No, no. It's not loaded." He tucked it back under his

jacket. "I just wanted to let you know that I am able to protect you. The next time you and Mrs. Kelley must make that kind of visit, I can help. I will go with you. Then we will see what Hanrahan or that Weaver have to say."

I had once seen Weaver hold a gun to a man's head and had been convinced he would have pulled the trigger. I certainly did not want Mr. Bierly facing off with such a man over a gun barrel. But it seemed politic to ignore Mr. Bierly's offer at the moment and to consult Mrs. Kelley and Miss Addams about how to relieve him of such a dangerous weapon later.

Luckily, the performance ended at that moment and it was followed by an invitation for each family to wish Miss Addams good evening personally and to receive their gift from Hull House. When Mrs. Kelley explained the fresh birds had to be replaced by cash there was a round of applause that was reassuring.

As families formed a line, some of them bearing their own gifts for their patroness, I went over to where Michel Langlois was congratulating the little singer. A mere seventeen years old with a pale face and lustrous dark hair falling around her shoulders, the girl received praise from the musician with a look of devout adulation. I, too, was glad to hear him praise her. Too often I had heard his criticisms as they practiced her performance.

"C'est merveilleuse, n'est ce pas?" He greeted us. Mr. Bierly was trailing behind me. I saw Dr. Chapman look towards the line and then take a step to join us.

"Yes, it was quite wonderful," I began, but just then I saw the girl's eyes roll back as she began to swoon. I stepped forward to catch her as she fainted.

The two men beside me were immobile for a minute but

Dr. Chapman appeared and easily lifted her slight form in his arms.

"Here, bring her upstairs," I said, leading the way.

We took her to Miss Addams's room at the top of the stairs and the doctor laid her on the bed, checked her eyes and felt her pulse. Soon she stirred.

"It's all right, you fainted. It was probably the excitement." He made way for Michel who hovered over her with concern.

"She's exhausted," Dr. Chapman murmured to me.

"It's the work. She's in a sweatshop. Mrs. Kelley says that shop works them twelve or fourteen hours a day," I whispered.

"We should find her parents," the doctor said more loudly.

"They are dead," Langlois told us. "She lives with her sister and her sister's useless husband. I did not see them here tonight."

"No, no, Senor Langlois," Maria said, attempting to sit up. "Mike is not useless. It is just he must change the job all the time."

"Useless. The women work for the sweatshops to support him and the two babies. I will go and get them." He started to rise but she caught him by the arm.

"No, you do not know where."

"What, you moved again?" He looked at us. "Every month they are in new lodgings. The man is a disgrace. He cannot even care for his family. Tell me, Maria, where is it now, eh?"

"No, please. I am well. I will just see Miss Addams and then I can go home. I am fine. It was the excitement."

She resisted all of our attempts to persuade her that someone must take her home. She seemed terribly alarmed at the prospect of revealing where they now lived and finally she became so agitated I commanded the men to go down and get her gift of money and her coat. We would do as she wished.

"Thank you, miss," she said when they had left. "I will be good now. It is not Mike's fault. He loves my sister and the children very much and he works very hard."

I forced the men to remain when she stepped into the night. She was much calmer then and I was sure allowing her to go alone was the only way to get her home and into her bed that night.

In the morning almost all of us went to an early Christmas service. Mrs. Kelley and Mr. Bierly both declined to participate as unbelievers, and Alice Mooney, our cook, stayed to prepare a breakfast. It was a happy morning, since we had averted disaster the night before and could face all our neighbors with the knowledge that we had not let them down. On the way home, some of the children started a snowball fight and I joined in landing some good hits on the urchins and responding in kind to an assault by the male residents. Fleeing that group, I was first through the door. I tore off my boots and moved in my stockings into the front parlor, since the others were right behind me and we were all scrambling to get in to breakfast.

As I skipped into the room, I was annoyed to notice Mr. Bierly at the desk in the middle of the octagon room, but with a second look, I understood that it was not him. It is strange how the mind will try to refuse to see what is right in front of it. I had to drag my sight away from the merry figures pouring in the door and back to the figure slumped over the desk several times before I felt sick to my stomach and forced myself to step closer. The man was lying there with his head bashed in, a crust of red brown blood matting his hair. And it was Mr. Hanrahan.

SEVEN

No one screamed, or fainted, or burst into tears. There was no male audience for such a performance. Only one dead man. But then we were not such performers. I found myself frozen. The figure of the man at the desk inevitably brought the picture of my father's death to mind. He, too, had been sitting at his desk when someone came up behind him and shot him in the back of the head. And he, too, had fallen forward into a pool of blood. I had not been there. I had not seen it. But how many times had I imagined the scene in my mind. This man, Mr. Hanrahan, had not been shot. He had been beaten over the head and I realized the brass candlestick that sat on the desk beside the wisps of red hair matted with blood must have been what was used. It had been placed, almost carefully, right side up beside the head as if, after all the rage was expended, the brutal beating had ended abruptly and the weapon calmly placed where it could be found. So there would be no question.

I heard the clank of metal on metal irregularly hitting and a shiver of icy cold ran down my back. It was a muffled sound and I realized that it must be coming from the workshop in the basement. Someone was at work, nothing sinister, but it unnerved me nonetheless.

There was a rustle of skirts that brought my attention back to the doorway where Miss Addams was stepping forward. The others had instinctively turned towards her, all of them, like a field of wheat when a puff of wind passes over it, bending the sheaves in the same direction.

"Oh, dear God." Even the ever calm Miss Addams blanched at the sight. But she recovered enough to do something useful. "Jenny," she told the girl nearest the door, "run and fetch Dr. Chapman. He was just heading for the men's dormitory."

Suddenly ashamed of my own revulsion from this thing, that had been a man, and which was now planted in the middle of our peaceful octagon room, I pulled off a glove and tentatively grasped his shoulder, like trying to shake a sleeper. This was no sleeper, though, and there was no response. Trembling, I slid my hand to his throat trying to feel some sign of blood pumping through his veins. I felt nothing but the cold skin and I quickly withdrew my hand, my gorge rising at the thought that some of the gore from the wound at the back of his head might touch me. I had to look away and gulp for air.

Stephen Chapman pushed his way through the women in the doorway. "What is it? Oh." He was across the room in two strides, feeling the man's wrist, raising his eyelids, gently raising his head a few inches then letting it down. I was aware of the irregular clanging of metal on metal that still was going on somewhere below us. "He's dead, I'm afraid. There's nothing I can do for him." He turned to Miss Addams. "But who is he? And how did this happen?"

"I don't know him," she began, but I interrupted her.

"He's a Mr. Hanrahan. I have seen him before—only once. I was with Mrs. Kelley and Mr. Bierly. He was at one of the factories we visited last week."

"Florence Kelley?" Miss Addams asked. "But where is she? She was not with us this morning, Doctor. She does not attend church. Neither does Mr. Bierly. Let me ask one of the women to find them."

For one terrible moment I was afraid of what we might find in the rest of the house.

"No," the doctor told her. "You ladies must stay together, in the other parlor." He pointed to the other side of the house. "Let me and some of the men check the rest of the house." Miss Addams looked grim but she firmly took my arm and began to shepherd the women from the doorway into the large parlor on the other side where Jenny Dow taught the kindergarten. Meanwhile Dr. Chapman sent one of the men for the police and led the rest on a quick hunt through the house. We settled uneasily as we listened to the heavy tread of their footsteps tramping up and down the stairs. It felt as if our normally feminine sanctuary was being invaded.

At last they returned leading Alice Mooney, our cook, and a red faced Milton Bierly and I realized the sporadic clanking sounds had finally ended. He held a hammer in his hand.

"We could not find Mrs. Kelley," Dr. Chapman told us.

"Of course not," Alice told him. "She left less than half an hour ago. She's spending the holiday with her children up in Evanston. She said to tell you, Miss Addams, she was taking the earlier train." Our cook seemed very put out. It was obvious no one had told her about the dead man in the octagon room. "I've got to get back now. I've things on the stove and some of you ladies can come help lay the table."

"Just a moment, Alice," Miss Addams took charge. "Something has happened. Were you aware that a Mr. Hanrahan was in the octagon room?"

"Yes, yes." She looked across at me. "Did he find Miss Cabot all right, then? He rang the bell asking for her just as I was putting the bread in to rise. I told him to come back but he insisted on waiting so I put him in the front room there."

"He asked for me? Not Mrs. Kelley?" I found that hard to understand. Everyone was looking at me.

"That's right, miss. Is something wrong? Has he left then? What's the matter?"

Miss Addams stood up. "Something very terrible has happened, Alice. A man has been found dead in the octagon room."

"Dead? Good Lord Almighty! Did he have a fit or something then? I wouldn't have heard a thing; it's that far to the kitchen."

"I'm afraid he is dead and we will have to have the police look into what happened."

"The police? God Almighty, and on Christmas Day?" Alice was distressed.

Dr. Chapman looked at Miss Addams, who had put an arm around the cook. Mr. Bierly stood in the background with his mouth open.

"Can we ask you to come in and just verify that the man is the one you let in earlier, Alice?" Dr. Chapman asked.

She nodded and he and Miss Addams led her into the other room while the rest of us sat in silence. My mind was racing trying to think of why Mr. Hanrahan, whom I had met only the one time the week before, would have come to Hull House on Christmas Day looking for me. He had seemed to know my father, or at least to know of him. Had I met him before in the past in Boston and not remembered? My eyes wandered around the room, stopping at Mr. Bierly. Even on such a holiday he wore a long sleeved work shirt and workmen's dungarees with a clean red kerchief around his neck. I shivered when I saw the hammer with a metal head in his hand. Whatever had he been doing?

"Oh, Lord, oh, Lord. What a thing to happen." Alice was led back into the room, obviously upset by what she had seen, as we all were. Miss Addams made her sit down in an empty rocking chair. "What a thing to happen on Christmas Day." She rocked back and forth wringing her hands in her apron. Then she stopped and stared straight into my eyes. "But, Miss Cabot, what about your brother?" She looked up and around the room, searching. "Where is he? What happened to him?"

"My brother? What do you mean, Alice?"

"He was a nice young man, with dark curly hair and the biggest blue eyes. He rang before Mrs. Kelley left but she wouldn't answer the door, not her. I had to leave my stove and go up. He said he was your brother and I told him to wait in the front room with the other man. Oh, dear, miss. I hope nothing has happened to him."

Alden. My brother Alden had been here.

EIGHT

"I haven't seen my brother since we saw my mother off at the train station more than a month ago. And I only saw Mr. Hanrahan that one time, with Mrs. Kelley and Mr. Bierly." I was repeating what I had already said ten times before but at least I was saying it to Detective Whitbread this time. I was grateful that he had been called to investigate this terrible thing. I thought Dr. Chapman must have arranged for it somehow. The tall, stern policeman had been my mentor the previous year and it was only because of his enthusiastic interest that we had compiled the lengthy report on police statistics. Incorruptible and relentless, I was relieved to learn the investigation was in his very capable hands.

It was a few hours since we had found the dead man. We spent most of that time in the north parlor as policemen tramped in and out and up and down. Alice insisted on serving the meal she spent so much time preparing and we were given leave to file en masse up to the communal dining room. Shock deprived most of us of an appetite and in the end Alice's concoctions were put to better use—the food seemed to put the policemen into a better frame of mind.

We were all questioned more than once but I was the person of most interest once it was known that the dead man had asked for me. Several uniformed officers asked me again and again what the man's business with me had been. But I had no idea. Finally the poor man's body was carried through the front door to a wagon. It was a spectacle witnessed by many of our neighbors. News traveled quickly and a crowd of people left their holiday merrymaking to try to find out more. We could hear the shouted questions and dismissive responses advising them to go home as the steely cold seeped through the open door. Then Detective Whitbread asked me to come to the front parlor again.

Miss Addams and Dr. Chapman insisted on accompanying me. The men had been dismissed to their lodgings some time before but the doctor refused to leave, pacing up and down as the rest of us sat waiting. Now the three of us returned to the scene where I had made the gruesome discovery.

The body was gone but the chair was still pulled up to the desk and Whitbread placed us on straight backed chairs in the parlor, facing the octagon room. It was there that he once again asked me about the two visitors and once again I denied any knowledge of what they wanted.

"You saw no one near the premises as you approached?" Detective Whitbread stood before us, his familiar lanky frame in a dark suit, his arms folded across his chest and a frown on his face. Three uniformed men lounged in corners of the room awaiting his instructions.

"No. We were having a snowball fight with some of the children." It sounded so undignified in view of what I had found in the room. "I was running to escape a final volley. I got to the door and took off my boots quickly to make room for the others. We were in a hurry to get into the warmth it was so cold. I moved into this room to get out of the way."

"And you saw Mr. Hanrahan?"

"Not immediately. I was looking back at the door. I saw someone at the desk from the corner of my eye. I had some idea it was Mr. Bierly because he did not come to church with us. Then I moved further into the room and I realized—I saw that it was Mr. Hanrahan covered with blood. We all saw and Miss Addams sent Jenny Dow to get the doctor."

"He had been dead long enough for the blood to stop flowing and to clot," Dr. Chapman told him. "Whoever did it was long gone by the time Miss Cabot found him."

Detective Whitbread frowned in concentration. He was not looking at us but at the desk in the octagon room, as if he saw the dead man still sitting there. He stepped over and picked up the brass candlestick, turning back to us with it in his hand. "Where did this come from?"

Miss Addams pointed to the mantelpiece of the fireplace in the front parlor. "It belongs there. You can see the other one that matches."

Cocking his head like an interested bird, Whitbread examined the mantel then carefully replaced the candlestick. He stepped back to look at the effect. Rubbing his long fingered hands together as if they were still cold from the outdoors, he said, "So, let us see what could have happened."

Dr. Chapman interrupted him. Like me, the doctor recognized the signs. Detective Whitbread was going to re-enact the crime. "Really, Whitbread, must you do this in front of these ladies? They have already suffered a shock." It was not the first time the doctor had disapproved of Detective Whitbread's methods.

As always, the detective ignored such disapproval. "It will not take long. They may be able to correct me. It is important that we reconstruct the man's actions insofar as it is possible. Now," he strode to the door. "Mrs. Mooney told us Hanrahan rang the bell not long after you all left for the service. She tried to tell him to come back later but he was insistent and she was anxious to get back to her bread so she sent him in here and returned to her kitchen. He entered." Whitbread stepped into the room and looked around as if he had never seen it before. "He removes his hat, but not his overcoat. No fires are laid and it is chilly. He places his hat, no perhaps he paces first," the detective walked up and down a few times. "He wants to see Miss Cabot. His desire is such that he comes to see her early in the morning even though it is Christmas Day. Whatever it is, it is important enough that he cannot wait. But he is left waiting." Whitbread continues to pace. "He realizes he may have to wait some time. He has second thoughts about the urgency of his mission." A look of surprise crossed the detective's face. He was a good actor. I knew it was a talent he frequently used when he went in disguise to investigate a crime. I was not sure that the other men in the room appreciated such a skill. But he continued, untouched by their skepticism. "Or perhaps he had another appointment. Unsure, now, of what to do, whether to wait, or to return later, or to abandon his task altogether, he notices the desk." Whitbread pantomimed surprise. Dr. Chapman moved restlessly in his seat and I could see two of the other policemen exchange a look. But Detective Whitbread was so immersed in his story he was impervious to their opinions. He continued. "He will leave a note for Miss Cabot. Now he puts down his hat, sits down and finds paper, opens the ink …"

I almost gasped to see him take the dead man's seat. I must have expected a protest from the shade of the murdered man. Despite the fact that the chair was empty now, I could not rid myself of the conviction that the man still sat there.

But now Whitbread jumped up. "But meanwhile someone else has entered the room." He strode back to the doorway and through it. Quietly he opened and shut the front door. Then he peered into the room, staring at the desk as if a man were there. I could see him, Hanrahan, and I could hear the scratching of his pen as he wrote whatever it was. But Detective Whitbread looked around cautiously and raised his eyebrows as if straining to hear if anyone was moving elsewhere in the house. We were all silent. He had captured our attention. We watched him tiptoe, noiselessly across the oriental carpet to the mantel where he carefully wrapped his fingers around the candlestick. Then, without hesitation he took a large step to put himself right behind the chair while raising the candlestick above his head in his right hand. Immediately he swooped it down where it would smash the head of the man at the desk. I flinched and felt a sickening contraction of my stomach as he swung the weapon up and down, up and down in rapid violent strokes.

"Oh, really, Whitbread," the doctor protested. Miss Addams and I had managed to contain ourselves but Dr. Chapman had no qualms about appearing weak in the face of such a demonstration.

Detective Whitbread ignored the protest but he stopped his flailing, taking a step back as if considering his handiwork. Satisfied, he looked at the candlestick in his hand and carefully placed it on the desk next to where the dead man's head would have been. Exactly where we had found it. The demonstration made me quite afraid of the person who could have done such a thing. I realized whoever it was must have beaten Mr. Hanrahan so quickly there was no time for him to even try to defend himself and the fact that the person who did this could then so coldly place the weapon right beside the bloody mass was very shocking. It had seemed a hot-blooded act when I found the dead man yet Whitbread's reconstruction had an inevitability to it that persuaded me. It was a cold-blooded act.

Detective Whitbread broke off then and turned back to us.

"And then what?" I asked. "He calmly went out the door?"

"You are jumping ahead, Miss Cabot." Whitbread had worked with me when I compiled a massive set of statistics on crime the previous year. In the course of our relationship he took on the role of teacher. "While I did open and close the front door to see if it could be done quietly enough there is no way of knowing whether the murderer came from outside or inside the house or where he or she went after the deed."

"He or she?" the doctor protested. "Surely you don't think a woman did this?"

Whitbread turned to him with interest. "Ah, is it your medical opinion then that a woman could not have done this?" He took up the candlestick and returned to the place immediately behind the victim's chair. "I was of the impression that with the weight of the weapon and the angle of the blow, it would be reasonable to assume a healthy woman could have delivered the blows."

"Of course, a woman could have," Dr. Chapman answered hastily, rising and taking the weapon from Whitbread. "A woman would be physically capable but I cannot believe there is a woman with cause to do such a thing." Ostensibly he was confirming his opinion by handling the candlestick but I knew it was the best, perhaps only method of preventing Detective Whitbread from repeating his dramatic rendering of the horrid death yet again. To Whitbread his re-enactment was nothing more than a scientific experiment. He had no inkling of the deeply disturbing effect it had on the rest of us. In his world such violence was merely a fact of life while the rest of us spent a large amount of effort building up the walls of our lives to block out such violence. That was why it was so inconceivable that such a thing could be found in the parlor of Hull House on Christmas morning.

"Detective, I hope you do not imagine that this was done

by a resident," Miss Addams spoke up. "It is a terrible, terrible act and we will do everything in our power to assist you in finding the truth of what happened to this poor man here in Hull House. But I am completely confident that no one here would have done this act. It is hard for me to comprehend anyone doing such an awful thing but I know it was no one here."

"It is too soon to draw conclusions, Miss Addams, but I must approach the task with an open mind. Until the culprit is found out all possibilities must be investigated. Now, we have talked to Mrs. Mooney. Who else was in the house at the time?" He pulled out a small notebook. "A Mrs. Florence Kelley and Mr. Milton Bierly. Is that all?"

"Yes, but Mrs. Kelley left before we returned."

"But only shortly before your return." He consulted his notes. "And then there was Mr. Alden Cabot who called and was admitted a mere half hour before your return. He was directed into the parlor. It would seem that either Mr. Cabot was the last person to see Hanrahan alive or else he must have found him dead. In that case, however, why did he leave without raising the alarm?"

"But, Detective Whitbread, you know Alden. He could not have…he would never…you can't believe he did this," I protested. Whitbread knew my brother but he would not let such an acquaintance prejudice him.

"What was the purpose of his visit today?" He held his pencil over his notebook as if I were someone he had met that day and not someone who had worked with him for over a year.

"I told you I have no idea. My brother and I argued after my mother returned to Boston. I have not seen him since then."

"Surely Miss Cabot's brother must have been coming to see her to make amends in honor of the holiday," Miss Addams suggested. "It would be the most natural thing in the world that he should do so."

Detective Whitbread concentrated on writing this down in his notebook but he spoke to me without looking up. "I believe I counseled you last summer, Miss Cabot, that you should warn your brother about the company he was keeping. Is he still associating with the men he met on the Midway? Do you recall that I warned you?"

I felt myself flush. "I—you did. And I did warn him against such associations. But he would not listen to me, that is why we argued. The truth is I only received information about where he has been staying from Clara Shea last week. I intended to contact him after Christmas. Clara told me, she said…Alden told her that he had stayed in Chicago to try to track down the man who is wanted for killing our father." That brought silence to the room. "Five years ago, my father was shot by a man involved in a case that was before him. He was a judge. The man got away and is a fugitive. My brother told Clara that he had information the man was in Chicago and he wanted to find him. He never told me that, and it is madness if it is true."

I looked around at them. "I don't know why he came looking for me today. I think he must have wanted to wish me a Merry Christmas and to make up our differences. We have neither of us ever spent such a holiday apart. I don't know why he left without seeing me. I don't know what could have happened. But why would he hurt Mr. Hanrahan? He didn't know him. Even if he did, why do such a thing? He wouldn't. He couldn't. You must know that."

"As you are quite well aware, Miss Cabot, we can assume

nothing in a case such as this until the facts are known. How do you know this crime is not connected to your brother's quest for your father's murderer?" he scolded me. Whitbread knew the facts of my father's death, as I had confided in him the previous year. But that had nothing to do with Hull House. "As for knowing Mr. Hanrahan, it appears that you have not been in communication with your brother so you cannot have any knowledge of whether or not they were acquainted. You must admit that Mr. Cabot's mysterious disappearance will have to be explained."

I did know from past experience that Detective Whitbread would be stubbornly insistent in his refusal to make any assumptions without proof, but I was appalled at the thought that he could really imagine Alden might have committed the horrible murder we had just seen mimed. My exasperation was such that I felt a knot rising in my throat and I clenched my hands tightly in an attempt to prevent tears from gathering in my eyes. I would not appear as a hysteric before Detective Whitbread of all men.

Dr. Chapman intervened. "If you will not make assumptions, then you cannot assume Mr. Cabot even saw Hanrahan, dead or alive. Alice Mooney said she told him he could wait in the parlor with Hanrahan but she rushed back downstairs. Perhaps he changed his mind and turned around and left? If he was here to broach a delicate matter, to admit he had been wrong to his sister, he may have found himself unable to go through with it in the presence of someone else. Even if he stepped into the room he might have exchanged a few words with Hanrahan and realized the situation was impossible and he would have to return when he could face his sister alone. Or, if the man was already dead, which seems very likely to me, he might have assumed the man was writing at the desk and left without saying a word. By your own professed methods you cannot assume anything."

I was grateful to the doctor. Detective Whitbread cheerfully acknowledged the validity of his argument. "Only too true, Doctor. We must speak to each of the people. Mr. Bierly has said that he arrived early and was working on a metal project in the workroom below. This appears to be substantiated by Mrs. Mooney who complained that the pounding went on all morning and was enough to give a body a headache. Mrs. Kelley we have not been able to interview as it seems she has not yet returned."

"She should be back tomorrow morning," Miss Addams assured him. "I hope you can wait until then. She has so little time to spend with her children who are in boarding school in Glencoe. They are dining at the home of friends in Evanston. I was glad to hear she took the early train as I urged her to do. I hope you will not feel you must disturb them with news of this today."

"We must not put off till tomorrow that which is better done today, Miss Addams, Christmas or not. However, the first concern must be to track the movements of the dead man. You say he was employed at a factory on Taylor Street?"

"Not employed, there no," I told him. "It seemed rather that he was employed by the owner and represented his interests. The owner is Mr. Franklin of Prairie Avenue." I knew the name of that prominent family and I assumed the detective would recognize it as well but Whitbread merely took down the information in his notebook. "Mrs. Kelley told me Franklin owns the buildings and rents space to the man who runs the sweatshop. Franklin is one of the main purchasers of the goods produced there. But he sent Mr. Hanrahan to advise the small businessmen when there were factory inspections. It was a rivalry that had gone on for some time, with Franklin sending Hanrahan to try to defeat Mrs. Kelley's attempts to enforce the eight-hour rule."

Detective Whitbread looked up and flipped the cover on to his notepad and slipped it into his pocket. "I see. So, Hanrahan was in the employ of Mr. Franklin. It would seem, then, that we must bear the unhappy tidings of the man's death to his employer. He should be able to tell us where Hanrahan was living and what would have brought him to Hull House on this day. Will you accompany me, Miss Cabot? Your former acquaintance with the inhabitants of Prairie Avenue will be invaluable." Whitbread knew of my connections with the Glessners through the Monday Morning Reading Club. I had met the Franklin family through them.

"No, Whitbread, what are you thinking of, man?" the doctor protested. "That is no place for Miss Cabot."

"Miss Cabot will be in no danger," Detective Whitbread told him. "I would anticipate that Mr. Franklin will not tell us anything willingly but Miss Cabot's presence may cause him to reveal what would otherwise not be forthcoming. There must be some reason that Mr. Hanrahan came to see Miss Cabot."

I welcomed the opportunity to assist the detective and to find out why the dead man had come looking for me but Dr. Chapman was still protesting.

"This is very unseemly, Whitbread, to say the least. You cannot expose Miss Cabot in this way. Miss Addams, can't you prevent this?"

"It is up to Miss Cabot, Doctor. She must do what she thinks right. We residents of Hull House must do everything we can to help Detective Whitbread to find out who has committed this horrible act."

Stephen Chapman stood there shaking his head, defeated. I stepped over to him. "It will be all right, Doctor. I will be with Detective Whitbread." I looked over to the desk, as if the shade of the dead man could hear me. "I have no idea what brought Mr. Hanrahan here asking for me. I really must find out why he came and whether that was the reason for his death."

NINE

Detective Whitbread had a small carriage with a driver at the front door. We were bundled up against the cold and he handed me into the trap. It was old, a police vehicle with a canvas covering torn in several places, but I settled my back into a corner hoping to avoid a breeze as Whitbread gave directions. We had to maneuver through a small crowd that was still gathered, looking for news. Whitbread ignored their shouted questions.

"I was so glad Dr. Chapman was able to get you to be the one to handle this awful situation," I told him as we began to clomp along.

"I thank you. I fear you are under a misapprehension, however. I am sure Dr. Chapman would have requested my assignment had he known it would relieve your feelings but, as it was, he had no say in the matter. As it happens, I was the only detective at the station today, and so naturally I was the one to respond to the call."

Christmas Day and Detective Whitbread was at the police station. I should have known. I rubbed my gloved hands together to keep warm. "I'm sorry to hear it. It must have been a very empty lonely place on such a day."

"Not at all. Although you might not expect it. As a matter of fact, with the weather so cold, the corridors were filled. The recent economic problems have led to the downfall of many and, when it gets so cold and they have nowhere else to go, they come to the police stations for shelter. I was on duty to allow those of my comrades with families to have the time. I would have spent a portion of the day catching up on paper work in any case, so it was no burden for me. And it turned out to be a lucky thing since you did not have to request my assignment to the case, you see."

He was quite honest in his satisfaction. I looked out of the window as we passed the saloons that lined Halsted Street. It was difficult to understand how they could be open and how so many could be patronizing them on such a day. But that was the very nature of the West Side where Hull House was located. The settlement was meant to be a bulwark against the tide of violence and filth of the area, yet today, unbelievable as it was, we had found a dead man in the parlor.

Clouds hung low and gray above the tenements looking like balls of dirty cotton pressing down. It was too bitterly cold to speak much and I sank back and watched as we passed through the empty markets of Canal and Maxwell Streets and crossed into the area of mansions on Prairie Avenue. Here the large houses stood apart from each other separated by lawns and black iron railings. I recognized the austere house of my friends the Glessners. It was all of stone, an almost fortress-like aspect that brought to mind the fears of the wealthy that had been aroused by the Haymarket bombing some years before. Yet I knew it to be a warm and friendly place inside, full of music and flowers. The Franklin mansion was more like the others on the street, being some sort of attempt at the re-creation of a minor palace, I thought, with a mansard roof and decorative carvings. We turned up the curved drive and stopped in front of the main entrance.

At the door the butler was going to refuse us entry but my presence confused him. It would not be proper to leave a young lady like me standing in the cold. It occurred to me that one reason Detective Whitbread brought me along was for this assault on the front door of the mansion. He had plenty of experience of being sent around to the tradesmen's entrance as a policeman but with me in tow he would receive a different treatment. The butler protested the family was at Christmas dinner but Whitbread insisted, so he left us in the ornate hall with a high ceiling and ferns in huge Chinese porcelain pots, finally returning to say Mr. Franklin would see us in the study.

We followed him to that room where we were directed to a couple of uncomfortable straight-backed chairs in front of the desk. It was a square room lined with bookshelves, the massive oak desk facing the door and a globe on a stand in the far corner. Soon a series of tapping and dragging noises announced our host was joining us. He came in from a door behind the desk, leaning on his cane and pulling along one lame leg. He was a tall, broad shouldered man with thinning gray hair that he wore long enough to brush his stiff collar. He had a wide forehead over deep sunk eyes with heavy drooping lids and jowls around a perpetually frowning face. He did not speak much and seemed to resent the need to put himself out enough to say anything. He sat down heavily in the armchair behind the desk and glared at us.

I was surprised to see Mr. Weaver leaning on the doorframe behind him. He did not come farther into the room. He seemed an unlikely guest for Christmas dinner at the Franklins and the fact that he still wore his broad black hat seemed to indicate he was not on hand for a social occasion. He wore a sardonic grin.

"What is it? What do you want that you come disturbing me on the holiday?" Franklin growled. He was looking at Detective Whitbread and did not acknowledge my presence.

Whitbread was unmoved. "I believe you have an employee named Hanrahan?"

Franklin moved, like some big animal bothered by a fly. "What of it? Why do you want to know?"

"I am sorry to have to tell you, Mr. Franklin, that a Mr. Hanrahan, believed to be in your employ was found dead in the parlor of Hull House this morning."

"Is that it? I'll take him off the payroll in the morning. What do you want from me?" The reaction was shockingly brusque. Yet it seemed calculated. Mr. Franklin wanted to shock. He used his wealth to insulate himself from society. He refused to acknowledge any obligation to display decency or feelings.

"We would appreciate your assistance. Mr. Hanrahan was bludgeoned. In order to find out who did this, we need to know what he was doing there, at Hull House. Since he was in your employ, perhaps you could tell us."

"Hull House? You mean that settlement house where those women try to civilize the great unwashed? Sentimental claptrap. They should be home with their husbands and children. A bunch of hysterical unmarried women who should be under lock and key." Hull House was well known and well respected by most of society but Mr. Franklin wanted to distance himself from that opinion. Again, I thought it was his wealth that made him think he could spurn anything he wanted.

"I understand you to mean that you did not send Mr. Hanrahan to Hull House on any business of your own. Do you know of any private reason that would have taken him there today?"

"He worked for me. I know nothing of his private life. He had a wife and children back in Boston, I believe."

"He was from Boston then? How did he come to be employed by you?"

"He's an account manager. He was recommended. He was with a firm, Talbot and Lawler, I offered him a better salary and he came here."

"But his family stayed behind? Why is that?"

"I have no idea why, nor do I care. As long as he showed up at the office why would I?"

"And the office he worked from?"

"The sixth floor of the Franklin Building on State Street. Is that all? I have guests."

Guests? He was in mourning. The black he wore did attest to that although I doubted it reflected anything in the man's heart. That he should have guests the first Christmas after the death of his only daughter would have been thought unseemly in the Boston society where I was raised. My acquaintance with the Franklin family had not been a happy one.

"A few more questions, if you would be so good." Detective Whitbread was cool as ice. "Do you know of any reason why Mr. Hanrahan might have wanted to see Miss Cabot? Had he ever mentioned her or her brother?"

Franklin had been preparing to rise from the desk but he growled at this. He had ignored me so far but now he leaned on his massive elbows on the desk and looked at me. It was a malevolent stare. "Miss Cabot. I understand from my friend, Professor Lukas, that Miss Cabot has been expelled from the university, which only goes to prove what the Professor and I have always said, that women are not suited for study at that institution." He was gloating. He had wanted to have his name on a building at the university but after the suicide of his daughter his money had been refused. He blamed me for that. "So now Miss Cabot has joined in the unnatural living arrangements of those women down there. No, Hanrahan never mentioned Miss Cabot to me. That Mrs. Kelley was his archenemy. But he was defeating her. He was winning." Franklin chuckled. "That woman with her factory inspections and her eight-hour rule, she thought she could dictate how a man's business would be run. But she was finding out that she may have friends down in Springfield in that disgrace for a governor, Altgeld, but we have powerful friends, too. And they aren't going to sit down to be told what to do by a bunch of women living on the West Side. Hanrahan was working with the lawyers to file the briefs that would bring down her eight-hour rule. Eight-hour rule! As if she should be able to tell people how long they can work. The women she's trying to impose it on hate her for it. She'll find out. And she'll find out like the rest of them down there playing house in the slums, business will not be tied down by the whims of a bunch of petticoats who don't know what they're talking about."

"I see. Did you have reason to believe Mr. Hanrahan might have gone to Hull House to talk to Mrs. Kelley, then?" Whitbread asked.

"Hah! That harpy. No. He would see her in court. I don't know why he would be looking for Miss Cabot here. Perhaps he knew something about her from Boston. Perhaps it was something she didn't want known. The spites and jealousies of those women are no doubt at the bottom of this. So one of them pounded him to death, did they? Don't come to me for reasons why. Ask them. Ask her."

I felt obliged to respond. "I never knew Mr. Hanrahan. I met him only once in a factory sweatshop where they were illegally working women beyond the eight hours allowed by the law. I was there with Mrs. Kelley in our capacity as inspectors of factories for the state of Illinois."

"Inspectors! What bullshit!" Franklin growled.

"There is no need to be offensive," Detective Whitbread told him. "If you cannot offer any reason for Mr. Hanrahan's visit today, can you tell me where he was living? Also, do you want to inform his wife of his death or do you want the police to do that?"

Franklin shuffled through papers on his desk and found a file. He read two addresses from it, one a hotel in Chicago, the other a street address in a genteel neighborhood of Boston. Whitbread copied the details into his notebook. The businessman leaned across the folder with an unpleasant smile on his face. "I expect Johnny Powers will be interested to hear a man has been found murdered in Hull House. I expect he might find that useful in his campaign."

Detective Whitbread ignored him. "Will you be contacting Mrs. Hanrahan, then?" he raised the issue again.

Franklin got up, ponderously leaning on his cane. "No," was all he said then he pulled himself past Weaver and out the door.

The butler hurried into the room to lead us back to the front hall. I had no doubt Franklin had growled at him to make sure we left without stealing the silver. When we reached the hall, the front door opened to admit Sidney Franklin.

He stopped, in surprise. I had the impression of a twinge of guilt but that might have been from the sight of Detective Whitbread and myself on a day when he must remember his only sister. He looked pale. He ignored the police detective and faced me. "Miss Cabot. Well, Merry Christmas. I cannot think how you have come to be here on such a day." He stared at me, his eyes raking over me up and down. "Surely a welcome sight compared to the others." I realized then that he was a little unsteady on his feet. I could smell it as he bowed over my hand in mock gallantry. He had been drinking. "If you've come to solicit from the old scrooge in there I suppose you are leaving empty handed. Let me see if I can make up the difference."

"No, no, Mr. Franklin." It was embarrassing. "There has been a death. Mr. Hanrahan, who worked for your father. He was found dead at Hull House this morning. We came to tell your father."

He frowned in an attempt at concentration. "Hanrahan? You don't mean the fair haired boy, god almighty manager Hanrahan, do you? Dead?" He looked at me, then the silent Detective Whitbread for confirmation. I nodded. Whitbread was closely watching the man, like a hunter, I thought, lying still to scout a prey. Suddenly the slightly drunk man before me started laughing. It was an awful response and I gathered my skirts and marched to the door, shaking my head. "Merry Christmas," he called after me. "Seems like it's going to be a Merry Christmas after all." I heard him slap the butler on the back behind me.

In the carriage, Whitbread was reading over his notes.

"Sidney Franklin was drunk," I stated. The detective was unimpressed by my observation. "What a horrible man the father is though," I added. "But I don't think he knows why Hanrahan came to Hull House and asked for me."

"Yet he did not seem totally surprised. It was very convenient that he had the addresses for Mr. Hanrahan already out on his desk, especially since he did not seem to want to concern himself with the man's personal life. And then he was already very well informed in the circumstances of his death before our arrival."

"He already knew of the death before we came? Do you think he could have had something to do with it?" It did seem to me that Franklin was the sort of man who should be blamed for such an action. I could believe it of him.

"I cannot imagine why he would want to dispose of a manager who was helping him to bring actions against the eight-hour law. No, I merely meant that he knew about it. I imagine it was Mr. Weaver who must have told him."

"But how would he know?"

"There was a great crowd outside Hull House, Miss Cabot. News of that sort travels fast on the West Side. I imagine Weaver heard of it, came and found out what he could, then took the information to Mr. Franklin. And was no doubt rewarded."

"I could imagine Weaver killing a man like that," I said.

"But, again, there is no reason why he should do so, unless there was some rivalry in their employment for Mr. Franklin. I will investigate. Meanwhile, I will go to Mr. Hanrahan's lodgings after I return you to Hull House. Then I must speak to anyone else who was there."

"You mean Alden. I'm sure he couldn't have done this, really."

"His absence must be explained. I will tell you, Miss Cabot, that there are others besides Mr. Franklin who will say that the existence of Hull House is to blame for the violent death there. I anticipate there will be considerable pressure to find and convict the killer. There are violent deaths in the saloons," he gestured towards those outside of the carriage as we traveled up Halsted Street, "and they are hardly noticed, it is expected. But to have such a death in a place like Hull House will be seen as an outrage. The women there are seen to belong more to Prairie Avenue than to the West Side, and their presence will be questioned. There will be a desire for a speedy resolution of this."

"But no one at Hull House could have done this," I protested. "Why would they? They wouldn't."

"That remains to be seen. But it is the case that anyone who was there from outside the settlement must be an obvious suspect."

"You mean Alden, don't you? But you don't really believe he would do something like this, surely you don't."

"It is not a case of what I might believe or be able to imagine, Miss Cabot. It is a fact that he was there and that he left for unknown reasons." I started to protest again but he stopped me. "The point I wish to make, Miss Cabot, is that it would be greatly to your brother's advantage if he would voluntarily come forward with his story rather than waiting to be found and questioned. I say no more. We are here." He hopped down and handed me out of the carriage. "I will be at the station after visiting Mr. Hanrahan's lodgings, Miss Cabot." He tipped his bowler hat. "I hope to see your brother there."

I watched him ride away and decided that now, if ever, I must find Alden.

TEN

I stopped inside the house only long enough to check with Alice to be sure my brother had not returned, and to run upstairs to get the card that Clara had given me with his address. I was particularly anxious to avoid Dr. Chapman as I knew he would prevent me from setting out alone to find my brother. But I wanted to be able to talk to Alden by myself, because I was uneasy about the whole situation. Somehow I couldn't face the other residents of the settlement house without at least trying to find out what connection there was between the dead man, and me and my family. I had a terrible feeling of guilt for bringing tragedy to Hull House yet I did not know of any reason why Mr. Hanrahan would have come there looking for me.

I hurried down Halsted, twice crossing the street to avoid men standing outside saloons. It was a sorry, disgraceful sight to see them there on a holiday when they should have been at home with their families. I knew from women of the neighborhood I had met at Hull House that the saloons were the downfall of many men. They would escape their crowded tenement rooms to socialize over alcohol and end up spending their hard earned money standing drinks in a ghostly imitation of some memory of hospitality from better times. They would return home inebriated and have to rise early the next day to do the work that barely kept them and their families alive. The women resented the saloons that took their men and hard earned money from them but there was nothing they could do about it.

Further south I entered the Bohemian section where some of the blocks were quite well built and prosperous. Alden was sharing rooms with Mr. Marco, a barrel-chested, deep voiced man who had run the concession for the Ferris Wheel at the World's Columbian Exposition. He had hair, moustache, and sideburns dyed the darkest black I had ever seen, an unpronounceable surname, and an English accent. As I looked around, it seemed likely to me that he was of Bohemian origins. He had also run the illegal gambling den where my brother's friend, Teddy Hanover, had been shot and Mr. Marco had been the young man's chief mourner. More than once Detective Whitbread had warned my brother Alden against fraternizing with these men, but he had followed his own inclinations in the matter and befriended them. Now the detective had made it clear that my brother must go to him at the police building on Harrison or he would come looking for him and that would not be good.

I found the alley which, by the card from Clara, was the address for the rooms inhabited by Alden and Mr. Marco. It was shabby and filled with garbage that overflowed the wooden boxes affixed to the ground. Surely they would not have stayed in such a depressing place on Christmas Day. I picked my way around the trash trying to save the hem of my good frock. It had been a present from my mother the year before, a wine colored taffeta trimmed with black velvet. I saw it was already spoiled and it reminded me that I could have been in Boston in a warm house surrounded by friends and relatives as I had been the year before. At that moment I deeply regretted that my brother and I had not returned to Boston with my mother on that train. I feared that Alden did know Mr. Hanrahan. I feared what I would find out when I questioned him and, perhaps even more, I feared what would happen if I could not find my brother before the police did. Apprehensive, and convinced this trip was in vain, I climbed a rickety set of steps to the second floor and knocked on the door. It was opened slightly and a single eye peered out.

"Emily." Alden pulled open the door when he recognized me. He looked pale to me, but so full of life, so much the Alden I remembered, I pushed open the door and hugged him. He returned the embrace as if he, too, had been worried.

"Alden, Clara gave me your address." I stepped back and held him at arm's length. "You came to me at Hull House but you left. What happened? Why didn't you stay?"

He looked over his shoulder and I could hear heavy breathing somewhere in the background but he motioned me in. It was a small room with a table and wooden chairs and a pile of bedclothes on the floor as if he slept there. A blanket was strung across a doorway.

"Is someone else here?" I could hear labored breathing.

"It's Marco. He's sick."

"I am sorry to hear that." I spoke quietly so as not to disturb him. The poverty of the room appalled me. It was a shock to see my brother's familiar leather suitcase standing in the corner of such a destitute place. I reached out and grasped his arm. "Alden, are you all right?"

He grinned. Then the worried look returned to his face.

"I'm fine, Em, really. It may not look that way, but, really, I am quite well. I came here with Marco. He wanted to be with his own people. This is just temporary. He hasn't been working since they broke down the Ferris Wheel and carted it away. He's done some work in saloons and, yes, some gambling, but that is just temporary." He followed my gaze around the room. I was trying hard not to be critical but I was alarmed at the broken windowpane and the peeling wallpaper. He grinned again. "I guess I haven't done such a good job taking care of myself, but it's all right, Emily, really. Marco got a job as a barker for a vaudeville show but then he got sick. He said it was nothing. He was just getting old. But I'm worried, Emily. He's been like this for a week. He has a fever and now he has a rash of some kind but he refuses to go to the hospital. He won't even let me in the room except to pass him a bowl of soup. He is so stubborn. I don't know what to do."

It was not like my brother to be so worried.

"Alden, why did you leave? Why didn't you wait?" I wanted him to tell me.

He looked down. "You weren't there. I promised Clara before she left." He looked me straight in the eye then. "She made me promise I would go and see you. But when you weren't there, I had second thoughts. When I heard you were at church services, I thought you would only scold me for not going, so I thought I'd better come back later." He turned away and motioned me in to sit on a dilapidated sofa pushed against the wall behind the door. "Come in, Em, sit down."

I took a seat as he closed the door. "Alden, a man was killed in the octagon room at Hull House this morning." I swallowed. "He was beaten to death. It was horrid. He was sitting at the desk. It's just through the left door as you come in. Alice would have told you to wait there. Did you see the man? Was he still alive when you got there? He was a Mr. Hanrahan, did you know him?"

With a sigh he sank into a wooden chair he pulled out to face me. "No. I didn't see anyone. Hanrahan? I don't think so."

"He was from Boston. He might have known Father. Think, did you know him? Do you recognize the name?"

"No, no."

"Oh, Alden, he must have been dead when you were there. You didn't see him? You didn't see anything?"

"No. I didn't see anything. I didn't go into the room. I turned around and left."

"Alden, you must speak to Detective Whitbread. You must go to the Harrison Street station immediately and if he's not there, wait for him. I'll go with you. If you don't he'll come looking for you and he said that would not be good. He said it would be much better if you came in voluntarily. We need to go now." I stood up.

"I can't leave Marco, Emily. He's sick. Worse than he was before. I'm afraid to leave him." The place was permeated with smells of sweat and sickness and I did not like the sound of Marco's breathing at all. I stepped towards the doorway.

"No, Emily, he'll have a fit if you go in there."

"Alden, I know you don't want me to interfere but, please, let me help."

He hesitated a moment, then nodded. I was at the blanket by then so I pushed it aside and stepped to the bed. Marco moved with a grunt but, as I couldn't see anything, I stepped to the window and shoved open the curtain to the dusk outside.

Turning back I had a startling glance of Marco's face covered with sores before he rolled away.

"Go away," he shouted heavily, his broad back to me.

"But Marco…"

"Go away. Take him with you. Go away." His labored breathing filled the room.

I hesitated then replaced the curtains and went out to Alden. "He needs a doctor."

"He'll throw a fit."

"He must have a doctor, Alden. Stay here, I'll get Dr. Chapman." I hoped the doctor would still be at Hull House so

I hurried as quickly as I dared on the ice-covered walks. When I found him, I took him aside and told him what I had seen. He looked grim and grabbing his satchel he came away with me.

Alden was waiting for us with a frown on his face. Dr. Chapman went in to Marco and we heard the older man shout and curse but the noise eventually dropped to a murmur. Finally, the doctor returned.

"It's smallpox," he said. "There have been the beginnings of an outbreak. I've seen four other cases, all of them related in some way to the Midway." He swallowed. "It is a disease that is horrendously contagious. Have either of you ever had smallpox or been vaccinated?" Normally the least anxious of men, he was agitated. He seemed ready to despair of our answer and I felt his horror as he looked at me with wide eyes.

"I don't think..." Alden began.

"Yes. We were vaccinated. It was before my father died, maybe seven years ago. There was an epidemic in Boston."

"Thank God."

"What must we do?"

"He will have to be moved to Cook County Hospital. They have an isolation ward. I will go and find a telephone. You and Alden gather up his clothes and blankets and anything that may carry infection. We will need to burn them."

When the sick man was taken away in a wagon, the doctor went with him. Afterwards, Alden and I started a fire in an empty lot two doors down from the building. We fed it with almost everything from their rooms and watched as it burned. The night was clear and still but very cold. The dirty clouds that had smothered the city during the afternoon had blown through. Looking up we could see millions of stars above the rooftops.

"Alden, you must go to Detective Whitbread. You must go tonight. I can come with you."

"No. It's better if I go alone, Emily. I will find him. I promise."

"But afterwards, what will you do? You cannot stay here." I was calculating how much money I had and how far it could be expected to go in supporting him.

"Dr. Chapman told me to go to Hull House. He said there is room there in the men's dormitory, at least temporarily."

"Oh, thank goodness. But, Alden, tell me, is it true that you stayed in Chicago because you thought you would find Michael Flaherty, the man who murdered our father? Clara told me you did."

He was pushing the burning materials around with a metal bar he found in the rubbish. "Yes."

"Why didn't you tell me?"

"I wasn't sure. There's nothing you can do anyhow, Em. This is for me to do. I heard it on the Midway. You know the man Weaver? Oh, I know, you think he's despicable. He probably is. He ran cattle out in the West you know. There were range wars and he rode with a rough bunch. When things settled down there was no place for him and he went back east with some of the others. They were rough and ready men able to handle a fight. They found work at factories where there were strikes, protecting the strike breakers, from what he told me." As always, I was amazed at what people would tell Alden. "Anyhow he was working for the horse trolley owners when they had the strike in Boston. He was protecting the nonunion drivers who were attacked by the men in that trial, so he knew all about it. He's the one who saw Flaherty on the Midway. He recognized him and knew he was a fugitive. But the man saw Weaver and he ran away. He's somewhere down here in the tenements. Twice I nearly got to him. He's a driver so when he's desperate he gets work doing that. I nearly got him, Emily. I will yet."

Looking at my brother by the light of the fire I saw a fierce determination I had never seen in him before. The man who had shot my father had never been more than a shadowy figure in my imagination, the embodiment of the results of a cruel and unyielding system by which he had been formed, a desperate man striking out in ignorance to destroy someone who would have helped him. The thought of my slight, agile, little brother physically face to face with such a monster was truly alarming. I wanted to warn Alden of the danger but to do so risked igniting the anger I had seen in the train station. I swallowed my words.

"You are sure you don't know Hanrahan? He and Weaver both work for Mr. Franklin."

"I don't think so, I may have seen him. What did he look like?"

All I could picture was the bloody head resting on the desk beside the candlestick. Suddenly I was very tired. "It doesn't matter. Just go and talk to Detective Whitbread."

"It will be all right, Emily. Don't worry. Come on. I'll take you back to the settlement. It's on the way."

As I took his arm to start the trek back to Hull House my mind was fuzzy with worry about the dead man and why he would have asked for me and who could have done such a terrible deed in Hull House. I thought vaguely that the coming days would be full of worry about that. I had no idea that soon enough we would all be too preoccupied with a smallpox epidemic to worry about almost anything else.

ELEVEN

"It's a note from Dr. Chapman. He has gone to the county hospital but he asks that we call a meeting of all residents tonight. We'll have to put a notice in the boxes. Oh, dear, I guess that won't do, will it?" Jane Addams received the note in the sitting room area of her bedroom suite on the second floor. She and I retreated there after breakfast on the day after Christmas to deal with the slew of telegrams, letters and visitors that began arriving as the news of the murder got out. Normally, we would have transacted this business in the front parlor downstairs and would have distributed a notice of the meeting to each resident's pigeonhole mailbox in the octagon room but a police officer was still guarding that part of the house.

"I'll print a big notice and post it in the dining room," I suggested. "And another by the front door. Dr. Chapman was very worried about the smallpox last night."

"I pray the Lord will spare us that. Things are going to be difficult enough as it is with that poor man's death." She was still staring at an editorial in the Tribune that questioned the whole idea of the settlement house based on the dead man found there on Christmas Day. *Was it really a breeding ground for fanatics?* the newspaper asked, as if one of the residents had battered Hanrahan to death in a fit of zeal. The incoming telegrams and letters were sorted into two piles in front of her, the thicker one being protests, while the slimmer one consisted of condolences and support.

"It's Alderman Powers that's behind that," I told her, pointing at the newspaper. "He'll have planted that idea or gotten somebody to write it, most likely." It angered me to see Hull House residents portrayed as a collection of crackpots and fanatics when I knew they were not. I might think them ineffectual but never evil like that.

Jennie Dow poked her head in the doorway. "The detective is back. He asked to see Mrs. Kelley downstairs, where it happened."

"The detective is well informed. Florence only arrived back a short while ago. Let her know." When Jennie had disappeared Miss Addams frowned at a third stack of unopened telegrams. "I really must go down with her. I cannot let her face this alone."

"Please, let me go. I know Detective Whitbread. I have worked with him." I was anxious to make sure he had spoken to my brother and believed him. I had not heard from or seen Alden that morning and could only hope he had done as he promised me the night before.

"Yes, yes. You go, Emily. I will see to this." She put her hand on the stack of negative letters, yet she seemed to be looking off at something far away. "It is a very terrible thing that has happened, Emily, and we must face up to the questions. What if, after all, they are right? What if it turns out that our very tolerance, our openness, our attempts to build a community without reference to any strict doctrinal faith, what if that has led us to this violence?"

"It hasn't, it couldn't. No one at Hull House is responsible for this terrible act. You'll see."

She turned towards me, looking into my eyes. "But *you* must see, my dear Emily, that if you are wrong and if one of us did do this, then we would have to question the very foundations of what we are doing here. I know that you yourself have sometimes questioned the value of the work here. You don't like to say it, but I can sense it. Don't you see that the very reason for us to be here is to demonstrate to the violent, intolerant world beyond our doors that it is possible to live in peace and civility, even among those who are most poor and most alien? If we cannot show this by our actions then we have failed and our critics are right." She sighed. "But go and fetch Florence. We must assist your detective friend to discover the truth of what happened here no matter what the consequences."

I hurried out the door towards the back of the house. This death was like a blot of ink that had been spilt on the surface of Hull House. No matter what the outcome of the investigation, I could not see how it could ever be expunged. It seemed as if in the matter of a day all the work and dreams of Miss Addams and her friends could be ruined forever.

I caught Florence Kelley at the back stairs that led down to a corner of the study. I clambered down ahead of her before I realized she had not intended to enter that way. To go by way of the front staircase and in from the front hallway might have been more correct for the formal interview that would follow but I was anxious to see the detective and gauge what his reaction had been to my brother. I wanted to be sure that Alden really had found Detective Whitbread and spoken to him as he promised. I feared he might have disappeared again instead. I was too impatient for formalities.

After a moment of hesitation, Florence Kelley followed me down the back stairs. Whitbread looked up from the desk in the front room and rose. There was a uniformed policeman with a notebook beside him. The beefy young man looked unaccustomed to his task, fingering a stub of pencil.

"Ah, Miss Cabot. And I assume this is Mrs. Kelley." Whitbread was looking beyond me to Florence.

"Detective Whitbread, my brother did find you last night, didn't he? We were delayed. Mr. Marco is very ill and we had to bring the doctor. He was taken away when it turned out to be smallpox." I noticed the younger man flush.

Whitbread pulled his eyes from his assessment of my companion. He was cool towards me. "I interviewed Mr. Cabot last night. He stated that he did not enter the rooms and that he went away without seeing Mr. Hanrahan, therefore he could be of no help. Please, be seated." He gestured towards one hard backed chair facing the desk and quickly placed another beside it. "Sweeney, since Miss Cabot has joined us, I will ask her to take notes." He removed the notebook and pencil from the policeman's hands. "You will go door-to-door to question the neighbors as to whether they saw anything of use yesterday. They were questioned before but it is always possible that someone was missed or someone has remembered a relevant fact overnight." He handed me the writing materials. When the young officer left, Whitbread turned his attention to Mrs. Kelley, who answered briefly that she left Hull House without seeing the murdered man. She took an earlier train at Miss Addams's suggestion and spent the day and overnight with friends and her children. She did not hear of the tragedy until her return earlier this morning.

There was silence when she finished her statement except for my pencil scratching on the pad in my hand. I caught up to the speech with my scribbles as Whitbread tapped his long fingers impatiently on a manila envelope placed on the desk in front of him.

"Did you know the dead man, Mrs. Kelley?"

"I have had dealings with him on several occasions in the course of performing my duties as chief factory inspector for the state."

The tapping stopped. "I see. And would you describe your relations as cordial?"

"Not at all. Adversarial, rather. Mr. Hanrahan represented the interests of the capitalists who own or profit from the work done in the factories. As such he opposed our attempts to enforce legislation that protects the workers from exploitation. His job was to thwart our activity."

"Would you say you were on bad terms with the man then?"

"No more so than you must be, Detective, when you enforce laws that are unpopular with some."

"I understand from Mr. Hanrahan's co-workers that the disagreements between the two of you were sometimes bitter."

I would have protested this statement but Florence Kelley looked him straight in the eye, a stone wall to his assaults. "There were certainly strong disagreements. I am not in the habit, however, of clubbing over the head those who violate the eight-hour rule or any other regulation in order to enforce compliance. No more than you are liable to use such methods, I am sure."

I could not tell whether she was being sincere or sardonic with that remark. Detective Whitbread opened the envelope in front of him and slid out some papers.

"You are not currently living with your husband and children, Mrs. Kelley. Is that correct?"

I was outraged at this question about her personal affairs but she seemed prepared for it. "I am divorced from my husband. My children are lodged with Mr. Henry Lloyd and his family in Glencoe where they attend school. I fail to see the relevance of this information to your current investigation."

Whitbread was fingering the papers in his hands and now he turned them around to be upright in her direction and offered them to her. "These papers were found in Mr. Hanrahan's office files. Perhaps you would like to look at them."

She took them without comment and for several minutes she read through them one at a time, shuffling each page to the back as she finished it. At one point she gave a very small snort. In the end she turned the set around and handed them back to Detective Whitbread.

"As you can see, Mr. Hanrahan was in communication with your husband. Were you aware that Hanrahan and his employers had approached your husband about these matters?"

It occurred to me that Whitbread had seized on the opportunity to dismiss the young officer and have me take notes in an attempt to keep a discussion of Florence Kelley's personal matters as private as possible in a murder investigation. But Florence disdained the effort. Her neck and back were stiff and her tones clipped as she responded. "My divorce decree was granted on the grounds of desertion, Detective. My husband abandoned me and my children while we were living in the state of New York. It was the fact that such action is grounds for divorce in Illinois but not in New York that forced me to move my family here. In view of that fact, I hardly think Mr. Hanrahan and his employers would have any success in appealing to my ex-husband's parental feelings." She nodded towards the papers. "Custody of his children can hardly be considered an enticement to a man who has already abandoned them." There was deep scorn in the tone of her voice.

I hesitated to transcribe her words but Whitbread folded his hands over the papers, ignoring me. "A man may be enticed by the opportunity to inflict pain in such a case, Mrs. Kelley, without regard to any actual outcome of his actions." She did move slightly at that, as if she had been pinched. "In any case, that was not my question. My question is, were you aware of these attempts by Mr. Hanrahan, on behalf of his employers, to contact your husband in an attempt to get him to commence legal proceedings to have your children removed from your custody, on the grounds that your current living arrangements and activities were unsuitable?"

How very unfair. I knew that it was a struggle for Florence. She needed the money from her job as factory inspector and at the same time she was enrolled in the study of law at Northwestern University. She was deeply indebted to Henry Lloyd and his wife for providing lodging and schooling for her three children. She had never told me that her husband had abandoned them. As I scribbled the notes my mind was seething with indignant protests. But I was not called upon to answer. Florence Kelley was, and her answer was "No."

"You are quite sure, Mrs. Kelley that you did not see or talk to Mr. Hanrahan when he came here yesterday? You did not, for instance, come down that back staircase and come upon him unexpectedly in this room?"

"No."

"Mr. Hanrahan asked for Miss Cabot when he came. I understand when he saw her in your company about a week ago he attempted to warn her about associating with you and others as something of which her dead father would not approve." My pencil slid off the page at this mention of my own name but I brought it back firmly continuing to write with clenched teeth. "Did you witness that admonition?"

"Yes."

"Do you think that Mr. Hanrahan's purpose in visiting Miss Cabot may have been to warn her against association with you?"

"I have no idea what the purpose of Mr. Hanrahan's visit may have been."

"And you are quite sure you did not see Mr. Hanrahan or anyone else leaving or entering this room yesterday?"

"Yes."

Silence reigned as Whitbread carefully returned the papers to the manila envelope. At last he spoke again. "I will assure you, Mrs. Kelley, that these letters will remain confidential and in my possession unless and until it is manifest that they are pertinent to the circumstances of Mr. Hanrahan's death."

"I am sure you will do whatever you need to do, Detective. I am sure that Alderman Powers and Mr. Hanrahan's employers will find it advantageous to use any means at their disposal to discredit my office, this settlement house, or any other institution or individual who dares to challenge their methods of achieving the profits which they consider their God given right to have. I am quite well aware of the powers arrayed against us and I will not be surprised if they are exercised. I will not hold you to your promise of discretion, Detective. I seriously doubt that you have the power to withstand the pressures that will be exerted upon you."

"You are mistaken, Mrs. Kelley. The investigation of a murder is not subject to the type of political influence you fear." I thought it was curious that he used that term since Florence Kelley did not seem to me to be afraid. She seemed cold, disillusioned and grim, but not afraid. He went on. "My power is the power of truth, Mrs. Kelley. I will discover the truth of Mr. Hanrahan's death. That I do promise you."

Florence raised an eyebrow but she stood up and nodded to Whitbread before exiting by the door to the front hallway. When she was gone I handed the notebook back to Detective Whitbread.

"You don't really believe she could have killed the man, do you?" I asked.

He stared after her, and with an uncharacteristic gesture the hardened police detective closed his eyes, shaking his head back and forth as he sighed.

TWELVE

I was unable to get away from my duties to look for my brother all day. At least I knew he had talked to Detective Whitbread but it was evening before I actually saw Alden again. The crisis meeting was held in the dining room of Hull House. Several of the long wooden refectory tables were pulled together for the twenty women residents and nearly a dozen men in attendance. Dr. Chapman spoke first.

"The physicians at Cook County Hospital report the isolation ward is full. Apparently the infection was first seen in the Midway and has moved to the West Side. They are especially concerned about the sweatshops since the number of garment workers infected is on the rise. The situation is out of hand and we are facing an epidemic."

"But haven't the local authorities been informed?" Miss Addams asked.

The doctor looked tired. "Apparently they are resisting taking strenuous action. With the state of unemployment that has existed since the financial downturn last summer there is a great fear that even more people will be thrown out of work and made destitute if quarantine measures are strictly enforced."

"But if the family members of the sick go to the factories they will only spread the problem," one of the men commented.

"Exactly. Inaction is leading to a crisis of terrible proportions."

"It is already prevalent in the sweatshops," Mary Kenney reported. She was a tall, imposing woman print setter who worked at a union shop. She and her mother ran a cooperative living arrangement with about twelve young working girls in a nearby tenement. It was called the Jane Club after Miss Addams. Like Maria Maglione and so many women of the area most of the girls worked in tenement sweatshops. "I hear of more of them getting sick every day. And of course if they don't work they don't get paid, so it is only when they are very ill that they stay home. And there is no vaccination going on."

"They all fear vaccination," someone else added.

"It is indefensible," Florence Kelley proclaimed. She had made no mention of her interview with Detective Whitbread after he departed. She had made no mention of the murder investigation at all. She refused to be drawn into speculation and spent most of the day at her office. "Well, we'll put a stop to that. As of tomorrow we will identify any workshop with infected workers and any that send out the work to homes where there is illness. As soon as we can prove exposure to infection we will destroy all goods on the premises. That, if nothing else, will produce action." There was a glitter in her eyes and, as one of her deputies, I foresaw long days tracking down stores of garments produced by infected hands. The fact that those who would be most angered by this type of rigorous enforcement would be the very employers of Hanrahan who were trying to attack her personally through her ex-husband was a fact that left her unaffected. There was a need to take measures against the epidemic and she would take them.

"What about the children?" Miss Addams asked.

"They are most at risk," Dr. Chapman told her. "Only those who had the disease in the old country or were vaccinated at Ellis Island on arrival here are safe. Children born here have no protection as there has been no enforcement of the vaccination laws."

"It is an outrage." People joined in protesting the state of affairs.

"It is the Board of Health then that must be alerted," Miss Addams continued. "We must discover as many victims as possible and report them to the Board so all of the family and neighbors in a tenement may be vaccinated."

This was considered a feasible course of action and it was discussed with excitement. Someone came up with the idea of marking the infected tenements with a yellow placard and this was also accepted. But Dr. Chapman sounded a note of caution.

"Unfortunately there is a great if unfounded fear of vaccination among the people, and Cook County is about to establish a pest house on the prairie west of here. Strict controls will mean infected persons will be taken there and many will fear that. I have seen it before in Baltimore. They even conceal the children in the fear they will be taken away."

"The children. We will have to require that all of the children in the kindergarten be vaccinated," Miss Addams announced.

"But some of them will resist," a voice protested.

"We must. Don't you see? Some may fear it and stop sending their little ones but eventually they will see that the vaccinated children do not become ill and they will give in."

"It would help for them to see that," Dr. Chapman agreed. He lifted up his satchel and placed it on the table. "They will set a good example, and in that line, since we are all so much abroad among the people here, I brought vaccine so that any of us who has not been vaccinated may receive that protection before another moment passes."

This announcement was followed by a vigorous discussion during which it was discovered that only three of the present residents required the procedure. A number of people including Miss Addams and Florence Kelley had been vaccinated before going abroad in the past several years. Mary Kenney, Jennie Dow, the kindergarten teacher, and Milton Bierly, our very vocal socialist, were the ones who lacked protection. Mary offered to go first, bravely rolling up her sleeve as we all watched. I noticed that Mr. Bierly appeared very apprehensive. Alden, who was seated beside him, took his arm. "You next, Milt."

I had been relieved to see my brother come in the door for the meeting. In the course of the day I had been able to discover that he was given a place in the men's dormitory but I had not actually seen him. In a brief exchange before the meeting he merely shrugged off my questions concerning his interrogation by Detective Whitbread. I suppressed my exasperation with him when I saw he was followed by Milton Bierly with whom he appeared to have struck up a friendship. How like my brother to become involved with yet another associate of questionable merit. The man who had so often spoken in ringing terms of the need for violent demonstrations by the workers appeared sick with apprehension now as Dr. Chapman prepared the next injection. But Alden assisted him to the chair that Mary Kenney had vacated.

"What of your mother?" the doctor asked Miss Kenney before turning to his new patient.

"She suffered the disease as a child."

Nodding, Dr. Chapman returned to his preparations. Only then did he perceive the apprehensions of Mr. Bierly who was watching him with wide eyes.

"Oh," he moaned as the doctor helped him roll up his sleeve. "Don't you have a smaller needle?"

They laughed and Alden slapped his knee. "Think of it as a bee sting. As for the vaccination I received, I can't even remember it. But I'll tell you about a bee I met one summer at the seashore. This was the biggest bee you have ever seen. I tell you honestly, it was the size of a robin. A very large robin."

Bierly squealed and turned to the doctor with an accusing stare. "You didn't warn me."

"It's done now, comrade. You see, it was nothing. Now, Miss Dow, if you will."

Alden grinned and slapped his new friend on the back. Somehow it made me uneasy to see my brother on such intimate terms with Milton Bierly. It was always thus with Alden. He made friends and sank into a new environment like water soaking into newly turned earth. But it was in just such a way that he befriended Mr. Marco and the other associates that Detective Whitbread warned against. He was never the least bit circumspect in his choice of companions. Mr. Bierly had been at Hull House for almost a year, but, aside from that, I knew very little about him.

As the room emptied out I blocked Alden's way, determined to speak to him about his interview with the police. I waited for him to end his conversation with Milton Bierly. When he finally could ignore me no longer, his companion showed no sign of leaving us. In fact, he hovered as if anxious to overhear.

"Alden, I must speak with you."

Alden frowned. He would have avoided me if he could. There were a few people lingering in the doorway now and Mrs. Kelley sat at the end of the table still sorting through a pile of papers she had brought with her and consulted whenever she lost interest in the proceedings of the meeting. I led my brother to a corner of the room. Mr. Bierly followed.

"What is it, Em? We were going back to make up the placards."

"Tell me about your interview with the police. You found Detective Whitbread all right?"

"There's nothing to tell, Emily. I went to the station and told the detective that I left without seeing anything. He questioned me for some time but I could tell him nothing of use so he let me go. I came back and Doctor Chapman fixed me up to share a room with Milton here. Milton Bierly, you are acquainted with my sister, Miss Emily Cabot, I believe."

Milton Bierly stepped forward eagerly. "Of course, Miss Cabot. I am happy to share lodgings with your brother. I hope to convert him to our struggle against the evils of capitalism and the oppression of the workers."

It seemed to me that my brother with his easy manners and love of entertainment was an unlikely recruit to Mr. Bierly's crusade. As I looked at the earnest young man in his too clean workingman's clothes, I saw the figure of Mrs. Kelley beyond him and knew she must be able to hear us. It seemed to me most unfair that she and my brother should be so obviously under suspicion by the police while Mr. Bierly must have had at least equal opportunity to do the deed.

"I suppose you must have been questioned by the police as well, Mr. Bierly. After all, you were acquainted with the dead man." I proceeded to recount to my brother the confrontation I had witnessed in the factory and I did not hesitate to describe the ignominious way in which Mr. Bierly had been dragged up the stairs and thrown onto the floor by Weaver. I saw the tips of Mr. Bierly's ears redden at my description of his humiliation. It made me wonder whether, after all, he might have come upon the unfortunate Hanrahan and taken his revenge.

"I suppose the police must know that if you wished to retaliate for that treatment, Mr. Bierly, you would have acted against Mr. Weaver rather than Mr. Hanrahan. Is that so?"

My brother was eyeing me warily and with disapproval. "I know Weaver," he commented as if making an excuse for Mr. Bierly. "He is not someone to be provoked."

Milton Bierly was quite red in the face now. "Hanrahan was as much at fault as the other, even more so. If it weren't for the machinations of the Hanrahans and others like him the owners could not succeed in oppressing the workers. It's no surprise he ended so. It is men like him who provoke violence by leaving the workers no other choice but to rise together and take what is rightfully theirs. He was a traitor to his brothers. He was a traitor to mankind. In fact, we would have to say that he deserved to die."

"This was no act of a mob of angry workingmen, Mr. Bierly. It was done singly and in secret in this house. You were here when it happened, though, weren't you? You were downstairs in the metal shop. We heard pounding when we came in. What were you doing down there on Christmas morning?"

His eyes opened wider and he looked at me as if he had had cold water dashed in his face.

"Emily," my brother began to reprove me.

But Mr. Bierly interrupted. "What I was doing had no relevance. That is what I told them."

"And you didn't come upstairs? You didn't talk to or see Mr. Hanrahan?" I hurried on before Alden could stop me.

Milton Bierly stared at me. He had a hurt look on his face as if I had slapped him. "No, Miss Cabot. I did not see the man. I assure you, I did not know he was in the house. You must excuse me now. I must go and tend to the placards your brother mentioned." He bowed his head slightly and left.

Alden was glaring at me. "Emily, you are a fool."

"I'm a fool? You are the one so easily seduced by new acquaintances no matter how little you know about them."

He snorted. "Emily, you saw he could barely stand the sight of a needle. Do you really think Milton Bierly could bludgeon a man to death and then hide it?"

"Someone did."

"Oh, I know how he talks. Don't you know bluster when you hear it? He didn't kill Hanrahan. Leave the interrogations to Whitbread, Emily. And leave us alone. At least we're trying to be useful."

I was seething with resentment as he turned on his heel and strode out of the room. But when I took a step to follow Mrs. Kelley called to me brusquely. She remained seated when I walked over to the table. "Miss Cabot, you were very harsh to Mr. Bierly just now. Was that necessary?"

"Necessary? You heard him. You heard what he said. He advocates violence. You've heard him say as much many times. Yet the police question you and my brother. Isn't Mr. Bierly by far the most likely suspect?"

She looked up at me from under her thick dark eyebrows. "Mr. Bierly has certainly mastered the rhetoric of those who would advocate violence but his actions are far from following the form of his notions. You saw him at that factory. Do you think him capable of striking out? He is not even able to defend himself, never mind fomenting acts of calculated violence."

"He could not defend himself against someone like Mr. Weaver, but might not his anger and frustration at his own inability there lead him to strike out against a lesser target like Hanrahan?"

"You think he struck down Hanrahan because he was incapable of striking back at Weaver? I see. Tell me, Emily, do you admire this man, Weaver? Do you think him superior to Mr. Bierly for his ability to act on his violent impulses rather than talking about them, perhaps? Is that it?"

"Certainly not. He is a vile man."

"Yet it is by the strength of men like him that the Franklins and Powers of this world are able to get what they want. That's what you think, isn't it?"

"Well, it's true, isn't it? How can we oppose men like that when they can employ men like Weaver?"

"How can we oppose them with only men like Mr. Bierly on our side, you mean. How can we oppose them without also employing men like Weaver ourselves?"

"No. I don't mean that at all."

"We will never succeed by recruiting champions equal in strength to the bullies employed by our foes, Emily. There can be no victory that way. There are no champions for us. We must do this ourselves, you and I and Jane Addams. All of us. We must do it with the forces of the law. It is only by creating and enforcing laws that we can protect the weaker from the stronger."

"Of course, I do know that. But the death of Mr. Hanrahan right here in Hull House has brought the violence to us. We must find out who did that awful thing and expel them. Don't you agree?"

She looked down at her papers. "You believe someone here killed the man, Hanrahan?"

"I don't know. But we must find out. And Mr. Bierly was here in the house. The rest of us had gone to church."

She looked up then, straight into my eyes. "I was also here and so was your brother. And before you assume that Mr. Bierly is the only one who could have done this, you should question why Hanrahan asked for you when he came to the door. And you should also question why your brother claims he came and left without seeing the dead man when I saw him standing over the body of Mr. Hanrahan before I left yesterday morning."

THIRTEEN

She refused to say any more on the topic and my urgent entreaties were met with stony silence. Furious with Florence Kelley, with myself, and most of all with my all too charming younger brother, I rushed to my room for my coat and hat. I would go after him and force him to tell me the truth that very night. As I hurried down the front stairs, suddenly Detective Whitbread stepped out from the front parlor, blocking my way.

"Miss Cabot, if I might have a moment of your time." His long arm gestured towards the room where the dead man had been found and I had no choice but to precede him into the front parlor. But I ignored the straight backed chairs in front of the desk and paced towards the library, past the opening to the octagon room. I knew that I should tell the detective what I had just learned. Both Mrs. Kelley and my brother had lied to him. Both of them had seen the dead man. Both of them had been in the room with the corpse, at the very least. What else had Alden lied about?

When I turned to pace back, the detective stood behind the desk leaning forward balanced on his long fingered hands splayed across the desk. "You are quite sure that you were not acquainted with Mr. Hanrahan, Miss Cabot? Beyond the meeting a week ago which you described?"

"Certainly." My mind filled with my doubts about Florence and Alden I did not know what he meant.

"I have had news from Boston, Miss Cabot. It would seem that Mr. Hanrahan was at one time employed by the South Boston Horse Car Company."

I stared at him, then reached for the desk and lowered myself into one of the chairs. The South Boston Horse Car Company. It was the strike and violence that accompanied it at that company that led to my father's death. Detective Whitbread knew that. I had told him the story. Suddenly I felt again that surge of regret and resentment about the act that cut off my father's life before his time.

"Five years ago," Whitbread summarized, "the drivers for the South Boston Horse Car Company went on strike. The owners brought in replacements and hired protection. The strikers attacked the carriages from roof tops where they had hidden bricks and rocks. Several people were hurt and three of the strikers were arrested and charged with the assaults. One of them was Sean Flaherty. The case came before Judge John Cabot, your father. During the trial your father was killed one night in the study of his home. Michael Flaherty, brother of the accused, was seen leaving the house but he fled before he could be arrested."

I looked at my friend and mentor, Detective Whitbread, unable to comprehend.

"Mr. Hanrahan, it seems, listed the South Boston Horse Car Company as a former employer. We will be contacting them, of course, but in the meantime I want to be assured that neither you nor your brother had prior acquaintance with Hanrahan when he was connected with that company. It is, you will admit, a rather startling development."

"Mr. Hanrahan worked for that company? He was involved with the trial?"

"That I cannot say yet, Miss Cabot. There has been another strange development. Our attempts to contact Mr. Hanrahan's family have failed. The address at which his wife was supposed to reside has been vacated and there is no news of where the family has gone. We have asked for assistance from the local authorities but so far they have been unable to help us. It seems a most suspicious circumstance, you will agree."

"I don't know what to say, Detective. I had no idea that Mr. Hanrahan was in any way connected with that case."

"What about your brother, Miss Cabot? He said he remained in Chicago in order to track down this man, Flaherty. Is it possible that he did not know Hanrahan? Could he have forgotten such a connection? Of course, it is possible Hanrahan was actually known to him under another name. But since your brother did not see the man yesterday, perhaps he could not recognize him from the name alone."

Alden. Alden had lied about seeing the dead man. But I could not tell Detective Whitbread that. I swallowed. "As soon as I see my brother I will ask him to contact you," I promised. "I do not know what this connection of Mr. Hanrahan to the past can mean. I will write to my mother," that seemed an inspiration. "Perhaps she will know the name."

"That could be most helpful, Miss Cabot. Please have your brother contact me at the precinct station house. We will be releasing these rooms back to Miss Addams tomorrow. I see you were on your way out. Do not let me keep you."

It was cold and dark outside and my urgent enquiries at the men's residence eventually led me to a building a few blocks away where Alden, Milton Bierly and another man were attempting to post a yellow placard indicating quarantine. They shushed me at my arrival and Alden jumped down to usher me out of hearing.

"Come away, Emily. We don't want to be heard. They had someone moved out to the hospital from here today." He took my arm and led me to the next corner.

"Alden, you lied to me."

He frowned, glancing over his shoulder but the others were busy attaching the sign and we were out of earshot.

"You went into the room. You saw Hanrahan dead. You lied to me, to the police. Mrs. Kelley saw you, Alden."

His brow furrowed and his bright blue eyes regarded me sharply. I could not imagine what he was thinking. That he could lie to me was bad enough but if he could lie to Detective Whitbread, I didn't know what he might not do. "Did you know that man, Alden? Did you recognize him and lie about that, too?"

"Emily, calm down." He glanced over his shoulder again.

"Alden, what have you done? Why did you lie?" I was trying to stave off an awful doubt. I was trying to block out an image of my brother Alden raising and lowering his hands over the dead man, beating him with the candlestick as Detective Whitbread had acted out the deed.

Alden grabbed me by the shoulders. "Stop it, Emily. I didn't kill that man. I didn't know him. Yes, I did go into the room, but when I saw that man …" He let go of me and shook his head. "I just thought how like my luck that when I came to see you, only because I promised Clara Shea, when I finally came, that I should find such a thing, such an awful thing. I know you, Emily. I know what you would think. You'd think I was responsible somehow, even though I had never seen the man before. You'd think it was my fault again, that my coming had caused it. I knew it would only bring you trouble, that I would only bring you trouble, so I left. I didn't know the man, Emily. I swear it to you. It had nothing to do with me. I left. I thought by leaving it would spare you. I can see it was another mistake but that is all it was, a mistake."

"You still say you never saw that man before? Oh, Alden. How can I believe you? How can anyone believe you when you lie so easily?"

"I'm not lying. I did not know that man."

"But Detective Whitbread found out he worked for the South Boston Horse Car Company, Alden. You told Clara you were looking for the man who killed Father, for Michael Flaherty." I grabbed his arm. "Was that who he really was, Alden? Was he really Flaherty? Did you kill him when you realized it? You have to tell me."

He was staring over my head. I grabbed his other arm and shook him. Finally he pulled away. "Stop it, Emily. No, I didn't kill him but I'll bet I know who did."

"Alden?" I was appalled. I was relieved to hear him deny killing the man. It was my worst fear that I had blurted out—that Hanrahan had really been Michael Flaherty and that my brother had killed him. But I was appalled by the fact that he seemed to know what was behind this.

"Silly Emily, don't you see? Flaherty must have done it. If Hanrahan really did work for the South Boston Horse Car Company he would have recognized Flaherty. He was a driver, along with his brother. Hanrahan must have recognized him. He knew you were the daughter of the man Flaherty had killed. He was going to tell you Flaherty was here, in Chicago, but the man found out and killed him. Don't you see?"

FOURTEEN

This time, I did not have to plead with my brother to speak to Detective Whitbread. On the contrary, he was so convinced that Flaherty was in Chicago and that he must have been responsible for the death of Hanrahan that he insisted on racing off to find the police detective that night. I wanted to believe him. I wanted to be reassured by his reaction. He made it clear to me before he left, however, that he had no intention of exposing his own former lie or that of Mrs. Kelley. He insisted it would only confuse the issue to admit that either of them had been in the room with the dead man. I could do nothing to convince him otherwise and I dreaded facing Mrs. Kelley on the topic again. Reluctantly, I withdrew my demand that he tell the truth about that. He was convinced the phantom Flaherty was the villain but somehow I was uneasy with this assumption. I trusted Detective Whitbread to sort out the truth of it however, and I wanted to believe that the act had been committed by someone unconnected with Hull House.

We had begun to see a decrease in participation in the Hull House classes and entertainments. At first I was grateful for the respite that allowed me to work on the maps and papers but it worried me. I feared it was because of the murder of Hanrahan. I thought it was ungrateful of our neighbors to desert us now that this terrible thing had happened. I was severe with some of the men in the English class I taught later that week. Only six of the twenty workingmen had appeared.

Usually the broad shouldered men, with heavily lined faces and sweat stained shirts filled the room's rows of wooden chairs, hushed and obedient, ready to repeat after me in a deep masculine chant. But now the few men were scattered across the empty room. Exasperated, I scolded them about how necessary it was to attend regularly and not to miss the classes. They looked down, abashed. Convinced of my correctness and wanting their embarrassment to cause them to tell the missing students of their disgrace, I took up my list and began a roll call. They shifted uneasily as there was no one to respond to the first two names I called out. At the third, one of the men moved in his seat and muttered something.

"What was that?" I was sharp.

"His daughter, she die of the sickness. It's why he not here."

"Oh, she had smallpox?" I had been so concerned about our own problems I had nearly forgotten the epidemic. "How awful, I am so sorry."

"He, too, Pepito, he sick," another man added. Soon they were eagerly naming the sick in the families of all of the missing men. I was amazed the sickness had spread so quickly and ashamed that I had assumed our neighbors were staying away on purpose. The men's faces were creased with worry and their eyes were sorrowful. They made me understand that if they did not show up themselves, it would be because they had been struck down as well. I could tell that each of them was burdened with apprehension.

Soon the activity of the settlement house was consumed by the epidemic. The first few days were spent in a furor of reporting cases to the Board of Health. It was an activity that did not make us popular with our neighbors. We also announced the regulation requiring vaccination for the children of the Hull House kindergarten. More than half the mothers would not be persuaded and kept their children away. Little Angelica's mother gathered her daughter into her arms and rushed away when I tried to explain. At the same time we began to hear of those who had taken to bed with a fever and later developed the blisters and ulcers of the disease. Attendance fell off sharply in all our classes and meetings. Now on a daily basis, Alden and Milton Bierly began to go out to visit and report back about buildings where the infected were living. Volunteers were dispatched in an attempt to persuade family and neighbors to practice quarantine measures but the yellow placards that we posted were quickly pulled down by angry residents.

Now that use of the front rooms was returned to us I worked regularly on the study in the octagon room and began a correspondence with the publisher. The desk and chair at which Mr. Hanrahan was found had been moved away. At some point a table was set out in the front parlor with a map of the neighborhood from the still unpublished Hull House study. Alden and Mr. Bierly conscientiously added a small yellow flag to mark each infected building. Names and addresses were compiled and submitted to the Board of Health but still no action was taken. Our efforts were greatly resented by many in the community and when we met again after dinner one night it was agreed that our plan was not working.

"It is completely ineffective," Florence Kelley exclaimed in disgust. "Even when the infected buildings are marked, the milkmen come and go, and the nearest relations report to work where they must spread the disease, and sick and well alike trot down to the local market endangering the very food there. And still the authorities refuse to enforce the vaccination laws."

A tired Dr. Chapman agreed. "There is a need for special inspectors armed with the vaccine," he told us. "The county doctors are overwhelmed. But as long as the local politicians oppose it, the Board of Health will do nothing."

"Detective Whitbread has offered to arrest anyone who breaks the quarantine," Alden told us. He had been dogging the detective's steps trying to convince him to find the fugitive, Michael Flaherty. "But his Captain has forbidden it and said he will discharge him if he does it."

"It is a high minded offer on the part of the detective but it would be useless," Dr. Chapman pointed out. "He would arrest some poor soul who would only be released and he himself would lose his position for nothing. There is nothing we can do if the City will not stand behind the regulations."

"Alderman Powers opposes it," someone mentioned.

"The alderman resides in a part of the district little affected," Miss Kenney pointed out. "Can't we get the local ward boss to petition him? He'll listen to Fitz."

There were groans. No one believed Fitz would go against his powerful boss. Florence Kelley was disdainful. "Fitzgibbons. Not only does he not assist in the effort to track down infected stores of garments, he attempts to impede it. He sends runners to warn them we are coming and to hide the merchandise."

It had been a frustrating week for all of us.

But Miss Addams did not propose to give up. "Surely there is someone who could impress him. Anna, who have we invited to lunch next week?"

Anna Farnsworth was a woman of wealth and leisure who resided at Hull House and most days she took on the duties of hostess. This was no small task. It seemed every dignitary visiting Chicago must come to visit Hull House. Every week there was at least one luncheon that included prominent scholars, foreign ministers, important politicians and even royalty.

"We have the archbishop."

"Oh, he is Anglican. I'm afraid that would be the worst thing for an Irishman like Mr. Fitzgibbons. Could we put him off and invite Monsignor Feenan?" Miss Addams asked.

"There's also Mr. Small and Mr. Gingrich from the university."

"Yes, he will be impressed by academics. But, Dr. Chapman, do you think you could invite your Professor Jamieson from his laboratory? He might help us to persuade Mr. Fitzgibbons."

"Certainly, in such a cause."

They continued to review and refine the list until they had, as my brother put it, "stacked the deck." Included were two state senators of Fitz's party and a dignitary from India where they had suffered a terrible epidemic the previous year. A formal invitation was specially produced on a thick card with Anna's beautiful calligraphy. To my surprise our local ward boss accepted. Alden claimed no politician could pass up such company.

Knowing of my prior acquaintance with the man, Miss Addams had insisted on my inclusion. I thought she was overlooking Dr. Chapman but he was not offended, relying completely on the outspoken elderly Mr. Jamieson to set Mr. Fitzgibbons right about the situation. I usually avoided this kind of social activity at Hull House. Like Mrs. Kelley I tended to disdain the efforts to curry favor. But this was a lesson in a type of tactical foray that I never appreciated until I was older. The friends Miss Addams cultivated could be useful in forcing actions from reluctant politicians and officials.

When the day came, the discussion was heated. In no uncertain terms Mr. Jamieson predicted the spread of the disease and the numbers of fatalities that could be expected unless there was change. The visitor from India described the annihilation suffered there in terms so touching the state senators, who represented distant counties, warned that action would be taken in Springfield to segregate the city if something was not done. And little Monsignor Feenan made a thundering appeal in a mellifluous brogue to his fellow Irishman to do his best to contain the spread of the disease. I saw Miss Addams conceal a look of quiet satisfaction at how things were going and, by the end the poor, beleaguered Fitz wore a pained expression.

He left us with the promise that he would meet with Johnny Powers in the morning and "see what he could do." He also mentioned gruffly that he did not appreciate the efforts of Mrs. Kelley and her deputies (here he looked directly at me) endangering jobs of the working people by confiscating garments.

But I had some doubts of our success even before the visit was over. At the end of the day I found myself alone with Mr. Fitzgibbons as the others were ushering out the dignitaries to a waiting carriage. He stood turning his bowler hat in his hands as the others went down the stairs. Broad shouldered with a deeply lined face under large sideburns and bushy eyebrows, he blocked my way to the door as if intent on a word with me. I liked the man when I first met him, but time had shown that his loyalty was all to his party, no matter the right or wrong of the situation. He was devastated by the assassination of Mayor Carter Harrison and lost much of his power with the change of administration. I could not trust him to do the right thing, but I attempted to follow the lead of Miss Addams and Anna Farnsworth. Their plan was to use their social graces to steer this powerful man to do good. He could influence the city to do something about this epidemic if he chose to, so I waited patiently for him to speak.

"'Twas a fine meal you ladies provided." He gestured to the table. "And in the several hours of pleasant and informative conversation, not a word has been spoken about the man found murdered in your parlor, on Christmas Day no less."

I was startled by the introduction of this topic, which had been carefully avoided during the lunch.

"No, no, I understand. You desired to impress on us all the seriousness of the sickness. I know. But you, Miss Emily Cabot, you must not have forgotten that bloody scene." His eyes narrowed. "I understand your brother is after the police now to find the man who murdered your own father as he claims he is responsible for the death here. Is it not so?"

"My brother believes so. He thinks the dead man may have recognized the fugitive, Michael Flaherty."

"Michael Flaherty, is it?" He sighed and smoothed a large hand over his hair. "Shot your da, did he then? A judge he was, your father?"

"That's right. Yes. It was five years ago now but they never caught the man. I do not know the truth of it. Detective Whitbread is investigating." I was uncomfortable with the way that Alden insisted the fugitive he sought must be responsible for the death of Hanrahan. I was uneasy about my role in keeping the fact hidden that both Alden and Mrs. Kelley had found the man dead. I was living in the hope that Whitbread would find the truth of it, but in some way I dreaded what revelations he might come up with. So I did not want to discuss the unsolved murder with Fitz. "But, Mr. Fitzgibbons, we will be truly grateful to you if you can do anything about the epidemic. The Board of Health must act on the names we give them. They must enforce quarantine and vaccination. Alderman Powers has been obstructing them." I was too blunt. I knew it immediately. But it had to be said.

He frowned. "Alderman Powers is very busy these days. He has to campaign hard to keep his seat, you know. He's mighty distracted as you might imagine. Now, if the good ladies of this house were to withdraw support for his opponent, I have no doubt he would have more time to tend to other serious matters."

That was it. He wanted us to give up the progressive candidate in return for his assistance in controlling the smallpox epidemic. It was outrageous. "But surely Alderman Powers cannot hope to be re-elected if he cares so little for the lives of his constituency that he cannot see how serious this problem is. People are dying of this disease, Mr. Fitzgibbons. You cannot expect us to support a man who stands by and lets this happen." I could not sustain the patient, gracious approach of Anna and Miss Addams. Florence Kelley was right. One had to work against men like Johnny Powers and it was a mistake to ever let up on the fight.

Fitz heaved a huge sigh at that, and he shook his head like a dog shaking off a gallon of water. "Miss Cabot, you do not know of what you speak. What are you doing here, you and the others? What in the name of God do you think you can accomplish with your tea parties and lectures?" He gestured towards the abandoned lunch table. We had covered two of the tables with a damask tablecloth and set out Miss Addams's own silver, crystal glasses, and Limoges china. "Why didn't you stay at the university where you belong?" I started to reply but he put up a hand to stop me. "No, just hear me out. The man who was killed here worked for powerful business interests in the city. Your Mrs. Kelley and her crowd disrupted their business. They know he was contacting her husband about suing her for the children. She had every reason to hate him. And your brother has been bothering everyone since he came here, looking for the man who killed your father. The dead man had a hand in that, one way or another. Do you really think the men with interests, business interests, in this part of town will let your friend Whitbread keep all that buried? They will not, Miss Cabot, I promise you, they will not. Oh, yes, I will go to Johnny Powers and I will tell him what they all said here, the monsignor and the scientist and all. But the best thing you ladies could do to help the people would be to pack up and leave. You will be squeezed by this. You will be squeezed until you are gone."

Shaking his head one last time he turned and pounded down the stairs. When I followed I heard him saying polite goodbyes to the ladies there, as if the outburst above had never happened and when I closed the front door after him I saw him stomp over to a light post across the street where the black clad Mr. Weaver was waiting for him.

I seemed fated always to be at odds with Mr. Peter Francis Fitzgibbons yet I sensed his warning had been given in part out of a sort of care for me and my brother who had once spent considerable time in his company. It did not bode well for Hull House, however. I was especially afraid for Mrs. Kelley.

FIFTEEN

Most of the residents were elated when Anna Farnsworth reported to them at supper that evening and there were great hopes that the problem would at last begin to be addressed. I followed Miss Addams out after the meal to warn her of what Mr. Fitzgibbons had said to me. Mrs. Kelley, who was with her, snorted in disgust but Miss Addams refused to take it seriously. Neither of them would even think of supporting Johnny Powers in this political campaign. Fitz must have known that. We three were not surprised when another week passed and still there were no signs of inspectors or any efforts to enforce the vaccination law.

I soon found the tragedy brought new and different duties to some of us at Hull House. As I came in the door early one evening planning to put some finishing touches to an article for the study, I surprised Miss Addams, who stood at the foot of the stairs, dressed to go out. Amelia Gyles, our keeper of the gymnasium, was thrusting something into the older woman's hands. Startled, she glanced up at me then turned and raced up the stairs.

Jane Addams turned towards me rather helplessly. She had a basket over her arm and she was clutching in her hands the bundle that had been thrust at her. She sighed. "Miss Gyles is not feeling well," she explained. "I know you have been at the office all day, Miss Cabot, but do you think you could accompany me? It is Lisle Pedersen."

"Oh, no." Lisle was a student in a business writing class for young working women that I had been teaching. The youngest child and only daughter of Swedish immigrants, she had been proud of her ability to translate for them. "Not Lisle?"

"I'm afraid she passed away this afternoon. We just heard. Apparently her mother is inconsolable and one of the neighbors sent to ask if we could help."

"Yes, of course. I'll come with you." I took the bundle from her hands.

She looked at me doubtfully and glanced up the stairs. In the end she judged me not so faint hearted as Miss Gyles. I had, after all, survived the excursions behind the garbage trucks without deserting her. I should have known by then that no outing with Miss Addams into the Nineteenth Ward was for the faint of heart.

We quickly walked to a three-story brick house a few blocks away. The Pedersens lived on the middle floor. Friends and neighbors on the stairs parted for us, shaking their heads and pointing to the second floor. Already I could hear the weeping of Lisle's mother. It came in waves, rising to a crescendo of near screams then falling to a whimper.

The doorway and hall leading into the kitchen where the poor woman wailed was filled with the lanky large-boned arms and legs of the dead girl's brothers. There were some six of them, I remembered, all employed in the stockyards, all with square-jawed faces and fringes of yellow hair falling over their eyes and toothy smiles that proclaimed their lack of comprehension. Lisle had been the one who learned English and acted as interpreter for all of them.

It was unnerving to see Mrs. Pedersen, normally a cheerful, smiling soul, bent over in a chair in the kitchen panting sobs before another wave of terrified crying began. Her stocky husband with a fierce brush moustache knelt beside her, holding her hand. His face was white; the shock of his daughter's death followed by his wife's descent into this madness clearly had fogged his own wits.

A neighboring couple stood across the room with crossed arms and worried looks, unable to do anything to ease the woman's suffering. The wife rushed over when she saw us and led us to a little bedroom in the back, shooing us in and turning away herself with a sob.

On a small cot lay Lisle's body. The pretty white skin, golden braids and bright blue eyes of the lively young girl we had known were gone. She had been sick for some time. The room reeked with a smell of decay. Her body blotched with the sores of the disease and drenched with sweat was wound untidily in stained and twisted bed clothes. A stool pulled up to the bedside must have been where her mother had spent a useless vigil watching her beautiful daughter suffer and die. A basin of dirty water with rags had dropped to the floor. No doubt she had tried to soothe the fever on the girl to no avail.

The stench of the room made me anxious to turn around and leave but when I did turn I saw Jane Addams put down her basket and begin to remove her hat and coat without removing her eyes from the dead girl. Her lips were moving in a silent prayer.

What could I do? A surge of wailing came from the kitchen. One of the gawky brothers looked in expectantly from the doorway. I felt smothered by the smell of the room. But what could I do? I couldn't just leave her. It was clear they had sent for us to help prepare the poor girl for burial. I had never done such a thing before.

I stepped to a small window across from the door and forced it open. Sticking my head out, I took a gulp of fresh air. Turning back I removed hat, gloves and jacket. I retrieved the bowl from the floor and took it to the young man in the doorway, motioning him to fill it with water.

It was my first experience of washing the dead. We pulled off the bed clothes, wadding them up and I thrust them into the corridor. The brother returned with the basin and fresh linen. Miss Addams unwrapped a bar of soap, and the smell of lilacs filled the room, as we carefully removed the dirty shift and washed the flaccid limbs. Without speaking we helped each other move the body, and when it was clean we shifted it to place her on a clean sheet, then Miss Addams unwrapped the package and shook out a white frock. Miss Gyles had been able to contribute that much, even if she could not bear to participate in the laying out. I sighed and helped to pull it over the head of the girl. Then we used one of Jane's silver backed brushes to brush the yellow hair and laid her back down. We even found stockings and slippers to cover her feet.

Lying there, the blemishes of the awful disease still marred the fresh face that we had known, but at least Lisle looked peaceful, not like the writhing mess she had been when we entered the room. I gathered up what clothes were still strewn around and shut the window. It was cold but at least the air felt clean.

We retreated to the outer room and in a few minutes two of the sons half carried their mother into the stool where she had spent so many hours helplessly watching the girl die. Her weeping became more muffled and regular, so it seemed to comfort her somewhat. She tearfully directed her boys and soon they had lighted candles at the head and foot of the cot. The neighboring woman went in and said a few words to the grieving parents then came out and thanked us. At that a procession started. People from the stairs began to come in a few at a time.

"Oh, dear," Miss Addams looked vexed. "They don't seem to understand the danger of contagion."

We pulled aside one of the brothers and tried to explain the need to vaccinate everyone and the danger that others would get sick. I wasn't sure if he understood us, although he nodded his head and said "Ja, ja." Finally, he went to his parents at our urging, but soon he came out to say, "Tak, tak, we thank you very much." He started to say something else, something about Hull House. I thought it was about the man found dead there and I was preparing to reassure him, but an older brother came up then and snapped at him in an angry tone. They turned away to argue in private. Twice more we tried to explain the need to limit contact with the dead girl but finally we had to give up. They would wake the girl for two days before burial and who knew how many would become infected in that time? But there was nothing more we could do about it.

As we left, someone, a woman, was entering the rooms on the upper floor. From the corner of my eye, I thought I recognized the embroidery at the edge of the hem although by the time I had looked up, the woman was gone, the door closed. Miss Addams had been behind me with a clear view.

"Was that…?" I was going to ask if it was Florence Kelley but Jane Addams patted my arm.

"It is not our business. It has been a long day. You must be tired. Come along." For some reason she did not want to discuss the matter and I was left wondering whether it was really the chief factory inspector that I had seen and, if so, what she might have been doing there that would be so secretive she would not acknowledge us. It made me uncomfortable, but I could not confront Miss Addams about it. She was clearly tired out by our experience.

After that, when Jane was called to help prepare the dead, I would get a tentative inquiry from her that I could not refuse. I must have attended her several dozen times in the following weeks on more of these dreadful errands.

The funerals had begun. Every day we heard of the death of someone among our friends and neighbors. It became a daily duty to decide who would go and represent us at the latest batch of funeral ceremonies.

The doctor's prediction was fulfilled as it soon became apparent that it was the young people who were falling sick while the aging looked on helplessly. Sons and daughters died before the eyes of parents who had passed through Ellis Island on their way to Chicago. We had to intercede for one poor elderly widow faced with eviction when her vigorous son passed away. Unable to understand what the bailiffs were saying, she was clinging to a massive trunk of possessions when we arrived to try to prevent them from putting her into the street. We found a place for her with a neighbor but the look of dull confusion in her eyes was eloquent testimony to her sorrow. There were no words in any tongue to explain the sudden loss of her only son.

I stopped working on the study. It seemed useless. Where suffering had already been great, due to the lack of employment, the epidemic created a disaster. Often it was the single wage earner of the family, the young girl who toiled in a sweatshop or the young boy who had a job in a factory, who was the very one to be cut down. Mary Kenney reported that at one sweatshop every girl and woman in the place had fallen ill and every place had been filled by another only to have the illness strike down each one until they were all replaced again.

Soon the clubs and classes of Hull House ceased to function altogether as the faithful participants fell ill themselves or cared for family members. Instead, we found ourselves operating a relief shelter, soliciting food, clothes and money from our wealthy friends. Stores were piled up all over the house and were doled out to the same people, desperate now, who used to come to Hull House to study or socialize.

When we would visit, to bring stores to those too ill to even come to collect them or to help to lay out the dying, it was the smell of sickness and sweat that assailed us. The crowded dirty rooms were stale with the stench of it and the eyes of the people, sick or well, were narrowed by fear. Every corridor was haunted by muffled sounds of moans, or weeping or the piercing cries of children in pain. They helped each other as best they could but the unseen enemy was running rampant, and it seemed that no family was spared.

I had thought that finding a dead man in the parlor of Hull House had been the biggest shock of my life. But now we were so surrounded by death it was little wonder that the image of Hanrahan faded from my memory in the following days.

SIXTEEN

One cold evening I was returning late to Hull House having been called out after dinner. I stumbled at the foot of a streetlight and, looking across, I saw a woman leaning in a doorway. The blanket wrapped round, hiding her face, did not disguise the nightclothes she wore. Beside her an older woman stood weeping and clutching a corner of the blanket while she smoothed her hand across the back of the sick woman. I thought to cross to them but just then I heard the clanging of a little bell and saw a covered wagon come around the corner. It stopped in front of them and the sick woman climbed in. The older woman stood forlorn, still weeping. When the wagon started to trundle on, she walked a few steps after it.

I heard the crunch of snow behind me. "It's one of the carts from the pest house," said Dr. Chapman who had come around the corner. He took my arm. "I think they are beginning to understand. They hate the idea of the pest house and the authorities won't enforce the regulations, but some of them are beginning to understand that by staying they only spread the infection. The carts go out at dusk and they return full. Some of the sick voluntarily part with their families to try to save them." We began to walk the three blocks to Hull House.

His hand under my elbow was comforting and I found I was longing to tell someone about my recent errand. "If only they would listen. I wish I could make them listen. I have been to see little Angelica. We learned her mother had fallen ill last week and I took them food as soon as I heard. I tried to get her to let me take the child away. She already had a fever. But she said her neighbor could care for Angelica." I stopped to look into his kind brown eyes. "That poor woman had lost three little daughters in one week and I could see she longed to care for the child from missing her own. When I returned tonight with food, Angelica had died. She was only three years old, Stephen. Her mother still lives but her baby has died. If only they had allowed us to vaccinate her. I should have explained it better. I should have made her understand. She should not have died."

He closed his eyes and sighed, squeezing my arm. "You must not blame yourself, Emily. You did what you could."

"Not enough. She is dead. At three years old she is dead. I should have convinced her mother. If she had let Angelica be vaccinated she would still be here. To see her lying there, so empty…not even like a doll. A doll is made of sturdier stuff…the material lasts. She was so white, so sickly looking but so empty." I gulped. There was a pressure pushing up from my throat into my head. I could still see the little girl's body laid out in a white dress, with candles all around. They couldn't hide the awful smell of decomposition that had already started to permeate the room. I clenched my jaw, and afraid to try to speak, I kept my eyes screwed closed.

Suddenly I felt the doctor's arms around me and he pulled me to him. I sobbed into his chest. He let me weep, stroking my hair. Finally, I pulled away sniffling. He took my arm again and led me to the steps of Hull House. My head was pounding as we took off our coats and stepped into the study where the map on the table bristled with yellow flags.

"Alden and his yellow flags," I snapped. "I wish he wouldn't do that."

But the doctor was standing across the table from me, looking down at the map in the pool of light from an overhead lamp. "It is good to chart the course of the disease so we can see how fast it is spreading."

I had to force myself to really look at it. "Oh, no, look at it. It can't have gotten that far so fast." It was appalling. The little box of toothpicks was half empty and the nasty little paper flags were stuck all over the map. It was the one from the unpublished study. It showed the streets of the whole ward in carefully colored blocks representing the nationalities that lived in the different buildings. The green and blue and purple rectangles were all bristling with a little forest of flags. "Where will it end? Look at it. The numbers double every day. Look here at Taylor Street. In these blocks it is almost every other house. How do we stop it? It can't go on much longer than this, can it?"

He shook his head and spread his hands over the forest. "It's far from over. This is only where the infection has shown itself. In reality it has spread further but it is incubating and hasn't shown itself yet."

I stared. How could it continue? I thought of Angelica. Dr. Chapman had been so right about the children being most at risk. There were so many of the little ones going down. Suddenly still. Suddenly gone, life escaping like the wisps of breath I had seen coming from my mouth as I walked back in the freezing cold of the night. "I don't understand. Where will it end? How will it end?"

He was leaning on the table, brooding over the map. "There won't be any children left. Twenty years from now there will be no young people to have more children. They will all be gone." He wasn't looking at me.

"We have to stop it. Surely it will stop soon?"

He looked up. "It's like a fire, Emily. It will spread through and fan out. It's contagion. It will only be stopped when it comes to areas where the people have been vaccinated. You must prepare yourself, my dear. It is not going to be over soon." His shoulders slumped and his eyelids seemed heavy and there were shadows under his eyes. "Only stringent enforcement of vaccination and quarantine will even slow it. What you see is really only the beginning, Emily."

I felt tears rising, more from fear than anything else. I shut my eyes for a moment wanting to shut off the experience. When I opened them I perceived how pale and drawn he looked. Glancing into the library, I saw a fire was still burning in the grate. "You must eat, Doctor. I looked for you at dinner, you weren't there. You cannot keep missing meals. You will make yourself ill. There will be food in the larder. Go in to the fire and I will bring you a plate."

"I am not hungry."

"You must sit down and eat. Just add a log to the fire, I will return immediately."

Hull House was uncharacteristically cold and quiet with all of the clubs and classes abandoned. I stepped around piles of supplies wondering if the place was haunted now by all those souls who had once found comfort here. I realized if it were haunted, I would be much too practical and literal to notice. Ghosts would slip by me without a nod. But I imagined more sensitive souls might have to place pitchers of water all over the place, on every stairway to ward off the ghosts before this was over. I still could not imagine how more and more of the people we knew could die off as they were doing. I shied away from the thought. I couldn't contain it in my mind. At least I could busy myself putting up a plate of cold meat, cheese, and bread and pouring a cup of cider to take to the doctor.

When I returned he had stoked a small blaze and was sitting on the leather couch, legs sprawled out and head resting on the back, his eyes closed. Exhausted, he had fallen asleep and he probably needed the rest more than food. I placed the food before him and sat down quietly, not wanting to wake him. I knew that being here was not what he really wanted. He wanted to be in the nice sterile laboratory doing experiments that allowed him to chart progress. There, he could believe he would accomplish something. That was where he belonged, yet here he was. He had been spending long hours administering the vaccine and seeing to patients who feared removal to the pest house. It gave me comfort to hear his breathing warm and alive beside me and I almost feared to leave as if, like the little girl, Angelica, he would be gone when I came back. But it was late and I knew I should leave him in peace. I moved to rise but, just then, he reached out and touched my arm. I felt the pressure of his grip. I wanted nothing so much as to feel his arms around me, comforting me. I felt a thrill of danger. I had only to reach out and touch him, but it was impossible.

"No, don't go." His eyes were still closed but I felt the pressure of his grip. I could see where gray had begun to speckle his sandy hair. He was badly in need of a haircut and his normally clean-shaven face showed a stubble of beard. I sat back and put a hand over his, willing him not to release his hand. I realized suddenly how much I dreaded going up to my cold room alone. I needed the closeness of him, warm and alive, beside me. I had seen too much of death that week. I looked at his square face and realized how dear he was to me. I was shocked by the strength of a sudden longing but I sat, afraid to move, just wanting to prolong the moment.

"I never would have imagined it," he said, his eyes still closed. "But this place, this house has come to mean more to me than any home I have ever inhabited." He opened his eyes and looked into mine as if he were searching for something. "I suppose it is because my mother died when I was very young. I barely remember her. I only remember sitting on the floor under a grand piano while she played a sonata. It was many years later that I heard that music again."

I knew enough of his story to realize he must have heard that music from Marguerite Larrimer when she was still Marguerite Ramsey. She was a woman he was engaged to marry, long ago, before I met him. She had been a music student when he knew her before she married a wealthy man and moved away. I thought sadly that music was not one of my accomplishments.

He shifted, turning his head to look into the fire. Sitting forward he put his forearms on his knees still talking of his mother. "Her family was wealthy. But after she died my father insisted on moving to the poorest parts of the city—to preach. We moved from one set of rooms to another, occasionally living in the houses of wealthy benefactors or the homes for the indigent where he did his work.

"He is a cold man. He thinks only of his mission to save the souls of the fallen. I never knew the kind of warm home you and Alden must have had. It was not until my university days that I realized not everyone lived as we did. But by then, I had my own mission and I dismissed thoughts of such a home as the ground for cultivation of people who were both soft and selfish. I told myself I was above that, more committed due to the hardness of life I had witnessed.

"It is only since I have been here that I have realized what I must have missed not being part of a real home. It feels a haven for me. I know you will not completely understand, but always before I have been alone and self-dependent."

Such loneliness seemed unbearable to me. "But here you know anyone would help you in any way you needed. You only have to ask," I agreed with him. "Yes, I can understand it," I told him naively. "As much as I quarrel and disagree with my brother it is true that I would never doubt that, if I needed to, I could call on him and he would respond without question. Well, not without question, but he would never deny me. Nor I him, I suppose." For a moment I was racked by a doubt about that. Alden had lied to me and he had lied so easily. I wanted to believe he had nothing to do with the death of Mr. Hanrahan, but I still could not be sure. Nonetheless, he was my brother and it was true that I could not betray him.

"It is the source of that great generosity which you bestow so easily. You don't know how rare that is." He squeezed my hand. "Oh, Emily. You should not be here. You should be safe at the university pursuing your studies. You do not know how much I regret my part in that. If it weren't for me and my troubles, you would never have been expelled. Neither you nor your brother belong here. It is not the place for either of you."

I felt slightly self-conscious. He saw my brother and me as mere children. He still thought of me as the young student who had come to study at the university and I knew he still felt it was by attempting to help him that I had been expelled. But he was wrong. It was all due to my own headstrong actions, yet he thought of it as a form of generosity. I felt guilty that he attributed such unselfish motives to me. As for my brother, he did not know Alden at all. Should I confide in him about how Alden had lied? Should I let him know how I could not be sure how deeply my brother was involved in the death that had happened here? I hesitated. How could I betray my brother? What if the doctor insisted on telling Detective Whitbread? Sensing my hesitation, he pulled his hand away and rested his head on the back of the couch again. Somehow I had spoiled the moment, thinking of Alden and his lie to the police. I couldn't tell him Alden had lied. What would he think of me and my brother then? It was on the tip of my tongue, then, to confide in him, to tell him that Alden had lied to the police about seeing the dead man. But surely he would want to tell the police the truth. What would happen to Alden, then? And what about Mrs. Kelley? She had lied as well. I had no doubt he would feel obliged to tell Whitbread the truth. I knew it was the right thing to do. But I could not do it. I could not put my brother and Mrs. Kelley at such risk. I just couldn't.

He regarded me through the slits of his almost closed eyes. "You shouldn't be here at all. You would have escaped all this at the university."

The thought of Clara and the others in the cozy parlor of Snell Hall was conjured up before me. I did miss that. "How could I leave now? Miss Addams says we can do no good cut off from the more than half of mankind that must struggle to survive. 'Any good we secure for ourselves is precarious and uncertain. It is floating in midair until it is secured for all and incorporated into the common life.'" I was quoting her directly. "You don't think I could abandon you all now, do you?"

He shut his eyes firmly and his jaw jutted out. "There is one here who admires you, you know. He admires you greatly. He has spoken of it to your brother and me."

This was so unexpected a change of topic that I was speechless as he continued.

"You must have noticed the admiration you have inspired in Mr. Bierly."

"Mr. Bierly?" I was horrified.

He was gazing at me intently now. "Milton Bierly is a good man, Emily. He may be a little young and foolish but he has a good heart."

I stared at him with my mouth open. *Milton Bierly? What was he talking about?*

He cleared his throat and stood up to use the poker to stir up the fire. "Did you know he is from a ranching family? He has been telling your brother and me all about it, and I asked Miss Addams. His father raises cattle in Wyoming. He married a woman from the East. She was never comfortable in the West despite the fact that she married a very rich man. As soon as Milton was school-age she insisted on taking him back East to raise him in a cultured manner. His father stayed on the ranch. He comes to Chicago once a year to sell off his herd. He looks for his son then. He has never insisted that Milton return to the ranch. He has let him seek his own way. But someday it will all be his."

He carefully replaced the poker in the stand and wiped his hands against each other. I could not believe he was going on like this about Milton Bierly and I think he flushed a little and refused to look at me. But he insisted on continuing. "I think Mr. Bierly is a little embarrassed to admit the wealth to which he is heir but he quietly contributes a substantial amount to Miss Addams and Hull House. But unlike many who donate only money he is not content with that. He is determined to be an active participant in the good works done here. He is a good soul, Emily, and he admires you greatly."

"Dr. Chapman. What are you saying? Why are you telling me all of this?"

He had the grace to look embarrassed, then. "Mr. Bierly has confided in me, and in your brother," he told me. I saw a flush rise on his cheeks and he cleared his throat. "He confided in us how much he admires you and he asked me—and your brother, of course—he asked us to speak to you about him. To speak for him. He is afraid to speak up himself." Now his face was truly red.

I felt my stomach lurch and a heated flush rose uncontrolled up to the roots of my hair. This was how Dr. Stephen Chapman saw Milton Bierly, and no doubt this was how he saw me as well. We were as children to him. Good hearted, foolish young persons who meant well but bumbled. And two such souls belonged together. To him we must be like Jack and Jill bumbling up the hill. He had no sense of me as I really was. I was totally embarrassed and angry when Alden entered followed by Mr. Bierly.

"We heard. Fitz still has done nothing. That is it. We have tried plan A; we have tried plan B. Now we must try a new plan. My plan. Our plan. Right, Milt?" He reached out to that man who staggered slightly.

"Alden, have you been drinking?"

"Only beer. You have to hear me out, Em."

"Oh, Alden, go to bed." I glanced at the doctor. His face was still flushed but he was smiling.

"No, Emily. I'm telling you. I am not drunk, although Milt here may be feeling his cups a little. I am not drunk and for once in your life, Emily Cabot, you are going to listen to me." He punctuated his last remarks with stabs at the air in front of him and, resigned, I sat back to listen to Alden's plan.

SEVENTEEN

It was snowing and bitterly cold as I made my way to the ward office the following evening. We had been alerted, by two of the children assigned the task, that Fitz was alone and had not yet left on his usual excursions to saloons, parties or funeral homes, where he kept in touch with the voters of the district each night.

A bell tinkled as I opened the door and stepped into the space filled with desks and filing cabinets. On one side, a large map of the district hung on the wall. At the back of the narrow room Mr. Fitzgibbons sat in shirtsleeves behind a cluttered desk. When he saw me his look of welcome evaporated and he did not rise. Instead, he poured himself another shot from a whiskey bottle in front of him.

"Miss Cabot," he acknowledged me before throwing back his head and swallowing.

I moved forward slowly. Poor Fitz. It was a much smaller and dirtier room than his office in City Hall had been and by the number of desks lined up it was clear that he shared it with others. I saw the same framed photographs of his family and himself with Carter Harrison perched precariously on two cabinets stacked high with bound notebooks. Fitz himself looked weary with red-rimmed eyes and stains on his shirtfront. This would not do. I marched down the room and stood in front of him, forcing him to look up into my eyes.

"Your constituents are dying, Mr. Fitzgibbons. We still have no enforcement of the vaccination law and the smallpox is spreading. You must convince the Board of Health to assign special inspectors and enforce the law. You must rouse yourself and do something about it."

He frowned. "Indeed, Miss Cabot, my constituents are dying. Do you know where I have to go tonight? Eh? To another wake. And tomorrow to another funeral—for Bobbie McClain. Oh, no, he is not a victim of disease, Miss Cabot, at least not the smallpox. Bobbie McClain grew up with me in the Back of the Yards. Oh, excuse me, that's not an area you would be familiar with, miss. It's rather dirty, it is. Not really suitable for the likes of you and Miss Addams with her great distaste for garbage. There's plenty of garbage in the Back of the Yards.

"But Bobbie and me, we got jobs, don't you see. Working for the machine. I know you don't approve of that but for Bobbie and me, 'twas a salvation. So for years now Bobbie worked as a clerk for the city government like. But he got laid off in the changing of the guard and with no job he come looking for help. Well, the only jobs for having were down digging the canal, so I sent for him and I told him. 'But I've never done anything but office work, Fitz,' says he. 'Well,' says I, 'you've got Maggie and the four kids to feed and this is it, man, this is all there is.' So he hung his head and he went away and did it because he was out of work for three months now. And it killed him. It killed him because he wasn't strong enough for it. He got the pneumonia, and he died of it."

"I'm so sorry."

"Sure, you're sorry but you want to put more of them out of work with your laws and your regulations and your vaccinations. You think you're saving the people but if they lose their work they die. You and that Mrs. Kelley on your high horses wanting to close down these shops now. What do you think you're doing? You think you're saving them from the smallpox, but for what? So they can starve? Because that's what they're doing out there. They're starving. It's all well and good for you Hull House do-gooders. You've got a hot meal every night. But look around you, woman. There's thousands of them without jobs I'm telling you, and they and their families are existing on stale bread."

"We do know that unemployment is a serious problem, especially this winter, Mr. Fitzgibbons. But people are dying of the smallpox and there is no other way to stop it than to close down infected places and isolate those sick with the disease."

He waved me off, too angry to speak and took another drink. The doorbell tinkled again and as he raised his glass he shot a glance at the door. What he saw made him put down his drink untasted. "What are you doing here?"

Detective Whitbread stood there holding the door open. This time he was neatly dressed in a woolen overcoat and a bowler hat with a long grey scarf draped around his neck. "I bring you petitioners, Fitzgibbons. Constituents. Voters. Citizens who come seeking your aid."

Fitz frowned at him glumly. I thought he was grinding his teeth. "Well, bring them in, man, don't leave that door open. It's freezing." He stood and capped his bottle as if to put it out of sight. Although he was always willing to listen to potential voters, it was clear he was unenthusiastic about this particular intrusion.

"They ask you to step outside," the detective informed him.

"Who?"

"Citizens, Mr. Fitzgibbons. A Mr. McCaffey, a Miss Sheehy, a Mr. Jacob," Whitbread announced solemnly. "They beg me to tell you without your present assistance they will be unable to offer their votes or those of their male relatives in the coming election."

"Oh, for God's sake, stop posturing, you clown. Bring them in." Impatient with the policeman, Fitz was at the door in three long strides, shouldering the man aside and stepping out into the cold in his shirtsleeves. The detective followed him and I hurried to catch up.

Fitz came to a sudden stop as his way was blocked by a covered cart that had been backed up to the sidewalk directly in front of the door. As he balked at two lanterns swinging on poles almost in his face, the canvas flap of the cart was thrown back revealing half a dozen bodies lying on pallets. A stench of corruption issued from the inside accompanied by sounds of groans and whimpering.

"What is this?" Fitz attempted to step back but Whitbread was close behind him. Alden and Mr. Bierly each stepped forward from the shadows carrying lanterns on long poles. Dr. Chapman stood close to the side.

"Your constituents, Mr. Fitzgibbons. Mr. McCaffey, Miss Sheehy, Mr. Jacob," Detective Whitbread announced.

Gulping and squinting, Fitz leaned forward. Alden shoved his lantern into the wagon to illuminate it. A young girl squealed and there was a brief view of what had been a pretty face, the smooth flesh now studded with pink and yellow pustules pushing up in streaky mounds. Then she buried it in hands wet with extrusions from more pustules and curled her body trying to dig into the pallet on which she lay.

Fitz put up an arm as if to ward off the sight but it was grabbed by a strong hand attached to an arm festering with blisters, as a man on a stretcher laid across the back of the cart attempted to sit up. Wiry gray hair sprung out from a face covered with more swollen blisters and when he opened his mouth to try to speak you could see ulcers inside. Only a mewling sound came from the mouth full of sores. Fitz tried to pull away but Detective Whitbread was close behind him again, forcing him to stay.

"These are your voters, and their families. This is what comes of spurning the law, Mr. Fitzgibbons. The law would have had these people protected by vaccination, but you and Alderman Powers prevented it. Behold the consequences of your actions. It's Mr. McCaffey. It's one of your own men."

"Mack?" Fitz froze, staring at the man who had fallen back with a groan, then he pulled his arm away and turning, thrust Whitbread aside to stumble back into the office. The detective would have followed but Stephen Chapman held him back with a hand on his shoulder. The doctor stepped forward himself to follow the ward boss and I trailed behind him.

Fitz had rushed to the end of the room shoving desks and chairs out of his way. He was attempting to pour another drink now but his hands were shaking. As we approached, he banged the bottle down. Glancing around with a look of panic, he knocked over the chair and backed up until he was against the wall. He had his hands up as if to ward us off.

"Stop. Don't come any closer."

When my brother had suggested trying to shock Fitz with such a revelation, I had been skeptical. Alden had proposed drugging the ward boss, bringing him to the pest house and allowing him to awaken surrounded by victims of the disease. Dr. Chapman had forbidden the kidnapping but he had seen the possibilities of the plan and, when I saw they were determined to go through with it, I had taken up the plan and revised it until it was something we could actually do. Dr. Chapman arranged for the pest house wagon to stop and I had recruited Detective Whitbread. Now the doctor stepped forward, carrying his satchel.

"It's all right, Mr. Fitzgibbons." He dropped the satchel on the desk with a thud. "You have never had smallpox, have you?"

Fitz looked at him as if through a cloud. He still had one hand up. Dr. Chapman reached for it.

"It is all right, Mr. Fitzgibbons. If you will allow me to vaccinate you, now, you will be protected from contagion." Gently, he pushed Fitz back into the chair which he had righted. The stunned man nodded and the doctor took vaccination materials from the bag and laid them out.

"It's a curse, a terrible curse," Fitz mumbled. "It shouldn't happen to anyone."

"We're trying to stop it. That's all we're trying to do," I told him. "We just want to protect people. The vaccine will keep it from spreading."

Fitz looked at me vaguely then down at the doctor's implements. Dr. Chapman was rolling up his sleeve. Fitz shivered. "Don't you have a smaller needle?"

"It won't hurt much," the doctor told him and I tried to distract him.

"Mr. Fitzgibbons, you must let the Board of Health send vaccination teams. So many people will be saved. Yes, those who already have the disease will be found and moved to the pest house but it is the only way to stop it."

He winced at the scratch of the needle and looked at me. At that moment the doorbell jangled again and a figure strode down the room. It was Weaver. The eyes under the shadow of his black hat were glittering. "What's going on, Fitz?" He stopped in front of the desk, his long coat dripping on the floor.

"Weaver." Fitz was unrolling his sleeve and fastening a cuff link as the doctor packed up his paraphernalia.

"Not afraid of a little pox are you, Fitz?"

Dr. Chapman looked at him mildly. "Mr. Fitzgibbons has just been vaccinated. Perhaps you would also like to receive this protection?"

The tall rangy man laughed and, slowly, he pulled off his broad brimmed hat. Ugly scars covered his forehead and ran down the side of his cheek and neck.

"I see you have already suffered the disease," Dr. Chapman commented, snapping shut his satchel.

Weaver replaced the hat and stood waiting. Fitz looked up at him as if he found the man repulsive. "You'll have the vaccination teams," the ward boss said.

Meanwhile Detective Whitbread had entered and stood by the door. "You'll not regret it, Mr. Fitzgibbons. If responsibility confronts you, seize it. Do not throw it aside—responsibility represents opportunity."

But the glittering eyes of Mr. Weaver narrowed and he fingered a sheet of paper on the desk. Fitz looked at him.

"But you won't get any help from us trying to confiscate goods you claim are infected," Fitz said to me. "We'll not help you take people's work away. And you, Detective, you had better be arresting someone for that murder, a murder right there in that settlement house. It's your job will be on the line if there's no arrest for it. It was one of them did it and you'd better find out which one."

"But…" I tried to protest.

"That's it now. It's over." Fitz pounded the desk and rose. "Now, out with you, all of you." He pulled a coat from a peg and began putting it on. "I have to close up now. I have a wake to go to." He glared at me.

Weaver smirked and with a final cold glance at me and the doctor he turned and pushed his way past the detective at the door. We all headed out into the falling snow. As Fitz locked the door, I saw Alden across the street in the shadows talking to Weaver. How he could tolerate the man was beyond my comprehension and once again I felt a pang of doubt about my brother.

The doctor, the detective, and I stood for a moment watching the bulky figure of the ward boss retreat into the hushed stillness of snow that was falling heavily now.

"Will he do it this time?" I asked. "Will anything change?"

"I think he meant it this time," Stephen Chapman said. "As far as enforcing the vaccinations and quarantine at least."

"But not shutting down infected sweatshops." I was sorely vexed by this. "He won't enforce that."

Detective Whitbread glared after the retreating figure. "He is still a believer in the great god Graft. He and Powers are beholden to the men who profit from the work of those shops. Weaver is their agent. He is a scoundrel. We have gone some ways towards stemming the epidemic tonight but disease itself is nothing to the rank corruption that infects the body politic in the form of graft. It is a plague for which no vaccination exists for the likes of Mr. Fitzgibbons and Mr. Powers. Nonetheless, we must congratulate ourselves on achieving some progress."

"He threatened you," I reminded him.

"There is much pressure to clear up the circumstances of Mr. Hanrahan's death. We must find the truth. Do not fear, Miss Cabot, I have no intention of allowing justice to be thwarted in order to assist Mr. Powers in his election. Miss Cabot, Doctor, I bid you goodnight."

We watched as he marched off into the night.

"At least Detective Whitbread believes they will enforce the vaccinations now," I said as we watched him disappear into a curtain of falling snow. Everything was hushed.

"Fitzgibbons will not want to disappoint you."

"Me? Me? I don't know what you mean." But I felt myself flush. I tried to look into his eyes but his face was in shadow from a streetlight.

"You have no idea how much a man may do for the good opinion of a woman he admires."

I nearly slipped when I had the impulse to stamp my foot. I caught at his arm. "I have never felt unduly admired by Mr. Fitzgibbons, I am sure you are wrong," I said stiffly.

"Perhaps." He took my hand and tucked it under his arm. I was annoyed by the impression that he was quietly laughing at me and it made me stiffen. But I allowed him to lead me back towards Hull House. An uneven layer of ice under the newly fallen snow made the footing treacherous. I clutched his arm several times to avoid slipping down in a graceless lump. It was several blocks before he spoke again. "He knows you are right and it shames him, Emily. Like most of us, he lives by the compromises necessary for his survival. He would not choose to go against Powers and the alderman's backers in the city. But he will do it. He could not bear to have you see him as such a little man. He will do what he can and still protect his position. He will release the Board of Health at least."

He nettled me. "Of course, he will. He must, but not to impress me." I had pulled my arm out from his and turned to face him but suddenly I felt my feet slipping out from under me and I was cursing my imprudence when I felt his arms scoop me up. I felt his breath on my cheek and he groaned. I shivered as his mouth moved over mine. We hung there for a moment then he buried his face in my neck. I relaxed then, and bent into his shoulder, grateful to finally be close. Suddenly he pulled back and held me at arm's length. "Stephen…"

"No, no. I am so sorry."

"Don't apologize, I…"

"No, come." He put an arm around my waist and hurried me the half block to the steps of Hull House. I tried to look up at him but he purposely looked away. I tried to cling to his coat when we reached the steps but he took my gloved hands and forced them on to the railing.

"Wait, Doctor, don't go."

His face was in shadow again. His gloved hand was under my chin. "You are so very young. You must forgive me."

"No, wait. I don't have to… I'm not… I…" but he was gone into the night. I stamped my foot in frustration and mounted the steps to Hull House.

EIGHTEEN

I looked out for Dr. Chapman in the coming days but he was successful in avoiding me. I even went in search of him at the men's lodgings but I was only frustrated. He was either at the clinic or the laboratory. After several attempts I came to believe I was being childish to insist on attention. I would have to bide my time. We were still dealing with the crisis.

Fitz was true to his word this time and the next day half a dozen special smallpox inspectors from the Board of Health appeared. Miss Addams offered them the use of Hull House, where they were fed, and at the end of each day they rigorously washed and changed their clothes so as not to take any infection to their homes. The most experienced and vigilant of them was a Mr. Wall who left his family altogether and moved into the men's dormitory for the duration of the epidemic in order not to endanger his own family.

Realizing there was nothing more I could do to stem the epidemic, and nothing I could do to confront the doctor until he was willing to be found, I returned to the stacks of papers of the study. I worked out the details with the publisher and finally packaged up the finished work and posted it to New York. I told Dean Talbot I would get the study to publication, and at least I kept my word on that.

There was some resentment in the neighborhood as people were forced to submit to the dreaded vaccinations and loved ones were promptly removed to the pest house when they were found to be infected. We tried to explain the need for these actions but too frequently were met with the hard stares of anger.

There were grumblings about the lack of an arrest for the murder. Detective Whitbread would appear at odd hours and take one of us into the study to ask questions we had answered before. It was too late to tell him about Alden and too dangerous. Meanwhile every time he came Alden would wait outside the door to try to convince him to look for Flaherty. He insisted the phantom fugitive had been recognized by Hanrahan and that had led to his death. Knowing how he and Mrs. Kelley had lied, his insistent protests made me uneasy.

I became aware of certain absences of Florence Kelley. Between her job and studies, it was hard to imagine how she could have time for anything else, but I began to notice how sometimes there would be a knock at the door and whispers and she would slide away into the night with no explanation. When I tried to ask Miss Addams about it, she looked pained and asked me to refrain from mentioning the circumstances. I could not bear to raise suspicions in the mind of Jane Addams but the fact was a man who was an enemy of Mrs. Kelley had been killed in the study. This was not a time for secrets. But neither Miss Addams nor Mrs. Kelley seemed concerned or at all willing to change their behavior based on the infamy of that event. Florence Kelley pursued her goals as ruthlessly as if Hanrahan had never been found bludgeoned in our home.

As the official chief factory inspector of the state, Mrs. Kelley was still determined to find and confiscate any goods that could have been infected by the sickness. But it was not an easy task. When the smallpox inspectors found a victim they would trace back the patient's contacts to administer vaccinations. If they were able to locate a sweatshop they sent word but all too often, by the time we arrived, the garments being worked on had disappeared from the premises.

It was during these searches that I became familiar with the truly terrible working conditions in the tenement sweatshops. The way the system worked was that the clothing establishments in the city's downtown took a client's measurements and chose the fabrics. They cut the cloth to the pattern and contracted out the actual sewing. It was a fearsomely competitive business as they sent out the work to the lowest bidder who promised the least amount of time to complete the work. As a result, the contractors were usually immigrants who rented the cheapest tenement spaces, in the back or over the stables, where they installed as many sewing machines as they could in the ill lit and poorly ventilated spaces. Here young women like Maria Maglioni came in the dark of the early morning and worked until late at night. They suffered the long hours not only because they were paid by the piece but also because their employer required it in order to satisfy the schedules of the downtown proprietors and, with so few jobs available, they could not afford to lose their places. For every woman at one of the machines there were ten begging to be hired.

They were paid pennies for each piece and the small contractors received very little profit. They could not afford to raise prices, competition for the work was so fierce. Efforts to enforce the eight-hour working day for women, which had been passed into law the previous year, were thwarted by the efforts of the workers themselves, so much did they fear a loss of employment. And some of the work was sent out to the homes of workers where women would finish garments with the help of the children. Children as young as three or four were taught to sit and pull out basting threads for hours at a time.

With the smallpox epidemic the sickness of one of the girls in the crowded sweatshops soon spread to the others and the garments they worked on. Goods sent out to homes for work might lie on the very sickbed of an infected family member. The danger of spreading the disease by infected goods was something that everyone at that time believed in, except for the sweatshop proprietors, and the girls who worked there were desperate to save the goods. They would risk infection in order to receive the meager payments that were so often the only thing that would save whole families from starvation, especially this cold and cruel winter with its sickness and unemployment.

As I became familiar with the truly dreadful nature of these establishments I remembered with shame times spent before the mirror in dressmaking shops admiring or criticizing the cut of a new gown. The fact that the only thing keeping so many of these families from actual starvation was the satisfaction of the vanity of their well-off fellow citizens was fearful to contemplate. Yet they must find some way to live and with this work they could manage, barely.

So it was that they struggled desperately to hide from us, in fear their work would be confiscated. It became a cat and mouse game, trying to track down and destroy the goods that might have been infected by sick workers. Occasionally the supply was found and destroyed but more often than not the trek through the snow-laden streets to a tenement sweatshop ended with disappointment and a long walk back empty-handed, as was true one afternoon in early February when I met my brother Alden and Milton Bierly at the small factory inspection office on Halsted.

"We found something for you. Come on, we'll show you," Alden told me. But I was tired.

"Alden. I have just tramped several miles and found an empty filthy sweatshop without a scrap of material in the place. I am worn out."

"But you'll want to see this, Em. Won't she?" He consulted his companion. Then with a conspiratorial nod, Mr. Bierly rushed away and Alden grabbed my hand. "Come on, Em. You won't be disappointed. I promise."

In all this new found world of sickness and dirt and endless toil, I could not understand how my brother seemed never to run out of his boundless supply of enthusiasm. Reluctantly, I allowed him to lead me some ten blocks south and west, winding through alleys and streets caked thick with snow-covered ice.

Finally, he stopped at the end of a narrow alley we had traversed, blocking my way.

"Hush. Stay back. Here, take a look but be careful not to be seen."

I leaned across him and looking out I saw a cart and horse being loaded with crates by several men. Standing by, watching, was the lanky figure of Mr. Weaver. He was leaning against the wall beside the door where a yellow placard plainly marked the premises as infected by disease. I made a move forward but Alden held me back.

"No, wait," he whispered. "We can't do anything alone, and they'll be gone by the time we could get help. Besides, don't you want to see where they take it?"

I began to protest but he shushed me until they started to move away with the horse drawn car. I was exasperated with Alden. We had walked ten blocks to see the culprits in action. In all that time he could have gone for help or found someone to stop them. It was obvious to me that my brother had another plan in mind. He had never wanted to stop them.

"But, Alden, how do you propose to follow them?"

Just then another horse came walking up behind us, drawing an open wagon. With some effort the driver managed to convince the animal to stop and, grabbing my hand, Alden pulled me out into the street. It was Milton Bierly looking very out of place on the seat of the wagon and clutching the reins as if for dear life.

"Where did you get the wagon?" I asked as Alden pushed me up to the seat.

"Simms. Milt managed to borrow it, right, Milt?"

But Mr. Bierly was completely occupied as we jolted to a start and he began the fearsome task of directing the animal in such a way as to avoid running over pedestrians while at the same time preventing sudden changes in direction from overturning the cart. I was soon too much in fear for our lives to attend to our direction but eventually, as we headed north on the wider Halsted Street towards downtown, I protested. "But we have lost them. I do not see Weaver's cart. Where are you going?"

Someone shouted a loud curse as we nearly ran him over and the horse slipped on some ice nearly sliding into a cab in front of us.

"You'll see," Alden told me. "We're pretty sure we know where they were headed. Aren't we, Milt?"

Our driver was breathless with concentration pulling on the reins to avoid yet another collision.

"You've followed him before?"

"Right. You'll see. Watch out, Milt."

We turned our attention to yelling warnings to Mr. Bierly about obstacles until we were well into the Loop and had turned east. When we reached State Street Alden demanded we stop, then jumping down he offered me a hand.

"Just keep driving around the block until we return. Pick us up out front," he told Mr. Bierly. I watched with some concern as he jolted away nearly hitting a police van.

"He'll be all right," Alden insisted. "Come on."

He led me down a side street to an alley that ran behind the storefronts. Sure enough, the cart was being unloaded. We waited until they were done and Weaver came out of the door and climbed on to the cart. As they pulled away Alden and I crept along the brick wall of the alley. It was like a cavern, that alley between the tall buildings that rose on either side. We reached the door they had used and over it hung a newly painted sign "Franklin Clothiers." My mouth dropped. Boldly, I knocked on the door.

"Emily, what are you doing?" Alden protested but it was too late. By then the door had been opened and who should it be but young Mr. Sidney Franklin himself.

"Miss Cabot?" He was stunned. He must have expected the knock meant the return of Weaver or one of his associates. It took him a moment to regain his composure.

But he covered his surprise well as I introduced my brother and he invited us in, eagerly leading us out of the dim storeroom where we saw the open crates that he must have been unpacking. I noticed he had a garment draped over his arm as we emerged into the lights of a men's clothing store that gleamed with varnished wood and copper fittings.

"Welcome to my newest venture, Miss Cabot. Franklin's—the finest men's clothing in the city. Or, at least, that is the name we aspire to. I see you are surprised. I have left the university to join my father in business. At first, I found it rather dull stuff, as you can imagine. But it was Professor Lukas who helped me to convince my father that, in addition to the garment manufacture and wholesale business in which he had invested, an entry into the retail side was just the sort of expansion needed. At first he grumbled. You know how he is. But when Lukas pointed to the accomplishments of Mr. Marshall Field, Papa grunted his approval. He's skeptical, of course, but I told him we had to do it with style and talked him into all of this." He waved his hands at the gleaming surroundings with pride. "So, here we are and I'm so grateful to your Professor Lukas, I've even had this coat made specially for him." He smoothed the fabric that hung over his arm then held up the garment to show us. "Do look at this collar. It's mink. Wonderful, isn't it?"

He laid the coat on the counter and continued to smooth the fabric.

"Mr. Franklin, I must tell you, as a deputy to the chief factory inspector of the state that the goods just delivered to you in those crates came from a shop which has been closed down due to smallpox. Those goods are in danger of spreading the infection and by law they are subject to immediate destruction."

He glanced at me sharply. "Deputy? Is that what you are doing now?" He smoothed the coat again then walked to the other side of the counter and, facing me across it, he calmly folded his hands. "Infected goods? I don't know what you mean, Miss Cabot. No goods have been delivered today. I am afraid you are mistaken. Oh, those crates in the back? But we received those weeks ago. We've been so busy setting up we simply haven't had time to unpack them."

"We saw them delivered, Mr. Franklin. We saw them loaded from a tenement sweatshop that was found to be infected and brought here."

He looked me in the eye. "I assure you, Miss Cabot, you are mistaken. I'm sure, if necessary, I can produce the bills of lading that will prove those crates came from no such place."

"Mr. Franklin, surely you do not wish to spread this awful disease. If you could see the terrible effects of it you would understand better the need for such stringent enforcement." He grimaced. "Mr. Franklin, I have heard you sympathize with the plight of the workers in your father's factories. If you could see the conditions under which these garments are made, I am sure you would be appalled."

"Miss Cabot, this is business conducted under the rules of business. It is ruled by competition. We simply use the same suppliers as every other merchant in the city."

"But I have heard you express sympathy for your father's workers in the past. Do you not want to see those who work for you now treated fairly?"

"You have heard me complain when my father cut my allowance as he cut the salaries of his workers. I am glad to say I am no longer dependent on that stipend. I have become a businessman myself and, as such, I am subject to its laws." He chuckled. "We must change with our circumstances, Miss Cabot. Then, I could afford sympathy. Now, I must seek out the cheapest form of manufacture in order to be able to compete with every other clothing establishment in the city. You must go preach to Mr. Field and the others, Miss Cabot, not to me." He grinned at the thought.

"I am very sorry, Mr. Franklin, but if you will not destroy the infected goods I will have to report them to the authorities and they will be confiscated. The law says that they must and the law also prohibits the women who work in these sweatshops from more than eight hours of work a day. Mrs. Kelley, who has been appointed chief factory inspector by the governor, will see that these laws are enforced."

He frowned at that. "You must do as you choose, Miss Cabot. But I do assure you there will be no proof that anything in this shop has been infected. Furthermore I think you will find that law challenged which allows the destruction of perfectly good garments on the whim of women inspectors. It is clearly unconstitutional. Professor Lukas has proven this argument and you will find that you are not the only ones who can organize to influence the lawmakers in Springfield. Soon you will find out that the manufacturers have banded together in our own association to protect our rights. Lukas has convinced them and the constitutionality of this wanton destruction of goods is even now being challenged in court. After that, the eight-hour work rule will be next." He pointed a finger at me. "Those people at Hull House have the ear of Governor Altgeld but we'll see what happens when the most powerful businessmen in the city start showing solidarity on these issues. You might want to throw in the towel, Miss Cabot, and return to your books."

I looked around at the varnished wood and the thick woolen coats that hung in a corner. The well-lit room was such a contrast to the tenements we had seen and it was nothing to the lavish mansion that Sidney Franklin would return to that evening. He would be waited on and fed a meal of many courses while those who produced the goods on his neat shelves went to bed hungry.

Alden was leaning against the wall, arms folded. He had a slight smile on his face. "So this is Mr. Sidney Franklin, Emily. I had heard you were acquainted with him. But did you know he was at odds with his father's business manager? That would be the unfortunate Mr. Hanrahan."

Sidney Franklin started at that comment. With his red hair and pale complexion he suddenly reminded me of the man I had found dead in the Hull House parlor. I was shocked at the sudden thought. Before I could speak Sidney was snarling at my brother. "It was that woman at Hull House, Mrs. Kelley, who had a standing argument with Hanrahan. The man must have provoked her, and see what happened."

"But I understand you had argued with the man. He had been hired to manage this very nice shop, hadn't he? I have heard he was not pleased to have his place usurped and to be given the task of thwarting Mrs. Kelley and her inspectors instead."

Sidney Franklin smoothed the material of the fur coat again. He smirked. "The right of blood, don't you know. I am my father's heir, after all. I am rightly the one to choose my place. Hanrahan was only a hireling."

"But I heard he was the better manager," my brother continued. I wondered where he had gathered this information and whether he had shared it with Detective Whitbread. "I heard that he bragged you would not last in your current comfortable position if you continued to lose money for your father." Alden looked around the sumptuous fittings of the room. "I heard Mr. Hanrahan had totted up the cost of this place and weighed it against the sales and he was confident that he would start the new year right here in your place. So much more comfortable than hurrying around the West Side at the beck and call of the sweatshops. Lucky for you he's no longer in your father's employ." I looked at Alden. Where was he coming up with all of this?

Wherever it came from, his comments were hitting their mark. Sidney was red in the face. "Lies, all of it. Nothing but lies. My father would not replace me with that slimy little snake. I'm his son. I'm flesh and blood."

I couldn't help asking, "Alden, how do you…"

"Everybody knows it. They had arguments. Everybody who worked for Franklin heard it. They were all just waiting to see the father kick him out and make him work for a living.

They were expecting it, as soon as the new year came around." I remembered Alden talking to Weaver. He cultivated the man in public, even if he followed him secretly as we had today.

"Get out. Get out of my store or I will have you arrested. You'll see. It's those women at Hull House who killed Hanrahan." He spit out the name as if it put a bad taste in his mouth.

"There's Milt. Come on, Em. There's no talking this boy around. He's scared if he doesn't turn a profit his father will throw him out." Alden held open the door and outside I could see Mr. Bierly struggling to keep the horse from walking on. I did not wish Sidney a good night but only rushed through the door into the cold of the falling darkness. I was angry as my brother handed me up into the seat of the cart. We had followed Weaver in secret yet I was sure that all the information Alden had about disagreements in the Franklin's company must have come from that source. What was Alden playing at? It must be a very dangerous game.

NINETEEN

As we had another exciting ride back to Hull House, Alden sensed my anger and tried to excuse himself. "Weaver works for Franklin—the father. He arranges the contracts with the sweatshops, so he's been moving the goods when one is shut down and Fitz gets a kickback. His people warn them so they can move the stuff before Mrs. Kelley's people get there. Weaver is getting a bonus for every lot he saves. He worked for Hanrahan directly. I know you think he's craven. He's a hard man, Emily, from a hard life. He told me about how Hanrahan came expecting the job that the son took. He was not happy about it but there's a professor from the university who advises the father and he backed the son." I frowned at him. He looked over my shoulder at Mr. Bierly but that young man was fully occupied with trying to handle the horse. "Oh, Emily, don't be so…Yes, Weaver told me when we were in a saloon. There's nothing like drink to make a man confide in you."

"Alden, you have no business going to saloons. How can you?"

"Oh, Emily, don't be such a prude. There's things to be learned in the saloon that you will never learn where you are. Besides, it's my life. Mrs. Kelley will be less scrupulous on how the information gets to her. Just tell her what we saw. It's probably best if you and Mrs. Kelley complain to the authorities although Whitbread says the police won't do anything as long as the alderman is against it. But that's where the goods are going." He shrugged.

"And what about the death of Hanrahan? Hanrahan worked for the Franklins," I pointed out. "What if he was coming to me to tell me something about them?"

"Emily, Hanrahan was killed by Flaherty. The man recognized him and he was coming to tell you."

"But how do you know that?"

"Because Weaver told me. He said Hanrahan was the one who spotted Flaherty, not him."

"Weaver! He's the one who told you Sidney Franklin was at odds with Hanrahan." It wasn't worth arguing with Alden. He would not listen to me. But I had trouble believing in the fugitive. He was a phantom that my brother was chasing, always just around the next corner.

I was cold through and through by the time we jolted to a stop in front of Hull House and I was deeply discouraged. I had no hope for a solution to the murder investigation, only fear about how it could turn out. I didn't believe in the figure of the fugitive. And I could not help remembering what Mrs. Kelley had told me about seeing my brother standing over the dead man. I felt as if I hardly knew my brother any more. If I did not know him, how much less could I say I knew the others I had met at the settlement? It seemed impossible that one of them could have hammered in the skull of the dead man but I had seen the result and no matter how I tried I could not purge my mind of the image. Somehow the red hair of Sidney Franklin had brought back the gruesome sight. I shook myself to try to rid my mind of the thoughts.

I had been trying to concentrate on the job of assistant inspector that I had taken on. Those in power were finally allowing enforcement of the vaccination and quarantine laws but they would not prevent infected goods from being sold, much less enforce the eight-hour working law for women that had been passed the previous year. Without their cooperation, how could the rule of law be effective? In this, too, it seemed impossible to achieve anything.

Alden was holding the horse's head as I hastily jumped down and headed up the walk to the steps. I heard my brother say, "You go ahead, Milt. I've got it. Emily," he called out to me, "wait for Milton. He has something to say to you."

Oh, no. Alden, how could you? I waited as Mr. Bierly stumbled on the curb and then hurried to catch up to me. How little I knew of him. Despite the words of Mrs. Kelley and Dr. Chapman, I could not rid myself of a suspicion of Milton Bierly that ran very deep. Nonetheless, I followed him up the steps. Inside he gestured me to go into the front study. There was no one around. We were late for dinner and they would all be in the refectory. I could not dash away from the patently nervous young man so I busied myself with removing my hat.

"Miss Cabot, I spoke with your brother…" He paused as if uncertain what to say. I waited impatiently hoping my stomach would not make noises. I hadn't eaten since breakfast. Remembering again what Dr. Chapman had said about this young man's intentions and desires, I was in no mood to encourage him. Alden had planned this rendezvous and I had fallen into his trap. "Miss Cabot, you asked me what I was doing Christmas morning when that man was killed here, in this room." This was not what I had expected, not at all. Unfortunately his words conjured up the scene I had witnessed in this very room and the bloody mess that was the dead man's head. I shut my eyes to try to block it out but it only became more vivid. "I am sorry if I have brought back painful memories of that day. Won't you sit down?"

"No, I'm fine." I snapped my eyes open and they were filled with the sad round face of Milton Bierly. I stepped back. He was too close.

"I'm sorry but it is this." He held his hand out with a small package covered in brown butcher's paper. "I wanted to give you this. To explain why I was down in the metal workshop that morning."

I took the package and, balancing it on the edge of Miss Addams's desk, I untied the string and folded back the paper. Inside was a short chain of dull hammered silver. It was made up of small leaves each no bigger than a fingernail, strung together with tiny links.

"It's a bracelet, you see. I wanted to give it to you as a Christmas present. I've been learning from Herr Glock, he teaches the classes. He had a jewelry shop in the old country. It's not very good, and I am not very skilled so it took me a long time so I wasn't finished, you see. And I was trying to finish it." He was looking me straight in the eye, as if trying to make sure I would believe him. His round face was still red from the cold. He was so earnest I had to swallow before I could pull my eyes away to look again at the gift he had forced upon me.

"It is very beautiful. Very nice. Thank you."

"Do you really think so? Herr Gluck helped me, of course. I think I spoiled one corner, the tip here but we smoothed it. I knocked a piece off." He rubbed his fingers on one of the leaves near the catch.

"No, you didn't spoil it. It is very fine," I told him. It was only the truth. Much as it wasn't what I would have expected, much as I would have predicted that he would choose or make some object quite clumsy or even ridiculous, I had to admit the little bracelet lying in my hand was a miracle of skilled workmanship.

He took back his hand and looked at me. "I just wanted you to see I really was working on something that day. I had no idea Mr. Hanrahan was being murdered in the room above me. I swear to you, Miss Cabot, I had nothing to do with that man's death."

I was appalled with myself. What had I been thinking? That this gentle, voluble, awkward young man had grasped that candlestick and beaten that man until he was dead?

"No, of course not, Mr. Bierly, you had nothing to do with it. Of course not…I am so sorry if I was suspicious it's just that I was worried about my brother, or Mrs. Kelley. I don't know what I was thinking."

"It's all right. So long as you know now. I wanted to tell you. I want you to think well of me, Miss Cabot. In fact, I would do anything in the world for you, Miss Cabot."

"Thank you, Mr. Bierly. That is very kind of you." I interrupted him firmly. What had Alden told him to encourage him so much? I was very much afraid of where this was going. "It is a difficult time for all of us between the epidemic and the murder investigation. It is good to know we have loyal friends."

His face was completely red now and drops of sweat gleamed on his forehead. "I hope—I hope to be more than that to you one day, Miss Cabot."

Oh, no. "Please, Mr. Bierly," I tried to forestall him.

"I—I must tell you, Miss Cabot—Emily." His round red face filled my vision again. I saw a little bead of sweat roll down the side of his face. I took another step back but his hand, like a little paw, gripped my hand still holding his present. "Please, allow me to speak, Emily." He cleared his throat. "You are the most wonderful woman I have ever met. I admire you so much. I have never known a woman who was so intelligent, who could understand what is going on here, what we are all doing here. Your brother…"

Yes, my brother Alden, wait until I could get my hands on him, this was his doing.

"Forgive me, but your brother told me, he believes, well, he thinks, anyhow, that your affections are free. That they are not engaged elsewhere."

He harrumphed to clear his throat again. "I wish…it is my dearest wish that you might consider placing your affections in me. Mine are already most tender towards you." His big brown eyes behind the owlish spectacles held my gaze.

"Oh, Mr. Bierly."

"Milton. Surely we are on such terms that you can call me Milton?" He gulped. "Emily, I know I am not a handsome man and you are far more intelligent than I am." I blushed realizing how vain I must be in this area for him to think so. "But I have a great love for you. I would be so proud to be able to use my family resources to make sure you never want for anything."

"Mr. Bierly, I really don't know what to say. Please, stop."

He withdrew his hand from mine and looked down. "I know I am not worthy of such a woman."

"Please, Mr. Bierly. It is not that at all. I am sure you are worthy of any young woman."

"I could not care for just any young woman, Miss Cabot. Only you would understand my work, such as it is. Only you would not ridicule such efforts. You are the only woman of my acquaintance who could share a life doing what I want to do."

I could see then that he had a little dream, a very nice little dream of how he and his helpmate would spend their lives working with the less fortunate, advancing the theories of social justice that he treasured and believed in. I felt ashamed of myself. I was even more ashamed that he thought me capable of such unselfish motives. Here I was, anxious to get word from the publisher that our study was published so that it could restore me to the place at the university that I had lost and Milton Bierly was inviting me to continue in settlement work. How wrong he was about me. But perhaps he was not so ignorant of my true self as I might have thought. His next comment made me wonder.

"I...I greatly admire your academic achievements as well, Miss Cabot. Dr. Chapman has explained to me how your studies were so unfairly cut off. If my fortune could in any way assist you in returning to those studies, nothing would make me happier than to support them."

I jumped as if he had hit a sensitive nerve. "Mr. Bierly, I don't know what to say to you."

"I would offer you my heart and any possessions I have, Miss Cabot. But if you do not believe in the institution of marriage, as I know some people do not..."

"No, no, Mr. Bierly." I had to stop him before he expounded a theory of free love or some other astounding thing from his reading. "No, I am most grateful to you, of course, and tremendously complimented by your interest, but I had no idea you felt this way. I mean to say, I had no idea of looking for that kind of attachment. Really, Mr. Bierly, Milton, I have no thought to marry at this time. No thought at all about such a thing."

He shuffled his feet and I dearly wished I could fly away and escape this confrontation. *Oh, Alden, wait until I get my hands on you.*

"I see. I hope you are not offended by my declaration, Miss Cabot."

"No, no, of course not, Milton."

"Perhaps you might think it over and, well, think about it."

"I would not want to lead you to hope for something that will not happen, Mr. Bierly. Please, let us remain friends. This will not come between us."

He let out a large breath and touched my hand. "I hope, if nothing else, I may always have your friendship, Emily." Then he hurried from the room.

It was my turn to expel a large breath. I wrapped the bracelet back up in its paper and hurried to the dining room where I was able to make a plate for myself just before the platters were removed. As I sat at the end of a half empty table, Dr. Chapman joined me. I pushed the brown paper package towards him. "Look at that."

He carefully folded back the paper. "What is it?"

"It's lovely, isn't it? It's from Mr. Bierly. He made it himself. That's what he was hammering on Christmas morning. A bracelet, a gift, for me."

He smiled and fingered the bracelet.

"Yes, I know, it's quite beautiful. Who would have thought that Mr. Bierly could make such a thing?" I shook my head. "But he did. And it was for me, and I have to admit…I do admit… it is very, very good."

"You are most fortunate to be the recipient of such a gift," he said still smiling.

I sighed. I was wrong about Mr. Bierly in this and perhaps in other things.

Dr. Chapman seemed a little sad as he fingered the silver bracelet. "And you accepted the tribute? Is there, perhaps, an announcement forthcoming, Miss Cabot? Something we should all know about?"

I blushed painfully, a huge rush of warmth flowing up my neck to my cheeks. I could feel it. "No, Dr. Chapman. There is no announcement. There will be none. This was a gift of friendship, nothing more. We are friends." Again, I was furious at my brother. What had he led them to expect?

He dropped the bracelet and was silent for a moment. I was becoming embarrassed by the awkwardness of it when he finally spoke, "I have come to ask for a favor, Miss Cabot."

"Certainly," I said, hoping he did not wish me to encourage any other awkward young men.

"I wonder if you would consent to leave the cares of Hull House behind for an evening? Mr. Langlois has asked me to bring Miss Maglioni to a symphony concert on Friday night. There is a singer he wishes her to hear and he himself will be playing. He has provided tickets and I would be most grateful if you would join us."

"That would be wonderful, Doctor." I was surprised and grateful.

"Good then. He has told Miss Maglioni to be here at seven. We will have to take streetcars, I'm afraid."

"I will look forward to it," I told him, and I felt happier than I had in months as I ascended the stairs that night. The thought of the evening to come lifted my heart.

TWENTY

So I pulled out the pink satin dress I had not used since the previous spring and carefully ironed it. And I found the blue velvet box with the single string of pearls that my mother had given me the year I began attending parties of the "season" in Boston. It seemed a time and place that were faraway from the West Side of Chicago.

When Maria came to Hull House on Friday night she wore the evening dress she had made for the Christmas performance and a thin shawl that provided no protection from the slicing cold wind of that evening. We admired the gown which Maria had made herself from flawed silk cleverly draped to hide the stains and I convinced her to accept the loan of a warm velvet cloak before Dr. Chapman arrived. He apologized profusely for the need to use the streetcar but neither Maria nor I cared how we escaped the world of disease and despair of the West Side tenements that night, so long as we did so. And I was happy to have time in his company at all after he had been avoiding me since that kiss in the snow.

In any case, it was a wholly different world we entered at the Auditorium Theater. As we walked through the low ceilinged lobby we were greeted by several people from the university. It reminded me of how much I missed the activities there and the whole atmosphere. I was gratified for each and every mark of recognition. Stepping into the golden hall among the throngs of people in evening dress was like stepping into bright sunlight from the shade. I had forgotten the impact of the huge oil murals and the gold metalwork that adorned the vast room, but to see them as for the first time through the eyes of my young friend gave me a shiver of excitement.

We sat on the main floor this time and looking up, I saw the Glessners in their box. When Mrs. Glessner waved an acknowledgement I recognized the woman sitting beside her.

"There is Mrs. Larrimer," I said to Dr. Chapman.

He looked up, pretending he had not noticed his ex-fiancée before. "Yes. She has moved to the city permanently."

This news gave me pause, but soon all that was forgotten as applause greeted the musicians. If the surroundings impressed Maria, the music quite overcame her. An Italian soprano sang arias from Mozart and Verdi, and we listened enraptured. When we joined the wild applause I looked at the faces of my companions and saw the doctor grinning with delight. It must have been a year since I had seen such an expression on his face. At the intermission we saw Michel Langlois step to the edge of the stage and peer out, smiling when he saw us. We waved. Then I received a note from Mrs. Glessner asking us to come up to their box during the break. I was touched and grateful that she would extend such a courtesy to me.

A look of dismay crossed Maria's face as we approached the glittering crowd outside the box. She whispered she had no gloves. It was true, all of the women wore gloves, as I did, but gloves were the least of it. All three of us might have passed for rag pickers in this company.

"No," I whispered back. "You have no gloves and I don't have any jewels." Every woman in the group wore a diamond choker and miles of pearl strings. "But that will not stop us, will it?"

I seized her hand and pulled her along with me to speak to Mrs. Glessner who greeted us warmly. Maria was soon drawn into conversation by Mr. Glessner and the Glessner's daughter, Fanny. Looking around for the doctor I saw him in conversation with Marguerite Larrimer. She had one gloved hand draped lightly on his forearm and another clutching his elbow in an almost proprietary gesture. When I looked at his face it seemed once again drawn and tired which made me angry with the woman. Marguerite Larrimer was the type of woman who always needed others, especially males, to lean on. For the doctor, this evening out ought to have been an escape from heavy responsibilities.

"Mrs. Larrimer makes a very decorative addition to society this year, doesn't she?" I was unpleasantly surprised to look up and see Sidney Franklin, who offered me a glass of champagne. "It is very daring of them to be seen together, isn't it? After the scandal surrounding her husband's death, I mean."

He didn't mention our last meeting, but it seemed to me he was getting his revenge for the suspicion my brother's questions had involved. He was obviously comfortable and confident in the environment of the boxes of the Auditorium Theater. Confident that nothing could touch him.

"Dr. Chapman was innocent in that matter. He would not shun her merely for the sake of gossip."

"Of course not. And then, she is a very wealthy widow I hear. That can make such a difference. I hear she has been invited to join all the best ladies' committees. Mrs. Potter Palmer herself has taken her under the gilded wing. And Dr. Chapman has even gotten her a seat on the board of the county hospital. No doubt her money will help to do much good for the hospital." He took a sip and looked at me across the top of his glass, "and for the doctor, of course."

I felt my face reddening. The champagne gave me a light feeling as if I were floating off above the glittering crowd under the chandeliers. Sidney Franklin had found the spot to touch that would irritate. I had come to believe that I understood the doctor, who was like me in so many ways. But I never understood quite what he felt about the wealthy widow, Marguerite Larrimer. Sidney was the type of person who could spot that uncertainty and press on it.

He smiled as if satisfied with a hit. "But have you left your friends at Hull House, Miss Cabot? If so, I must congratulate you on your escape. I am happy to see you exchange the company of those harpies for your charming companion. Who is she?"

He was looking at Maria, flushed with excitement as she talked to Fanny and Mr. Glessner. I took a sip of champagne wondering what Mr. Sidney Franklin would think if I told him she was from one of the sweatshops that made the goods for his store. "She is a pupil of Mr. Langlois, a singer. He invited us to accompany her tonight. And neither Dr. Chapman nor I have abandoned Hull House. We continue to live and work there."

"Ah, a pretty songbird." He tipped his glass to get the last of his champagne as chimes rang out calling the audience back to the seats. "I'm sorry to hear you have not returned to your studies. As for that settlement, I understand there will be an arrest soon that will end all that. You might think about leaving before the ax falls, Miss Emily Cabot." A smirk concluded this parting shot, and then he bowed and drifted away. I might have been alarmed by this prediction but I didn't believe him. How would he know what the authorities planned? And hadn't he shown himself capable of jumping to incorrect conclusions by his assessment of Maria? I smiled stiffly at his retreating back.

Sidney Franklin's understanding of the world was warped and corrupt. I had no reason to believe he could tell the future.

Maria was at my side and we went together to rescue the doctor from the woman who still clung to him. Marguerite Larrimer looked up into his eyes. "Stephen, won't you stay with me, up here? There's an extra chair in the box. I'm sure Mrs. Glessner would not mind."

I thought this was much too much to endure from the woman. "Oh, dear," I said, trying to sound pathetic, "I'm not sure Maria and I could find our way back to our seats without the doctor."

"No, certainly, I must accompany the young ladies," he gently removed her clinging hand and stepped forward between Maria and me, taking an elbow of each of us. "We had better hurry, those chimes mean they are about to begin. Good evening, Mrs. Larrimer."

"The next time, perhaps you could join me?" There was a note of helpless entreaty, as if she would be unable to come, herself, without him to escort her. Yet she had managed to attend this evening, I thought to myself. She did not want to let go of him. "I am thinking of taking a box for the rest of the season. The Glessners have been so terribly good to me. They brought me tonight."

She said it as if they were her dearest friends. She barely knew them. "Yes, Mrs. Glessner has been very kind to me as well," I told her. "I spent more than a week at their house when I was ill last spring. They are a very generous family." I was glad to see she looked a little startled by this information.

She reached across to touch my arm. "Any time, Miss Cabot. There will always be room for you and your friends in my box."

It was a promise I would have welcomed from Frances

Glessner, but coming from Marguerite Larrimer it seemed more like a threat. We thanked her and hurried away.

"She is very beautiful, the signora," Maria whispered to me.

I bit my lip. She was very beautiful. But I realized as I listened to the Schubert and Strauss of the second half that whatever Marguerite Larrimer might have to offer Stephen Chapman, she could not ease his spirit. The previous year I had assumed the doctor belonged to the world of the Glessners and Larrimers. Now I understood that I myself was much more at home in that world than he would ever be. It did not come naturally to him to wear evening clothes and attend supper parties. Knowing him better now I understood that it was his love of the music that allowed him to endure it. He had never belonged to Marguerite's world but I realized as I saw her gazing down at him that she would draw him back into it if she could. I stole a glance at his face and knew he had no idea of this at all. How much easier his life would be with the money Marguerite had inherited. But as I listened to the orchestra I realized with a lurch that I could not bear to see that happen. I would not lose him to Marguerite. I thought—I was almost sure now—that he cared for me. But he thought of me as a child. So young. Not that young. I would have to confess my feelings before he would ever say anything. He was only too aware that he did not belong in the society that I came from. That was why he had pressed the case for Mr. Bierly. Milton Bierly came from money and a family of status in Eastern society. It was all very alien to Stephen Chapman but he thought that was where I belonged, in the world of the Glessners which was also the world of Sidney Franklin.

Suddenly it was clear to me that he was very wrong in his assumptions about what I was, and what I needed, and I longed to set him right. Suddenly I could see myself at his side in a university setting. I would appreciate his need to spend time at his laboratory, and he would appreciate my desire to study and research and write. I thought if I could only talk to him about it, he would see how close our interests were and stop encouraging Milton Bierly. Our return from the concert would be my opportunity. I felt queasy at the thought, but having decided to speak, I put it from my mind and let go to follow the flight of the music with all my heart.

At the end of the concert we met Mr. Langlois briefly in the green room where he took the doctor aside and, I could see, pressed money on him to pay for a cab ride home.

In the cab, Maria leaned forward eagerly as we moved slowly away in the throng of carriages. "It was wonderful, wonderful. This is the most wonderful night of my life."

I added my thanks. The doctor looked tired but smiled at me. I was eager to speak with him alone but I was a little concerned at the way Maria shivered, more with exhaustion at the excitement than from the cold. I knew she would have to rise early to get to work.

"Thank you, thank you," she said again. "I will never forget tonight."

"We also enjoyed it, Maria. But won't you let us take you home? It is too late and too cold for you to walk alone from Hull House," I tried to persuade her. She was always so secretive about where she lived but I was afraid she would not be able to walk far, she was so buoyed up with excitement. "Even if you let us take you to somewhere close to it. We can let you out and not have to know exactly which house it is. I promise."

She turned to me, her dark eyes shining with reflections from passing street lamps. "You are so good, Miss Cabot. Your father, he died in the tragedy, it is true?"

I was completely surprised that she should know of this. I cold not imagine what made her think of it.

"Yes, Maria. That is so. It was back in Boston."

Impulsively, she took one of my hands in both her own. "I am so sorry. But, yes. I will take you to my family." She told Dr. Chapman the location and he gave directions to the driver. After that she continued to speak of her family, how her parents had come from Italy. How they had lived with her father's brother and how her father had died in a work accident at the stockyards and her mother had succumbed to consumption. She and her sister had lived with relatives until her sister married. It seemed their relations did not approve of the match. Since that time Maria had lived with her sister and her husband, helping to support the two children. Lucia, the sister, worked at home while her husband was in and out of jobs.

"But he is a good man," she told us. "You will see. Here, come, I will show you."

The cab stopped and she jumped down. I stepped out as the doctor asked the cabbie to wait.

We followed her up the stairs to the second floor of the two-story tenement. Like most of them it was divided into four sets of rooms, two on top and two on the bottom. She brought us into a single room where the door had been boarded up to further divide that set of rooms. The whole family lived in that one room. There was a bed in a corner surrounded by curtains strung from the ceiling and a straw mattress in another corner that provided a bed for Maria. A small carton on the floor served as an infant's crib. By a tiny stove near the door a big burly man rose from a wooden table. He looked at us with alarm as he clutched a toddler who had been sitting in his lap.

There was one oil lamp on the stove to light the room. "Maria, what is this? What are you doing?"

She answered him volubly in Italian that he seemed to understand although he replied in English, shaking his head.

"What do you think you are doing? You will ruin us all, girl."

But she spoke again, stamping her foot then turned back to me. "Here is my sister's husband. He is Mike, Mike Flaherty."

TWENTY-ONE

"Michael Flaherty. No, surely not. It cannot be." I was stunned.

Maria saw the shock on my face and stepped forward. "But he is not the tragedy. He did not hurt your papa. Come, sit. He must tell you now."

She pulled out a chair and insisted I sit opposite. The big man slid back into his seat, defeated. "She shouldn't have done it. She means well, but it'll be the ruin of us. Oh, Maria."

Taking the toddler from him, she went over to the box to look down at the baby.

"You are Michael Flaherty? I am Emily Cabot. Judge Cabot was my father."

He looked confused. "Oh, I know. She told me all about you. Yes, I am Michael Flaherty but I never harmed your da, miss. I didn't do it. But when they accused me of it, I had to run. I had no choice." He shook his head. "She wants me to tell you my story. She shouldn't have brought you here. She shouldn't have done it. I'm sorry, miss."

I felt Stephen Chapman's hand on my shoulder and looked up at him. "He killed my father," I told him. He glanced sharply at the man but Flaherty only seemed helpless, despite his large frame and the powerful muscles of his neck and arms. He must have been about my own age.

"I didn't do it," Mike Flaherty protested. "I didn't. It's a long story, ya see. But I didn't do it." He shifted his gaze from

Dr. Chapman to me. I felt the blood pounding in my head but I couldn't move, as if a heavy blanket had descended on my limbs. "It was back in Boston. Five years ago. My older brother Liam and me, we worked for the South Boston Horse Car Company but we joined the union. There was a strike and he was took in for throwing rocks at the scabs during the strike. We was on strike, ya see, and the owners they brought in scabs to drive the trolleys."

"I am aware of the facts of the case," I told him. "Bricks and stones were hurled at the cars. The police found piles of them on the rooftops along the way and witnesses testified that your brother and the two other men were seen throwing them."

"It's a lie, that was. They didn't do it. It was a man named Weaver and the others. You see, miss, the owners hired them to protect the non-union drivers. But that wasn't enough. They wanted to make the union look bad. So they did it. They put the piles of stones there. They threw some and then they testified as how my brother and the other union organizers did it. There weren't none of the people lived there said they saw them. It was only all these men paid by the owners."

"They weren't the ones who testified that you were seen on our street the night my father was shot," I told him. I could still hear the blood beating in my ears. "Those were neighbors. People I've known all my life."

"But that's just it, miss. I was there." I shifted in my seat, feeling nauseous. I didn't want to stay in this room. "No, listen, please, your da, he suspected there was something wrong when it all come before him. He could see there was something not right about it. So he sent the word out on the streets to find out secret like, what really happened. He knew the police were in the pocket of the owners. When I heard that, I went to him, see, and I told him the truth of it, how it really was. And he said, if those men testifying were in the employ of the owners, he could throw the case out. He told me to go to my brother's lawyer and tell him to ask them under oath did they ever work for the owners. And if they lied, they'd be the ones to go to jail.

"I was so happy, miss. I left there and I was going to go to the lawyer next day and make him do what your father said. But I should have known, when I left that night and I seen that someone was lurking across the street. I thought it was me they was after and I thought they was following me. I ran and I hid figuring I'd stay hid long enough to get to my brother's lawyer. Then next day they say your da's dead and they wanted me for it."

I clenched my fists together and closed my eyes. I could see it all again. I was in a classroom at Wellesley, being called out to the president's office where, in a voice choked with sobs, Alden told me the terrible news. Something had shattered then. It was the life I had known. After that day it had all been so different and my greatest regret was that I had never been able to speak to my father again, to ask him what to do about it. He would have known. I opened my eyes and the teary red face of the big man before me filled my vision.

"What could I do? Nobody would believe me, and, like you said, there were them that saw me there. I had no choice. I had to run or get hanged."

"You're still wanted then?" the doctor asked squeezing my shoulder.

"Oh, aye. I was a fugitive from that day. I had to run. So I came here where I had a cousin and I met Lucia. My poor Lucia." He hung his head, tears falling down his cheeks. "I love my Lucia but I bring her nothing but trouble. First her family cuts her off for marrying the likes of me, they wanted her to marry an Italian, see. Then I can't keep a job for fear that

Weaver or one of them others will see me and turn me in. Twice he nearly got me, nearly cornered me. I was going to move us all away out west but I ain't been able to get the money and then my Lucia got sick."

"And Hanrahan," I asked. "Did you know Hanrahan? He saw you and recognized you, didn't he?"

"Hanrahan?" He looked puzzled at first. "Oh, no, miss. Him that was killed at the settlement house. He worked for the horse company, sure, miss. I didn't know him but I seen him. But I didn't see him in Chicago. I didn't kill him. I swear that to you."

There was a pounding at the door that made me jump.

"Police. Open the door." I recognized the voice. It was Detective Whitbread.

Michael Flaherty stood up facing the door with wide eyes.

"Don't be foolish, man. Open the door." The doctor stepped closer to me as he said it. When Flaherty didn't move, he spoke to Maria. "Open the door, Maria. You must."

She hesitated but when more blows were struck against the door, she sidled over, unlatched it and let it swing open. Detective Whitbread stepped inside followed by my brother, Alden, and two uniformed policemen. They did not seem surprised to see us. All of them held pistols.

TWENTY-TWO

"Michael Flaherty, I have a warrant for your arrest for the murder of John Cabot."

Flaherty backed away until he was against the curtained bed but Maria rushed forward yelling "No!" and grabbing at Whitbread's arm. "No, you cannot do this. You cannot do this."

Whitbread merely looked down at her but Alden reached out to pull her off. She twisted away from him and faced Stephen and me.

"You, you did this. You trick me. I believe you my friend. You bring them here, you…" Her speech turned into Italian that I did not understand. Detective Whitbread waved off one of the policemen who took a step towards her. Michael Flaherty yelled something to her in Italian. Whitbread turned back to the man.

"Come now, sir. Are you Michael Flaherty?"

The man put his hands to his face.

I stood up. "Alden, what are you doing here?"

"We got him. I followed you. I never thought she would take you here. I thought she would go home from Hull House and I'd try to follow then. Every time I've tried before she lost me. But we were outside the theater and we followed. I sent Milt to get the police while I stayed." He was proud of his accomplishment. "Weaver tipped me off about Maria."

"Weaver. Alden, what have you done?"

"I've caught the man who murdered our father, that's what I've done."

"But what if it's a mistake, a terrible mistake?"

"Oh, stop it, Emily. Whitbread has a warrant. I knew Flaherty was here. I told him and he wired Boston so he would have it when we found him. Michael Flaherty is wanted for our father's murder. I'm sorry if you didn't figure it out first but there it is."

"But, he says he didn't do it."

"You don't know what you're talking about." He raised his pistol leveling it at Flaherty. "It's him. He's the one. He killed our father."

"Don't Alden!" I yelled.

"Lower the pistol, Mr. Cabot," Detective Whitbread demanded, holding up a hand to stop the uniformed men from moving forward. Alden's hand trembled and I held my breath. "Put it down, Mr. Cabot." With one step Whitbread closed his hand over the gun and removed it. The others grabbed Alden by the arms. While he struggled, yelling for them to let him go, Whitbread removed the bullets from the pistol and put them into his pocket. "Release him," he barked. Then he handed my brother the gun. "The law will take care of this, Mr. Cabot."

"But he says he didn't do it," I told the detective. "He says that someone else was there and that someone connected to the company did it."

Whitbread looked at me with a serious expression. "Be that as it may, Miss Cabot, this man is wanted in Massachusetts for the crime. Your brother has come to us with the information concerning his whereabouts and has insisted we take him into custody." Turning back to the accused man he said, "Come, Mr. Flaherty. You will have to tell your story in court."

"He's lying anyhow, Emily. Of course he would tell you he didn't do it," Alden snarled.

"Alden, you fool. It was Weaver who sent you here wasn't it? And Weaver works for the Franklins. They wanted you to find him."

"It's too late, Emily. He's taken," my brother blustered.

Suddenly Maria hurled herself at Detective Whitbread flailing and scratching. She had put the toddler down and rounded behind us so that she could launch herself between Flaherty and the detective. Whitbread struggled with her while telling the other policemen, "Stay back, stay back." He quickly had her encircled in his long arms and turned around facing us as she struggled, swearing in Italian. He had her arms pinned to her sides.

"Don't hurt her," Flaherty protested. "Stop it, Maria. Stop it, girl." When Whitbread had her subdued Flaherty tried to calm her. "Stop it. It's not your fault, Maria. I know you meant well. I have to go with them, now. You've got to stay and help Lucia. Let her go. She'll be all right now, won't you girl?" He pleaded with Whitbread.

"Calm down then and I'll let you go. You won't do any good fighting like this, young woman." Whitbread let her go then and she flung herself weeping into Flaherty's arms. "Come on, man, I have to take you to the station."

As Whitbread reached across to take his arm there was a wail from the bed and the curtains parted. A woman with arms and face covered with the blisters of the smallpox wrapped her arms around Flaherty, who turned to her.

"My wife, she's ill."

"Doctor," Whitbread nodded to the doctor who moved to the bed.

Stephen took one look at the woman and said, "Smallpox. Your wife must be moved to the pest house and you must all be vaccinated for your own protection."

"No. You can't take her away. I won't let you." Red-faced, Michael Flaherty grabbed the doctor by the coat.

"No," Maria wailed and both the children began crying.

"Mr. Flaherty step away from there." When the man did not respond Whitbread tried to ply him away. The two uniformed men stepped forward.

Flaherty looked at the advancing men with fear in his eyes and a wail went up from the sick woman lying on the bed. Dr. Chapman pulled himself away and bent to comfort her. There was a wild look in Flaherty's eyes as he faced the detective.

"I won't let you take her. I won't let you."

He swung a huge arm at Whitbread who ducked, then the others rushed forward to wrestle Flaherty to the floor. As he thrashed around, yelling and kicking, Maria screamed and Lucia called out from the bed. The table jumped and rattled in front of me and I pressed myself to the wall in an effort to stay out of the way.

"Here, now, calm down," Whitbread's voice rose above the melee. "Handcuffs," he ordered.

But Flaherty continued to struggle, yelling that he wouldn't let them take his wife away. Whitbread and the others raised him to his feet, hands manacled behind him. Head lowered like a bull, he kept trying to shake them off.

"It's not her we've come for," Whitbread tried to tell him. "The doctor will look after her. You must come with us. You know that. You're wanted for murder in Boston. Take him down to the wagon."

As they dragged him from the room I looked across at Maria clutching the baby and watching it all with huge eyes. Lucia Flaherty called her husband's name while the doctor held her back from trying to rise from the bed. "We must get her away from here to be treated."

"No," Maria cried.

"She must go to the pest house," the doctor told her. "They will be able to care for her. She is in a very bad way, Maria. She must have help."

Whitbread turned to Alden. "Mr. Cabot, go to Halsted Street. Quickly. We passed a cart from the pest house there. Bring them." Alden hurried out the door. "I must see to my prisoner, I will return." Detective Whitbread disappeared down the stairs.

I went to the bed and attempted to help the doctor calm the weeping woman. She was very weak. It was not long before we heard them coming back with the stretcher from the pest house cart. As they moved to her I stood aside and looked around. "Doctor, where is Maria? Maria and the children are gone."

When Detective Whitbread and Alden returned, the doctor faced them. "You must find Maria Maglioni and the children. They must be vaccinated if it is not too late or they too will fall ill. I will go with Mrs. Flaherty, she is out of her mind with worry." They moved aside as the stretcher bearers took Lucia out the door. Dr. Chapman was angry. Suddenly he turned on me and my brother. "You have frightened that girl into running away. You must find Maria and the children. I have to go, but you must stay and find them. They are children, all of them. They cannot survive out there alone."

He hurried after the stretcher and Detective Whitbread called an officer up the stairs and instructed him to start a search for the missing girl, then he turned back to us. "I'm afraid it will be too easy for her to disappear into the streets in this neighborhood."

"But, what if Michael Flaherty *is* telling the truth and someone else *did* shoot my father? You have taken Mr. Flaherty away to jail while his wife is dying and his children are lost." I recounted the story that Michael Flaherty told us.

"Why should you believe him?" Alden demanded.

"But isn't it more likely? Doesn't it sound exactly how Father would have acted?"

"You don't know that. I say he's lying."

"You say that because you listened to Weaver. He tricked you, Alden. He tricked you all along. He got you to track Flaherty down. He's working for the Franklins."

"I told you, Emily. Hanrahan recognized Flaherty. He told Weaver. Flaherty killed our father and he killed Hanrahan because Hanrahan saw him. You do not know. I have been looking for him for months. I had to get Weaver to tell me. I had to worm it out of him when he was drinking. He didn't care one way or the other. But he knew that Hanrahan regretted what had happened, especially when he saw you. Hanrahan was going to tell you the whereabouts of Flaherty. You don't want to believe it because I found it out."

Detective Whitbread intervened. "I have warned you, Mr. Cabot, of the evils of associating with Weaver. He is a dangerous man. As to Flaherty's story, the truth of it can only be proven by further investigation. Meanwhile, he is a fugitive. The valid warrant was rightly executed as you requested. Excuse me." He stepped to the door to confer with an officer who had come to report.

I turned to my brother. "Alden, how dare you follow us like that? I promised Maria we would not reveal where she lived. You caused me to betray her. Look at the terrible consequences." I gestured to the empty room.

"I wanted to capture the man who murdered our father."

"But what if you are wrong? You just don't want to admit you were duped by Weaver."

"Emily, think of what you're saying."

"But the Franklins…"

"You're a fool if you think anyone is going to accuse the Franklins of killing Hanrahan. Why should they? Don't you know that they and Powers and Fitz are all pressing Whitbread to arrest Mrs. Kelley?" He glanced at the door to be sure the policemen had not returned. "They want to call it an anarchist plot and have her arrested. Is that what you want? Or maybe you want them to arrest me for Hanrahan's death. Is that what you want?"

He would have gone on but Detective Whitbread returned to tell us Maria could not be found and he thought we should use the cab that was still waiting to take us back to Hull House.

"But we promised the doctor we would find Maria and the children," I protested.

"We have made our best effort, Miss Cabot. There is nothing more to be done tonight. We will continue the search tomorrow."

"And what about Michael Flaherty?"

"I will interrogate Mr. Flaherty and communicate his story to the authorities in Boston. They must investigate the truth of it. He will be returned to them in due course to stand trial."

Reluctantly, I allowed him to conduct me to the cab. I knew that in arresting Mr. Flaherty, he was only doing his job at the insistence of my brother. I thanked him for his care and asked him to inform me when Flaherty was to be sent back to Boston. Bitterly angry with Alden for betraying the trust Maria had shown in taking us to her home, I refused to talk to him further. When we reached Hull House, I ran up the steps, slamming the door behind me.

The evening that had begun as a respite away from the tenements of the West Side had ended in a nightmare. We were being swallowed up again by the hopeless sickness and poverty that surrounded Hull House. The house itself was an attempt to build a sort of bridge between the worlds of Prairie Avenue, where the Glessners and Franklins lived their lives, and the sweatshops and tenements of Maria's world. But it was as if the joy of the early part of the evening was an illusion. The two worlds were incompatible and it was a destructive mistake to try to meld them together.

TWENTY-THREE

I did not sleep well, haunted by the memory of Maria's frightened face and the wails of the children. I rose early and was sitting in the empty dining room, thinking about the story I had heard from Michael Flaherty the night before, when Dr. Chapman entered shoving my brother Alden before him. Both looked bleary eyed with lack of sleep and Alden's shirt was unbuttoned.

"He knows where she may be," the doctor explained curtly. Alden slumped into a seat. "He had been following her and he knows the whereabouts of the sweatshop where she has been working."

"I was trying to follow her home," Alden admitted reaching for a piece of toast. He loaded it with marmalade and shoved it into his mouth.

"Do you two have any idea what you have done?" I had never seen Dr. Chapman so angry. "How do you think that girl and those children will survive alone? Have you learned nothing about the dangers of life here? You think they all have family to fall back on as you do, as the people of your world do? You think to suffer a little disgrace is the worst that can happen. They die down here all the time, children like that. They die of starvation and sickness made worse by the lack of food and heat and care, things you have always taken for granted. You don't belong here, either of you. You have no idea of the dangers they face, so you let something like this happen. How could you return to your own warm beds last night without Maria and the children?" He rubbed a hand across he forehead, calming himself down. "Her sister is wild with worry. I promised her they would be safe."

"But do you think she will go to work?" I asked.

"She must, to survive. Come on." He grabbed Alden by the shoulder pulling him to his feet. He had already made it plain to my brother that his act the night before, betraying the trust of the poor working girl by following us, was despicable. I joined them, shocked by the doctor's scolding words and determined to prove to him that he was wrong about me. As I struggled into coat and overshoes the doctor warned us. "We must be careful. She will run at the sight of us. She has no reason to trust us now, thanks to you." He glared at Alden. "If we do not convince her to accept our help she will be sure to disappear. And once she knows we have found the shop she will never return to it. Without the money from that work she will be completely destitute. So we must not alarm her."

We followed Alden out into the biting cold of the winter air. A brisk wind blew shafts of snow as we struggled along the icy streets, climbing drifts frozen solid at the street corners. It must have been a two-mile journey before we reached the alley between a street of shops and a row of tenement houses.

"It's down there," Alden told us pointing. "It's over that stable about a third of the way down."

"Wait, there's someone coming out." The doctor pushed him to the side of the building and peered out carefully. "It's Weaver. Luckily, he's going in the opposite direction. Wait till he's gone." The doctor gave me a pleading look. "We must convince her that no harm will come to her if she accepts our help. And we must convince the others to be vaccinated." He had carried his satchel all the way. "Her sister was far gone with the disease. Not only Maria and the children but all of the other girls in the shop are in danger of infection. They fear the vaccination so much. I don't know how to convince them it will protect them." He was so much less sure of himself now, than he had been in the dining room. In some ways his lack of confidence was more alarming than his earlier fit of anger.

Alden stirred uneasily. "Maybe I should get help."

"What help? The police?" Dr. Chapman shouted. "Haven't you already done enough harm? No police. None. Do you understand?"

Alden nodded and the doctor led us down the alley.

The contract sweatshops rented parts of the tenements that even the most desperate did not want for living quarters. The rooms were at the rear facing the filthy alleys or, like this one, over stables where in the warm weather the sounds and smells would be unbearable. Even on such a cold morning we could smell the horses as we climbed the broken steps to the room above. The doctor stopped for a moment, then without knocking, he pushed open the door.

It was one room about twenty feet square in which a dozen girls and women were crammed at tables bent over sewing machines that whirred with the incessant pumping of the foot pedals. How they could see in the dim light was unimaginable but each one had stacks of fabric beside her from which she grabbed her work. At the front by a dirty stove stood a small man in a worn woolen suit. He was painfully thin and had a hacking cough. Standing beside a waist high pile of garments on the floor, he checked off a clipboard as he sorted them. He stopped and looked at us with alarm as we entered. It was quickly apparent that his English was not very good.

"We are looking for Maria Maglioni, please, we are only here to help her," Dr. Chapman told him, trying to scan the faces in the dim light of the room. The tailor stepped in front of his pile of clothes.

'No. No. No take. No take." He motioned with one hand.

"Doctor." I had spotted a child at the bottom of the pile of clothes. It was one of Maria's nephews. I realized with relief she must have come here the night before. At least they had found some shelter. But now the girl herself appeared, pushing her way through the rows of women from the back. Most of them had stopped to see what was happening.

"Maria," I told her, "we are sorry for what happened last night. We want to help you."

"Help? You take away Mike. You take away Lucia. Now you want to take away little ones. No, no. Go away."

The little tailor could not understand what was going on. He questioned Maria in a foreign language and when she snapped an answer he appeared alarmed and stepped behind a table in the corner.

"It's all right," Dr. Chapman tried to calm him. "I am a doctor. Maria's sister is sick. We want to help you. I bring vaccination." He held up his satchel. "It will help so you will not get sick."

The tailor looked even more frightened and there was another exchange between him and Maria. She stood, still wearing the evening gown of the previous night, her eyes blazing with anger and drops of sweat on her brow. I thought she looked feverish.

"Please, Maria, it will be all right." I tried to calm her. She held up a hand as if to keep me away.

"No. You no come here. No needles. No take clothes away." Her English deteriorated as her agitation increased.

"We want to help you. You don't want to get sick, like your sister, do you? We must vaccinate you and the children and the others here." A slew of Italian came from her mouth, none of which I understood except in tone. I thought she was cursing me.

"It is the law, Maria. We must do this to keep others from becoming sick."

"Bad law," she snapped. "No good. We no have to do." Communicating more to the little tailor she drew a folded paper from her bosom and opening it waved it in front of me. "Bad law," she hissed.

I reached out and took it from her then read it with incredulity. "It's a letter from the Illinois Manufacturing Association," I told the doctor. "It says a new law requiring confiscation of infected goods is unconstitutional and it is not necessary to obey it. I don't believe they have done this." I was disgusted.

"Look out," Alden warned.

We followed his gaze and saw the tailor had pulled out a rifle from behind the table. He held it unsteadily and it was obvious he knew little about guns.

"Weaver," Alden mumbled.

"No," the doctor tried to placate the tailor. "No. We are here to help." He bent over to his satchel on the floor. "It is medicine, only medicine."

But as he unlatched the case to show them there was an explosion. Screams and acrid smoke hung thick in the air. The doctor dropped to the floor.

I screamed. "Oh, no, Stephen!" I stepped to him. He had fallen against the mountain of garments and was bleeding all over them. "The gun, get the gun," he said but the little tailor had dropped the rifle and was crying hysterically, his hands held to his face. Meanwhile the girls were screaming and rushing for the door. Alden jumped across and grabbed the rifle.

"Get help," I told him as I tried to staunch the doctor's wound. His right arm was broken and bloody and he flinched with pain when I touched it, then fainted. I heard the wails of the toddler and I took him in my arms as Alden rushed out the door struggling to get by the women. When he was gone Maria stood in the doorway weeping.

"Maria, stay. It will be all right. I promise."

But she looked at me with horror as I hugged the toddler, then wildly at a box on the floor and I realized it must contain the infant. The poor tailor sat on the floor weeping over what he had done. Then she was gone.

"Oh, Maria."

I tried to comfort the child in my arms but the blood was flowing from the doctor's arm and he was still unconscious. I was nearly hysterical myself when Alden returned with a policeman and said help was on the way. By the time they were moving the doctor to a wagon to take him to the hospital, he had revived. He begged me to stay with the children and to find Maria and tell them it was an accident. He was worried about the tailor. I had to let them take him off without me.

I had promised him I would find Maria. I had promised him but once again I had failed.

TWENTY-FOUR

Even with Alden's help it was impossible. They dragged the poor hysterical tailor away and there was no sign of Maria. The policemen shrugged off our pleas that they find her. In the end, we were left with the children and the need to get them back to Hull House. There was a great stir of activity when we finally got there and many hands reached out to assist us. I couldn't help blaming Alden in my distress.

"Do you see what you've done?"

"I'm sorry, Emily."

"Sorry? Maria is gone with no way to support herself. She'll freeze to death or starve now. There's no one to take care of the children and Dr. Chapman, Dr. Chapman may be..." I couldn't say it. But he had lost an awful lot of blood.

"I'm sorry, Emily. I'm sorry." Alden rushed out of the room.

With the children in the care of Jennie Dow I changed my bloodstained dress for a clean one and before I left for the hospital I gave Miss Addams the letter that Maria had held out to me.

"The Illinois Manufacturers Association? I will find Mrs. Kelley and tell her. She had a letter from Governor Altgeld today. Perhaps it is about this. But I will see to it, Emily. Are you sure you do not want me to accompany you to the hospital? Please, send for me if there is anything the doctor needs."

I feared the worst about the doctor's condition but I knew he would not thank me if I took Miss Addams and the others away from their work. He had complained of the uselessness of relatives in the hospital waiting rooms where he thought they only hindered the staff.

But I could not wait patiently at Hull House for news. The amount of blood that had soaked my dress, and the groans of pain from the stoic doctor when he was moved, were unbearable to contemplate. I had to know the worst, so I took a horse trolley and walked through the city crowds to the county hospital where it took more than an hour of pleading with various busy persons before I finally found out where he had been sent.

"He got moved to a private room, miss. By the lady's order. She was here with a charity committee. I think the doctor had got her to work on it." I had found a nurse who knew him and knew of his injury.

"A lady?"

"A Mrs. Larrimer, miss. Lord knows he needs a lot of care. He was hurt bad. That arm is shattered. If he pulls through at all he's lost the use of it." She saw the shock on my face. "He's a strong willed one, though. I'm sure he'll make it. I have to see to this but if you go up those stairs and ask one of the nurses you'll find him." She patted my back and hurried off.

I climbed the stairs as if in a dream and got directions to a room down a quiet little corridor. The door was propped open and I saw Marguerite Larrimer sitting in a shaft of sunlight close to the bed. White faced, the doctor lay sleeping, his arm encased in bandages. She saw me and came to the door.

"Miss Cabot. He is very weak but they believe he will recover," she whispered. "But he may not recover the use of his arm." We stepped away from the door. "I was here when I heard. Stephen got me a place on the charity board, you know." When I said nothing, she felt compelled to explain. "I sold my husband's estate. I left that life behind me. Stephen knew I wanted to make amends."

It seemed such a very long time since I had come upon the two of them in the Music Building at the Fair. I had realized there was some feeling between them despite the years since she had broken their engagement and married someone else. As he lay there helpless, I realized that she believed it was obvious that she should be the one who stood at his bedside. She looked at me with concern.

"He would want to know of your visit but they have given him something to make him sleep. Do you want to sit with him?"

She appeared still as lovely as ever if a little sadder. But she seemed more peaceful than I remembered her. Perhaps it was because, at last, she could do something for him.

It flustered me. "I came from Hull House. To see how he is." I strained to see around her, into the room. "I was with him when it happened." I blurted that out.

"It must have been terrible for you." She looked over her shoulder at where he lay still asleep, but she did not move out of my way. "He told me of your work in the poor section of the city. I do so admire you, Miss Cabot, we both admire you—and the other young people who spend their time there."

I flushed. The thought that he had discussed me with this woman was embarrassing. What had he said? That I was some well-meaning little student with sanctimonious aims? How could he?

The work of Hull House in the poor section of the city sounded so clean and good in Marguerite Larrimer's description. If only that were true. I realized as I fought to stifle my anger that she and the other wealthy women in the city had no idea of the real circumstances. The dirt and desperate poverty—the hopelessness of the situation where people would freeze or starve without jobs or else succumb to the horrible disease contracted by going to work in the crowded tenements and factories where only illness thrived and spread with deadly purpose—these were all things they could not even imagine. And what power had we at Hull House, a group of well-meaning do-gooders, against the rich men who controlled it all? What had I accomplished but to lead my brother to Michael Flaherty whose arrest left his sick wife and helpless children abandoned? Dr. Chapman believed we did not belong to this world. And he had probably told her. It sapped my confidence to realize that.

"I came to be sure he is being taken care of. I—we all at Hull House, Miss Addams, Mrs. Kelley and everyone—we are all terribly concerned and want to be sure that he has everything he needs." I strained to get a view of him over her shoulder. She had braced an arm against the door jam quietly blocking the way.

"Have no fear about that, Miss Cabot. You must know that I will do everything in my power to make sure he gets the finest care money can buy. You of all people know what I owe him. I would do anything to help him, especially now that he has been so terribly injured." She shook her head. "I'm afraid it will be a very long recovery for him, if we are lucky enough that he survives and my fervent prayers are begging for that outcome. But I promise you, I will never let him want for anything. He will need much care. He is very badly injured. He may even lose the arm."

I was shocked to realize that she was right. He would need constant support and he had no money himself. Certainly I was not in a position to provide a tenth of the comforts that Marguerite Larrimer could afford. Suddenly I understood how he must have felt comparing his fortunes and resources with those of Milton Bierly and I was appalled. What could I offer him in comparison to this wealthy woman?

And this was just as my perceived stubbornness was causing her to give way. She dropped her arm from the doorway. "Would you like to sit with him for a while?" she asked reluctantly. "I'm sure I can find a little stool to sit on, or something. I couldn't bear to leave his side." She looked back at him longingly.

"No. I must return to Hull House," I told her. I had no desire to stay. The doctor had begged me to care for the children and Maria. The girl was still out in the cold with no money or home or means of support. How could I stay and report that to him when he awoke? How could I face him? But Marguerite Larrimer knew nothing about that.

"I must return. Please send word to us if there is any change in his condition."

She was relieved. "I will, I promise. You must assure all the people at Hull House that he is well looked after. He speaks so highly of you all." She reached out and took my hand. "We do so admire you, Miss Cabot."

"Thank you. I must go."

Blinded by tears, I found my way out of the building and trudged back to the trolley stop. In all honesty I had to admit to myself that I regretted ever coming to Hull House at that moment.

I remembered how sure I had been the night before that Stephen would never belong in the world of Marguerite Larrimer. I had a bitter laugh at myself. How could I think that the relief of being able to lead a life away from the hardships of the tenements could be anything but welcome? Of course he belonged with Marguerite in a world where there were not silly, foolish little tailors brandishing shotguns. Of course she could offer him the kind of comforts that only wealth could bring. It might even be possible that her wealth and position would allow her to have some effect on the ills the doctor had seen so much of and so wanted to remedy. It was clear to me at that moment that her wealth would be of far more use in that struggle than any of my inept attempts to help had been.

TWENTY-FIVE

The building was unnaturally quiet on my return. Somehow I felt it would always feel empty to me now. The ongoing ravages of the epidemic had brought much of the normal activity to a halt. Classes and clubs had stopped meeting and the people were still angry at Hull House for abetting the authorities in finding infected individuals, transporting them to the pest house, forcing vaccination of anyone who had contacted the sick person and destroying goods produced on premises that held infection. The fact that the special inspectors used Hull House to congregate was the final straw and lately we found ourselves shunned by the neighbors who had always been our friends. What was the use of the settlement house at all, if it was so hated?

I knew it was cowardly to let my personal disappointments rule my actions. Burying my doubts for the moment, I went to report on the doctor's condition after my return. I found Miss Addams and Mrs. Kelley at the desk in the front parlor.

"We are relieved to hear the doctor is recovering," Jane told me. "He will be well cared for there as he is so well known and respected. And we can know that we will be notified of any change. I thank you, Emily, for making the journey. But, come, sit down. You look tired. The children are with Miss Dow. We will keep them with us until we can make other arrangements."

"You were right about the manufacturers' association," Florence Kelley told me waving a piece of paper in her hand.

"I telegraphed Governor Altgeld and received his reply. It seems the most powerful owners have organized. Professor Lukas of the university and Mr. Franklin senior are the moving spirits. They have hired a prominent law firm to challenge the law in court. They attack not only the law requiring destruction of infected goods but the eight-hour day work rule for women."

"We thought it a great victory when that law was passed last year," Jane told me. Florence Kelley snorted.

"There was suspiciously little opposition at the time and we found out later there was no intention of enforcing it."

"But Mrs. Kelley has been diligent."

"True. We have managed to win some suits and to convince some employers by such legal harassment that it is less costly to obey the law than to pay the resulting fines. But now they will launch a major legal assault using their combined resources." She tapped the letter. "And the governor believes the statute will eventually be overturned."

"It is hopeless if even the governor predicts defeat," I said.

"We cannot give up," Miss Addams reproved me. "In the case of the infected goods during this epidemic, this group also plans a legal battle. So they have distributed copies of the letter which you gave me from this morning's incident to sweatshops and factories all over the infected areas."

"Governor Altgeld was already aware of that plan," Florence took up the story. "He is moving to counter it. He has announced he will call a conference of the governors of Indiana, Wisconsin, Iowa, Missouri, and Kentucky with a view towards instituting an embargo on all shipment of products of needle trades from Chicago. This action must force Lukas and Franklin and the rest to reconsider."

It seemed a game played at high stakes somewhere far above our heads. How it would play out must affect how many of our neighbors lived or died, yet there seemed nothing we could do to influence it. I listened silently as Miss Addams and Mrs. Kelley discussed the possible outcomes. Suddenly we were disturbed by the sound of the front door banging open and the cold draft it sent slicing into the room. An agitated Michel Langlois appeared in the doorway followed by Anna Farnsworth, who was in charge of answering the door that day.

"Where is she? Where is Maria? Maria Maglioni? What have you done to her?" He turned on me accusingly.

"She ran away, Mr. Langlois. Last night her brother-in-law was arrested, and her sister was taken to the pest house ill with smallpox. Maria panicked and ran away with the children. We went to try to find and help her this morning but there was a terrible accident. Dr. Chapman was shot. Maria was terrified and ran away again. This time she left the children. They are here, safe," I told him. It was obvious to me that he had already heard some of it before and blamed me.

"You tricked her, is it not so? You tricked her to take you to her home then you brought the police. Do you know what you do? She has no money. She has nowhere to go. Do you know what happens to a woman like that on the streets? She will die out there. You of all the people she knows. You she trusts. She trusted you."

The other two women intervened to calm him down. Mrs. Kelley took him in to see the children. The toddler recognized him and ran to him immediately. He had heard from a neighbor of the evening's upset as he was known to be a friend of the family.

He calmed down as he played with the children but he refused to look at me.

"I'm sorry, Mr. Langlois. My brother learned that Maria's brother-in-law was the man wanted in Boston for shooting my father. He did not tell me he was following us."

"He killed your father? Ah, I have always said he is no good that one."

"No. I think it is wrong. There is reason to believe he did not do it. But Maria's sister was very ill. Dr. Chapman took her to the hospital."

"The pest house. You send the poor woman to the pest house. You leave them with no mother, no father." He gestured to the children. "What kind of monsters are you?"

"We are not monsters, Mr. Langlois. We will care for them until their mother is recovered," Miss Addams told him.

"And what do you do if the mother dies and the father is in jail? You send them to the orphanage, eh? I know." He clutched the infant to him. "No. I will take them. Yes."

We began to protest but he became vehement.

"I take them. I take them. My landlady, she has children. I will pay. She will care for them."

Mrs. Kelley began to argue but Miss Addams intervened. "If you can make this arrangement with your landlady, Mr. Langlois, I see no reason why we cannot convince the local authorities that they are better off in your care than in the county orphanage." I realized that the musician was not just being high-handed in his demand that the children be entrusted to his care. It was that he, like Miss Addams, realized that the children were on the brink and could fall into a trough of misery. If not swept up and protected by someone with means, they could perish in that world of poverty on the West Side. It was the world that Dr. Chapman insisted I did not understand and a place where I did not belong.

While Jane Addams calmed Mr. Langlois with a discussion of the details of this plan, Mrs. Kelley took my arm and led me to the door.

"She will get him under control," she told me. "Why don't you go up to the dining room and get something to eat. We put out a cold buffet. Go along. There's nothing else for you to do here." I watched her slip back into the office, thinking of what Alden had said about the powerful men in the city who wanted to blame Hanrahan's murder on her and I shivered.

I climbed the stairs with a heavy step. She was right. My presence would only enflame the anger and hatred in the Frenchman's heart. He blamed me for the tragedy that had befallen poor Maria. It was hard to believe that only the night before we had all been so happy and excited to attend the concert. It seemed the malevolent spirit of the place could not allow us even one evening of such happiness without exacting a mercilessly heavy toll.

I had little appetite but I filled a plate from the sideboard where cold ham and potatoes had been set out. Then I joined Milton Bierly and Mr. Wall, the smallpox inspector at the table. Milton hesitated before he spoke.

"Miss Cabot, I am afraid I have some disturbing news."

I looked at him dully thinking there was little that could disturb me more than I had already been disturbed this day.

"It's about your brother. He's gone."

"Gone?"

"His things are gone and he left a note." He handed me a scrap of paper. It read, *Thanks for the bed. I'm no use here so I'm leaving. My sister will be glad. Alden.*

I stared at it. How like Alden to desert us now.

"I thought you should know, Miss Cabot. He has no money. I don't know where he can have gone. Shall I try to find him?"

Poor Mr. Bierly with his wispy beard had dropped the word "comrade" from his speech these days, so shaken was he by the desperate circumstances all around him. I pitied him his concern for Alden.

"I wouldn't if I were you. My brother will make his way. He always does." It sounded bitter but I was too tired to care. Ever since Alden had shown up at the door of Hull House one catastrophe had followed another. Embarrassed, the budding socialist mumbled his excuses and left us.

Mr. Wall appeared untouched by our exchange as he attacked his food in a businesslike manner. I looked at my plate and pushed it away from me.

"Mr. Wall, may I ask you something?"

He touched his napkin to his mouth and swallowed. "Certainly, Miss Cabot."

"How do you manage to continue your work? I mean, I think the people are very ungrateful to you. Here you leave your home and family to come and help to get this dreadful epidemic under control and the people, well, people…"

"Hate me? Yes, that is all right, Miss Cabot. It is quite true. People hate and fear me and the other inspectors."

"How do you stand it?"

"But someone must, Miss Cabot, someone must. You observe I leave my family to do this. But I know, even if the poor people in these neighborhoods do not, that I am protecting my family as well as them by doing this work. It is not their fault, Miss Cabot, if they do not understand but it is our duty, since we do, to take the measures necessary to stop this scourge. If we do not, it will only spread until no one is safe, including our own families." He crumbled a roll of bread with his left hand. "I can bear the hatred, Miss Cabot, because I know it will be forgotten. Oh, yes, when the disease has been contained and run its course, the people will return to their lives. Some will be gone. Others will bear scars and they will not forget, but the rest will return to work and play. They will not remember the inspectors who invaded their homes and places of work, I assure you. They will purposely put it behind them then, burying it in their memories as they should. And life will be that much better because they have survived. It is not really me who is their enemy, Miss Cabot, it is the disease. And even if they do not know that, you and I do."

"I suppose you are right."

I thought of the governor convening his meeting with other governors and sighed.

"You are tired, Miss Cabot?"

"I confess I am discouraged, Mr. Wall. The problems here are so insoluble. No matter what we do, it seems to have so little effect and even if something is accomplished, the next moment it may be undone again." I was thinking of the eight-hour day law, which seemed so certain to be overturned in the courts. Mr. Wall considered this as he chewed another mouthful.

"I think you must not look for quick results, Miss Cabot. These things take time and they must take their course. Consider these insoluble problems to be like hard rocks and your efforts to be as falling water streaming over them. Now it may seem the water has little effect but over time you will observe the rock is worn down."

"You are a philosopher, Mr. Wall."

"We must all be philosophers enough to discern some pattern in the world, Miss Cabot, or we would all become discouraged. You must not give in to it." Having completed his meal, he folded the napkin carefully. "Now, if you will excuse me, I will go to my rest. The more energy we can put into our work the sooner we can finish it." He gave me a cordial nod and left, carrying his dishes.

I sat for a while feeling frustrated. I had no idea how to find Maria, yet I felt unable to face either Dr. Chapman or Mr. Langlois until I knew her fate. I no longer even had Alden to blame. I had a terrible premonition about Alden. Flaherty had not killed Hanrahan, I was sure of it. Fear of what my brother might have done, in his frantic pursuit of the man he believed had killed our father, hung on me. It was like a heavy stone on a string round my neck. Somehow things had gone very wrong. I could see no way to right them. It was at that moment that I looked out the window and saw Florence Kelley sneaking out a side door. She carefully waited until no one was in sight before leaving. This time I wanted to know where she was going.

TWENTY-SIX

I had my overcoat with me, so I slipped down the stairs and out into the darkness in pursuit. It seemed to me that I had been avoiding finding out where Mrs. Kelley went when she left furtively like this. Now, I had to know.

There was no one else around. That was an advantage in that there was no one to see me, or hail me, or to tell Mrs. Kelley that I was there. On the other hand it meant I was alone following her when I was certain whatever she was involved in was bad. But who could I ask to come with me even if I had the time to seek someone out? No one in Hull House would believe her capable of iniquities. But if what she was doing was innocent why was she taking such pains to be secretive? It was very unlike the outspoken socialist. Three times I had seen her meet with a figure in the shadows and twice she had lied about it. What did it mean? And what did it have to do with the murder of Hanrahan? Whatever it meant I did not want it to mean that Florence Kelley had been involved in the beating death of that man in the study of Hull House.

But if Mrs. Kelley was not implicated in that death I was even more afraid that it would mean that it was my brother, Alden, who was responsible. Much as I desired to avoid either conclusion, I could no longer live with the doubt. I had to know what it was that made Florence Kelley, a woman normally so outspoken as to be rude, suddenly turn so secretive.

I had to hurry not to lose her dark skirts in the shadows of the alley. Where she was heading was not far, only a few blocks from the settlement. It was a narrow lot where a small house had been moved back to allow a four-story brick building to be constructed fronting the road. I saw her stop by a small tenement at the back of the lot. The figure I could barely discern now, turned down some steps to a basement level. She disappeared and when there was no further movement I crept forward. There was light from a window in what must be a basement room. I remembered Miss Addams talking about the socialist party to which Florence Kelley had belonged in New York. She claimed she had been expelled. But what if that was not true? What if it had been a ruse to cover her activities here? I knew there were socialist, anarchist and other groups especially in the Italian community of the West Side. But I knew nothing about their activities. There were those who claimed that Hull House encouraged such movements but I had never seen it. Some believed one of those groups was behind the Haymarket bombing in 1886 but it was never proven. What if Florence Kelley was involved with such a group? What if Hanrahan had found out?

A hand grasped my upper arm and I jumped but the grip only got stronger. Panicking, I tried to twist away but I felt my arm swept behind me. It hurt. “Let me go!”

“Hush.” A hand clamped over my mouth. It smelt of an herb—oregano? We were both breathing heavily when I realized it was a heavy skirt enveloping my own. I struggled but this was a powerful woman who had me in a strong grip. She was frightened. I felt her stiffen as she swung me around, back and forth, as if looking to see if anyone was coming. I felt myself flutter with panicky feelings, smothered by the rough hand. But I forced myself to be calm. I could smell sweat and garlic and her breath came in gasps. When she saw there was no one else she released me, shoving me down the steps by the shoulder. The basement door opened and she pushed me into a small room that flickered with candlelight.

There were murmured greetings. I knew enough to recognize Italian. With a rustle of skirts I was quickly surrounded by anxious faces eerily lit from below by candles. My heart still pounding, I forced myself to relax a little as I realized they were all women. My mind jumped to the conclusion that this could not be an anarchist den if the only participants were women. But then I took in the rest of the scene and felt the hair rise on my neck.

The women had beads draped from their fingers and a continuous murmuring of prayer rose and fell in the background. In the middle, on a stool, a woman was slumped, her shoulders held by one figure while another held a basin and attempted to wipe blood from her face. There was a continual moaning with occasional chirps of pain as the woman on the stool flinched from these attentions. This was followed by murmurs as if to comfort a child and the figure at her back rubbed with a circling motion.

Before I could take this in enough to understand it, my eyes were drawn to a table against the wall where three rows of small candles flickered. It was a sort of shrine. I noted the crucifix and then blinked and forced myself to look at it again. My first impression had not been wrong. The figure on the crucifix was not Christ, it was not a man. It was a woman.

I felt sick and weak at the knees. What sort of cult was this that I had stumbled upon? I shivered involuntarily with repulsion. I had never felt comfortable with the statues, paintings, and stained glass images of the Catholic immigrants in the area around the settlement. I had been brought up in Boston's Unitarian churches where clean white walls were ornamented only by simple copper chandeliers, austere benches, and a carved pulpit. Church, to me, was a place to leave behind the dirt and confusion of the world to contemplate the transcendental ideas of divinity. It was a serene and lofty place for thought of serene and lofty things. The first time I had entered one of the churches of the West Side I had been appalled. Miss Addams had squeezed my arm to remind me not to react as we were guests of the local priest with whom she had business. But I had not been able to look at the statues for long. I found I had to look away in embarrassment. The poses and depictions were calculated to move vulgar feelings, not lofty thoughts, and I found them offensive. Gruesome scenes of torture and death were interspersed with images of mother-like women, sad but comforting. Far from invoking thoughts of the ideal, these images were shocking in their immediacy. I found them repulsive.

"Saint Liberata." It was the voice of Florence Kelley. Several of the murmuring women looked up and then skidded sideways until there was an empty space between us. She was in a corner of the small room. Whatever could the cynical Florence Kelley be doing in such a place? Her voice was pitched low but I could hear every word. "She was the daughter of a king, according to the story. Her father wanted to marry her to the King of Sicily. But she had dedicated herself to her god, the new Christian god. So she prayed to her god to make her ugly so that the king would not want her. She got her wish, the king rejected her and her father was so furious he had her crucified. Saint Liberata." She moved quietly through the group to the figures at the center. She held her candle up to the face of the woman on the stool. The woman shrank back closing her eyes. Her face was badly bruised and swollen with blood dripping from the side of her mouth. She cringed a little as Mrs. Kelley's hand moved a strand of hair from her eyes and gently smoothed it behind an ear.

"What happened to her?" The murmurs of prayers had begun again after a pause during Mrs. Kelley's actions.

"She has been beaten by her husband. This is a place of retreat. Like Saint Liberata, these women have no control over their lives and like her they suffer for it. When they must escape their homes or face dying they come here, for a while. Don't look so shocked, Emily. What do you expect them to do? They have children. They cannot abandon them. They can only escape for a while and say their rosaries and pray for help from this patron saint of theirs. And then, when some time has passed, they can return."

"But how can she go back after that?"

"Where else could she go?"

"But you…"

"Yes, I have left and gone very far away to get a legal separation from my husband, but few of them can do that. There is nothing else for them to do but they can comfort each other. But it must be secret. It is a great shame and a great secret. When they meet each other in the street they do not acknowledge it. Only here can they admit it."

"But how can you, I mean…"

"Why am I here, you mean? Because in their secret world they recognized me right away as one of them. And when one is hurt and needs help they know I can find them a place. They move around. They cannot always meet at the same time and place. This is not a society club like the women's clubs of Prairie Avenue, you know. I can help them to find a place. I'm an organizer. That is what I do, Miss Cabot. So, although I cannot share their hopes for assistance from the martyred saint, I can usually find them a place to gather when some woman, like Livia, here, has had to leave her home before being beaten to death." She looked around at the women who still murmured together in a rising and falling chant. The she put an arm around my shoulders and moved me to the door.

"They will tend her and pray with her until she has the courage to go back." She looked into my face. "You do not need to worry, Emily. There are no bomb plots here. There is no evil conspiracy to overthrow the government. Yes, I know. No doubt you feared something of the sort. There is a secret, certainly. They live in fear that their husbands will find out about the group and find a way to destroy it. But you need not fear they will attack anyone, they cannot even defend themselves. Now, go. Leave them to their sorrows and shame. But before you go, you must promise me you will not tell anyone what you have seen." Her hand clutched my arm.

"But Detective Whitbread should know. They are trying to get you arrested for Hanrahan's murder. They want to accuse you of being an anarchist. He should know about this." I was whispering.

She was shaking her head. "No, Emily. Don't you understand after all? You would put these women in danger, real, terrible danger. Don't worry about me. I never hurt Hanrahan and they will never convict me of it. Although, I'm not sure whoever did it wasn't right. Promise me. Promise me now, you will tell no one."

I nodded and she released my arm. With a firm hand in the small of my back she pushed me out the door and I heard the latch click behind me. I took a deep breath of the cold crisp air and quickly mounted the steps to the alley, stepping into the shadows. I stopped for one look back at the flickering lights from the low set windows. I knew I would tell no one. How could I after bringing such bad luck to Maria? How easily the vulnerable could be hurt here when all of us ought to be protecting them.

I returned to Hull House and tried to be unobtrusive when I entered and went up to my room. But almost immediately Jenny Dow came to me and told me they had been looking all over for me. I had a visitor waiting in the study. She said she was Mrs. Hanrahan.

TWENTY-SEVEN

Nothing could have surprised me more than that name. I rushed down the front stairs and barely caught myself in time to stop and collect my thoughts before entering the front parlor.

I looked in and saw a slight, dark-haired woman in mourning slowly turning around gazing at every inch of the walls, ceilings, and fixtures. Of course, she must know that this was where her husband had died. The memory of his corpse flashed across my mind again and I had to grit my teeth to enter. But I did.

She swung round and lightly bent forward to regard me with obvious suspicion.

I cleared my throat. "Mrs. Hanrahan. I am Emily Cabot. I must tell you how very sorry I am for your loss."

She frowned, lines of care and worry marking a young face with a sharp chin and cheekbones. She stared at me for a moment, then fumbled in her reticule, drawing out several envelopes. She extended one towards me. "I came at your mother's request. She sent this."

I took it and quickly unfolded the sheet. My mother's writing was light and wavering. I strained to read it with the help of the desk lamp.

My dearest Emily,

We have had the help of some of your father's friends who found Mrs. Hanrahan at her cousin's farm in Worcester. As you will hear from her she retreated there at her husband's bidding and has been following his instructions to stay in hiding. She will tell you what little she knows of her husband's affairs before his untimely death. I beg you will enlist the aid of Detective Whitbread in helping her to retrieve her husband's body so she can return it to lie with the rest of his family here in Massachusetts.

Please, when you have a few minutes, send me news. I trust in God that you and Alden are safe.

Lovingly, your mother,
Catherine Cabot

"She is a good woman, your mother," Mrs. Hanrahan said when she saw I was finished reading. "Were it not for her kindness, I could never return Daniel to our home. She said you would help." The woman gulped back tears.

I sighed. How like my mother. Even with her own finances constrained, she would help poor Mrs. Hanrahan. "Yes. I can send you to Detective Whitbread. He can help you with any arrangements." I immediately wrote a note to the detective and put clear instructions for how to find him on the envelope. I handed it to her. "But, Mrs. Hanrahan, can you tell me anything about why someone would have killed your husband? I am so sorry, but won't you please, sit down and tell me anything you know?" I took her arm and led her to the couch in the library.

"It happened here, didn't it?" She had a handkerchief clutched in her hand.

"In the other room. Mrs. Hanrahan, did your husband know something about my father's death? Is that why he came to see me on Christmas Day?"

"Christmas Day, Christmas Day," she was rocking back and forth but with an effort she took herself in hand. "We should have been here. Christmas Day, all of us, Dan, me, our four children. We had made all the arrangements but then the week before, the week before he wrote me. He told me not to come." She took another envelope from her bag. "Here." She shoved the envelope at me. I took it and read:

My dearest Henrietta,

You know how much I depend on you, my dearest. I know it has been hard for you. You would not leave everything to come here if you had your wish. But I asked it of you and you have been so wonderful. I know that managing it all while I came ahead, selling the property, arranging shipping, all the while caring for the children has been hard for you and I thank you from my heart for doing it so well and with so little complaint. Truly I do not deserve someone as good as you are.

But now I must ask once more for your forbearance. Forgive me. Forgive me after all your hard work for asking you to stop. Stop. Do not come to Chicago. Please, I beg you. I promise you it is only to ensure the safety of you and the young ones that I ask this of you. For their sake, for my sake, go quietly to your cousin Millie in Worcester. I know she and her husband love you and they will never deny you. Only for a short while. But I must beg you to promise you will tell no one where you go. Let the world believe you are in Chicago. Do not leave the farm until I send for you. Do not contact me.

I am so sorry. It is the old business. I had thought to leave all of that behind. I had promised you it would be different if you agreed to the move. And so it will be. I stand by my promise to you. But, as I told you, the position here is not what was promised. Franklin has not fulfilled his contract. But I can make him do so—or else we will not settle here. I know he will come around.

But first I must straighten out the old business. How may it be anything but Fate that Miss Emily Cabot should be here? I take it as a sign. And there is another, one so dangerous that I cannot be quiet this time lest past sins be multiplied. I tell you no more for your own protection, my love. You know nothing, but even so I fear for your safety until this deed is done. I must expose the man who killed Judge Cabot and until that is done we must be parted.

You must do your best to arrange a happy Christmas for the children. Mine will be a sorrow without you all. But only if I do this can we really have a new beginning. Until then, my love,

Your husband,
Daniel

"Oh, Mrs. Hanrahan, your husband was coming to tell me that the man who killed my father was here. Did he tell you who that was?"

"No, never. You see. He says it. He wanted to protect me."

"Even at the time it happened didn't he tell you anything?"

"That awful strike. It ruined everything. It destroyed him."

"He worked for the South Boston Horse Car Company?"

"He had for seven happy years. But then the strike happened. Dan was a manager. He had to do what the owner wanted. They brought in men to take the strikers' jobs then more men to protect them. It got worse and worse. I could see Daniel hated it. He refused to talk about it. He didn't want me to know, I'm sure of it. Dan was a good man but the job was all he had, all any of us had. He would do anything to protect it." She took a big breath. "The trial was a turning point. But the company was worried. Your father had a reputation. They did not think he would rule in their favor, I guess. Dan's hands would shake when he just put in his cuff links. I had to do it for him.

"Then your father was killed by the brother of one of the men. He escaped but the others were convicted and that ended the strike. But Dan was never the same." She squeezed her eyes shut. "He began to drink. He was surly. I told him he would lose his job. He laughed. I told him I would leave him, and I did. I went to my cousin, Millie." She sobbed then took a breath and continued. "That brought him to himself. He quit that job. He had a hard time but finally he got offered the job out here.

"He was supposed to manage a store, a men's clothing store. He left me to make all the arrangements to move. It was going to be a new life. But then he complained the job was not what was promised. The owner's son wanted the job in the store. They had Dan doing other things. I don't know what but things he didn't want to do. Finally he said he would insist on the job he was promised or he would quit."

"But why was he afraid for you and the children?"

She shook her head. "He never told me."

"Mrs. Hanrahan, you must show this letter to Detective Whitbread."

Her back stiffened. "I showed your mother. I appreciate all her help." She carefully folded the letter and tucked it back into her bag. "But I must protect the children. I promised him I would keep them from harm."

"Please, Mrs. Hanrahan. I am very much afraid that the wrong man has been arrested for your husband's death. He, too, has a wife and children who need him. Please, help me to ensure a great injustice is not done." Of course it might have been Flaherty that Hanrahan had recognized. In any case, it seemed to confirm that it was not Florence Kelley or my brother who had killed the poor woman's husband and that gave me a great relief.

She shook her head. "I must take Daniel home. Then I must protect my children. You must do whatever you think is right but I will not let my husband's sacrifice be in vain. I must protect my children."

She was right, of course. It was not her responsibility to find out whether the charges against Mike Flaherty were true. But someone must.

TWENTY-EIGHT

"Are you quite sure this is what you want to do, Emily?" Miss Addams had taken the news of my defection with the same serenity with which she faced all the daily small catastrophes of Hull House. She seemed less surprised than I was by my decision.

"I am sorry to disappoint you and Dean Talbot." I struggled to explain myself. "But I am responsible for driving Maria away and for the misfortune we have brought on her family. I must go back to have my father's death investigated again. Only by finding out the truth of what happened that night can some of the harm be undone. My mother will support me in this, I know. At least we may be able to prove the innocence of Mr. Flaherty, if that is true, even if the guilt of others cannot be proven." I knew it would be a difficult task. If my father were still alive, he would be able to move the powers of justice to work for Flaherty rather than against him if he were innocent. But for me, a woman alone, the chances were that anything I would attempt would be without result. But I had to try. My mother would welcome me, even if I had failed at Hull House as well as at the university. And I knew Marguerite Larrimer had far better resources to assist Stephen Chapman to recover than I could ever offer. Much as I disliked the thought that he would depend on her, I knew it would be inevitable. I couldn't even find Maria now. Detective Whitbread would have to do that. The only thing I could do to be of any use whatsoever would be to return to Boston and at least attempt to help Mr. Flaherty.

For too long I left my father's death unresolved. For too long I tried to ignore my brother's futile efforts to avenge that crime. I left home without facing the facts of that terrible night and I knew the questions hanging over us about what had happened then had led my brother to do a terrible thing. I realized all of this during a restless night and made my decision in the morning. I sought out Miss Addams as soon as I could find her alone at the desk in the front parlor.

"You must do as you think best. But I should tell you that during all the activities to combat the epidemic, a vote was taken on your probationary period and I am pleased to tell you that they all wished to offer you a permanent place here. We cannot be successful in all of our attempts, Emily. Sometimes we fail. We must accept that. You are discouraged, it is natural. We all become discouraged at some point, but if you should change your mind, and wish to return, you will always have a place here."

"I thank you. I cannot see the future. I will probably need to find a teaching job and live with my mother as I did before."

She did not reproach me. It was not her way. I told her I planned to leave at the end of the week and she asked me to complete some simple assignments that would make the time remaining that much easier.

When she left to attend a meeting in the city, and I turned my mind to producing some replies to mundane correspondence, I was interrupted by Jennie Dow who ushered in Professor Albion Small from the university.

"Mr. Small. I am sorry but Miss Addams is away this morning and not expected back until after dinner."As Miss Talbot had told me, Professor Small was a good friend to Hull

House and a frequent visitor. However, since so many activities like the lectures had been curtailed during the epidemic, I could not imagine what would bring the chairman of the sociology department to us on this day. To my surprise I found he had come in search of me.

"May I have a few words with you, Miss Cabot?"

"Certainly, Mr. Small. Shall we go into the library?" I led the way.

"Miss Cabot, I have come to inform you of some recent changes at the university and to make you an offer that I hope you will find amenable. For one thing, I can tell you that the publisher has sent me the galleys for the Hull House papers and maps and they are very good, very good indeed. Well done." He was rubbing his hands together.

"Mrs. Kelley and the others collected all of the information, Professor Small. I merely completed the typing and made arrangements with the publishers."

"You are too modest. The publisher is well aware of the value of your editing. I tell you, Miss Cabot, this is going to be a very important piece of work, you'll see. We'll all see."

"Important enough to allow my return to the university?" I was beginning to suspect the true purpose of this call.

"That is not all. As you know, Professor Lukas has been a strong critic of the place of women at the university. In this and other matters his views have been so much at odds with those of President Harper and the majority of the faculty that he has at last decided to resign his appointment to take a permanent position with the newly formed Illinois Manufacturers Association. In fact he will lead that organization. In view of this, Mr. Reed has proposed your reinstatement. He would very much like you to return to continue your work with him. Having completed the initial study based on the information you collected last year, he plans more in-depth analysis and will require assistance. It is work for which he assures me you are uniquely qualified and I agree."

I looked at him. It seemed such a long time since I had lived at the university and worried about the fellowship.

"But I am suspended."

"I am happy to report to you that Mrs. Larrimer has been at great pains to explain to the university administration the distressing details surrounding the death of her husband and to insist that you and Dr. Chapman were forced to suffer unjustly as a result of your efforts to uncover the true circumstances. I believe the doctor encouraged her to make the explanations. Your reputation has been further enhanced by your work here at Hull House and the suspensions of both yourself and Dr. Chapman have been revoked. I can only hope you will accept our apologies for any difficulties this has caused you. And in restitution as well as recognition of your abilities, I am empowered to offer you the full fellowship which you were previously denied."

"The fellowship is restored?" It stung to think I might owe this change to Mrs. Larrimer, even if Dr. Chapman had forced her to do it.

"Completely, Miss Cabot. We look forward to having you rejoin us for the spring quarter. I have no doubt that the work planned by Mr. Reed—and your own efforts—will lead, at last, to the advanced degree in sociology which was your goal in coming here." He smiled.

"Mr. Lukas has left the university and I am invited back?" I could see the Dean's handiwork in this. It was not only Marguerite Larrimer's influence and money. "It would mean leaving Hull House, then?"

"I am sure you will understand that it would be impossible for you to remain here. I believe Miss Addams herself would agree. I assume you would be free to return at other times. Do not mistake me, Miss Cabot, you must be aware that I am a great admirer of the work done here. But our purpose at the university is somewhat different. While here you are immersed in the problems of the community, at the university we must take a step back in order to attain an objective view of the problems. Ours is to study, measure, evaluate rather than to initiate specific actions. It is these activities that brought you to the university in the first place and these continue to be our goals."

I tried to remember the fervor with which I had collected the crime statistics from Detective Whitbread the previous year. Now it seemed a rather whimsical thing to do, summing up all those little cards. And what a tragedy it had been when they were blown around the yard of Snell Hall. I remembered the dance and all the commotion about the propriety of dancing on university grounds. It made me wonder what they would think about the propriety of the sweatshops I had visited or the pest house. It seemed an odd idea that the nightly classes and discussions of mixed sexes that happened at Hull House would be deemed an impropriety in Hyde Park, yet I knew it was so. I knew Dean Talbot would consider it a great victory to have me return to the university completely vindicated and reinstated. I considered the man before me. At one time, not so long ago, he had seemed to be so eminent to inhabit lofty places of academic renown. Today, he looked like a very ordinary man to me.

"What if for any reason I should be unable to accept your proposal at this time, Mr. Small?"

He looked surprised. "I confess I had not considered the possibility, Miss Cabot. Of course you must give due consideration to your particular circumstances. I hope you will appreciate that it will be necessary to bestow the fellowship for the upcoming spring quarter. As I mentioned, Mr. Reed is counting on the appointment for assistance with his work. If for any reason you should decide not to accept, there are other candidates whose position would be greatly enhanced by this grant. Once it is given, it will not be available again until that person completes an advanced degree and moves on to another position. Two or three years, I should think. We would be very sorry to lose you, Miss Cabot, should you decide not to accept. Do not misunderstand me. I can appreciate it if you feel a commitment to your work here but I hope you will think seriously before rejecting this offer. I am afraid, if there is any question whatsoever, I must ask you to make a decision very soon. I hope that will be possible?"

"Yes, certainly." I was struck by a whimsical thought. "One more thing, Mr. Small. Suppose I were to marry. Would the offer be open to me then?"

He looked surprised and a little confused. "I had no idea you were contemplating such a thing."

"I am not. I merely pose the question." I was not planning to pursue Mr. Bierly's dreams for the future but something prompted me to ask nonetheless. Perhaps it was the thought of Mrs. Kelley. I wanted to know.

"Well, it is generally considered that on entry into the married state a lady has too many other duties, and neither the interest nor the time to devote to serious study. It is generally considered that a woman must make a choice of either one or the other, so, no, in that case the offer of the fellowship would have to be withdrawn."

"I see. I thank you, Mr. Small, and I am grateful for the efforts of Mr. Reed and Dean Talbot to restore the fellowship for me. But I find I cannot accept. I have decided to return to my home in Boston. There are duties that call me back there.

Things I must do. I hope you will forgive me. But I cannot accept your offer. I know you will find another candidate better suited for this honor."

He searched my face but found no chink in my armor. Standing, he extended a hand. "We are very sorry to lose you, Miss Cabot. I hope you will not regret your decision. Good luck then."

I shook his hand and felt no regret at his departure. I felt only a numbness and a desire to return home. There were things I had to do in Boston, truths that must be faced before I could go on. And suddenly I found the memories of the university which had loomed so large in my mind before had shrunk to something much smaller. Suddenly all those pictures were like pretty little miniatures hung on the wall to be seen as illustrations of some far off fairytale world. The world I had discovered beyond the walls of the university was so much harder and grayer and grimmer. But, like Miss Addams, I had discovered that once I knew of its existence it was a world that I could never again ignore.

TWENTY-NINE

*I*n the morning I received a telegram from Boston informing me that my mother was seriously ill and requesting the immediate return of both me and my brother. It was signed by my sister, and I knew if my mother were conscious she would never have allowed it to be sent. I had missed my weekly letter from Boston but I barely noticed it in the rush of events. Now I remembered an uncharacteristic complaint about what my mother had termed a slight fever in her last letter and I was very alarmed. I had been so sure that no matter what happened to me in Chicago, I could always return to my mother in Boston. Now I was afraid. I could not face the possibility that she could be gone from the world.

I took my coat and rushed out to knock on the door of the men's dormitory, asking for Mr. Bierly. He appeared in time, slightly disheveled as it was still early.

"Mr. Bierly, I am sorry to wake you. I must find my brother. I have had news. My mother is very ill and we must return to Boston."

"I am very sorry to hear it, Miss Cabot. It is no trouble but Alden did not tell me where he was going."

"Surely he must have said something. I really must find him."

"He did not. He returned late the night before and did not retire but spent the rest of the night pacing about. He was very upset about the fate of Miss Maglioni. He went out early, returned for his things, and left only the note I gave you."

"But where did he go?"

"He did not say but I had the impression he might have gone to see Mr. Fitzgibbons. He is always sure that man knows everything that goes on in the district."

"Thank you, Mr. Bierly. At least it is something."

"I wish I could help you, Miss Cabot."

"You have. Good day."

I walked through the streets crowded with people on their way to work until I came to the ward office. As usual, Fitz was at his desk already, surrounded by three or four men in shirtsleeves getting their instructions for the day. He was not pleased to see me.

"Miss Cabot. You've come to gloat?"

"Excuse me? I don't know what you mean. I am looking for my brother."

"You haven't heard of your victory then? Well, you will soon enough. The governor has threatened a boycott of goods coming out of the city if the so-called infected merchandise is not seized and destroyed. You and your Mrs. Kelley have won. I'm just instructing the boys here to assist and many a poor innocent garment will be put to the stake today, don't you worry."

The men grumbled. I knew this would be a great victory for Mrs. Kelley and I thought I should have felt some gratification. But my concern for my mother's peril had wiped every other care from my mind and I could not spare even a thought for this news—it meant nothing to me.

"I have not come about that, Mr. Fitzgibbons. My brother has disappeared and I must find him. I am told he came to see you yesterday morning. Can you tell me what it was about?"

"The owners have capitulated, Miss Cabot. Does it not make you happy?"

"Please, Mr. Fitzgibbons."

He waved the men off to their work. "He was looking for Weaver. I told him to stay away from the man. He's a dangerous character in case you haven't guessed it. Your brother was all in a flurry claiming that someone else had murdered your father and that after spending months hounding us all about somebody named Flaherty."

"It is true. There is reason to believe it. But that is not why I am looking for him. I have only just received news that our mother is very ill and we must go to her in Boston. But Alden left Hull House yesterday and no one knows where he went. Please, Mr. Fitzgibbons. Can you help me find him?"

He rose with a sigh and took my arm insisting that I take the chair. "Most likely he's looking for Weaver. He wanted to ask him something about the Franklins, although I told him he'd get nowhere trying to sully that name. They've a lot of pull in this town and that is the truth. I did tell him that Marco has returned after spending time in the pest house. He's still weak but well enough for them to boot him out."

"Where is he? Surely Alden will have gone to see him. He may know where to find my brother."

Fitz grimaced. "It's not a place for the likes of you, Miss Cabot. He was at one of the houses in the Levee where he knows the ladies."

"I must find him."

"I think not. I will go and see what he knows."

"Do you know where to find Mr. Weaver? If my brother is looking for him he may have seen him."

"We must hope not. He's not a man who would take kindly to being harassed. He's in the pay of the owners and he's been going about moving the confiscated garments before they could be destroyed. He's not going to like it that he's to be called off, you know. You cannot go looking for him, Miss Cabot. Go back to Miss Addams. When I find out something I will send word. That Weaver is like a wild dog. It's not safe to hunt him, as I told your brother. Your brother was looking for Marco; I can go and see him."

"Mr. Fitzgibbons, I will go with you."

"Miss Cabot, it is not right that the likes of you, a young lady, should go to such a place."

I stood up. "Nonsense. There is no time for delicacy, Mr. Fitzgibbons. I must find my brother and we must leave on the train for Boston tonight. If you had been to the places where I have been this last month, you would not think a visit to a brothel could infect me. Please take me to Mr. Marco so I may question him about my brother."

Fitz turned away with a jerk to reach for his hat. He marched down the office and out the door trailed by me to the sidewalk where he whistled and motioned with a sharp slice of his arm. Helping me into the carriage that pulled up in response, he kept his eye on my hand, then he growled a name to the driver before bounding into the carriage, shaking it to the frame as he dropped into the seat opposite me.

We were soon in the Levee, a district that was quiet and empty at this time of day compared to the moving crowds of people on their way to work on Halsted. As if they moved to the time of a different clock than the rest of the world, the inhabitants of the Levee came out in the nighttime and during the day they were all dug into their holes like little nocturnal animals.

The carriage shuddered to a stop in front of a large brick house more prosperous looking than the rickety tenements that surrounded it. A wide door up three steps was painted a shiny red. Fitzgibbons jumped down but he did not turn back for me; he just pounded up the stairs and pulled an iron knob bell keeping his broad back to me. I was out of the carriage and by his side before anyone responded.

We heard a bolt slide and the door opened slightly.

"Fitz." Stopping in mid yawn, a plump young woman who had a blanket pulled around her, and red hair in curls unraveling on her shoulders, stepped back. A round white arm slipped from the blanket pushing the door open. "Come in and let me shut the door. It's enough to freeze yer to hell out there. Brrr." She pushed us in and slammed the big door. "What're yer doin' here this time o' day? It's not mornin' even. You'll get nothin' from us this time o' day. An' yer lookin' for Madam, she'll not be up for sure. Not for hours yet. An' don't you expect me ter get her. It'd be worth a hard beatin' to anyone goes into her 'fore she's ready." The girl was throwing her words at Fitz who loomed above her all the while, but she was glancing over at me between phrases with her slightly protuberant eyes ringed with black smudges.

Fitz took a step to put himself between me and the woman. "It's Marco I've come to see. He's upstairs, I hear, recovering."

"Marco? Yes, Marco's here. He's up…Well I guess that's all right then." She stepped to a set of stairs opposite the door. The shape of the rooms reminded me of Hull House. We were in a hallway with stairs straight ahead and wide open doors to parlors on either side. Like Hull House it must have been built as a modest mansion for a wealthy family some time in the past. But the decoration was bizarre. There were large mirrors on the walls, framed in chipped gilt carved in fantastical whorls. The mirrors were shaded around the edges and speckled with blotches. Ebony chests and tables with heavy chairs that had stained velvet seats lined the hall. A huge Chinese porcelain vase at the foot of the stairs had been used as a spittoon and the scarred wooden floor around it showed brown pools of stain.

I could glimpse heavy velvet drapes on tall windows in the parlors, so the whole place was very dark. A gas wall light flickered but the large glass chandelier with a third of its pieces broken or missing was not lit. I supposed in the evening when they were at their business it gave a more flattering view of the place. The stair railing came down over a banister missing an occasional piece like a grin with missing teeth. The rail was painted gold and where it curved at the end a gold statue of a naked woman with wings sprouting from her back stood as if ready to fly off. As I followed them up the steep stairway I supposed the men who came here couldn't help but rub their hands over the body of the golden angel as they pulled themselves up the first steps. The whole place reeked of the smell of tobacco and sweat. The dirt that was ground into the edges of everything was probably easy to ignore in the lamp or candlelight of the evening. It seemed like some sort of fantastic parody of the mansions of Prairie Avenue I had visited.

Upstairs there were narrow hallways and the rooms had been cut up into smaller ones that barely fit a bed and dresser or bureau. Most of the doors were open and there were gentle snores from the mounds of bedclothes in the chilly rooms. There was clothing strewn on the floors or hanging on hard backed wooden chairs in the rooms.

The woman led us to a corner room with windows at the end of the hallway, then pushed back past us without entering. On the bed, Marco was being fed by a woman in a nightgown and shawl, sitting on one of the hard chairs. Another woman with dark hair falling around her face lay on the bed behind him, her chin resting on his shoulder.

Marco looked smaller than he had when he ran the

Ferris Wheel at the Columbian Exposition. He had seemed a big man then with a booming voice and a warm charm that engulfed you. Now there was more gray than black in his thinning hair and large handlebar moustache. His face was marked with scars from the smallpox and his whole frame seemed hollow where before he had been solid. But there were the same crinkles at his eyes, which had not totally lost their merriment.

"Fitz, Fitz, it's good to see you." I was reassured to hear the same deep timbre in the voice even if it had lost some of its force. "But what have we here? Dear me, is that Miss Cabot? Fitz, my dear man, I am overwhelmed by your concern for my well-being but you might have sent word ahead that you were bringing a visitor. What are you thinking?" His eyebrows were raised and he sat up. The women helped him arrange the pillows for his back.

Fitz chomped his teeth. "Miss Cabot is looking for her brother. Their mother is ill and they must both return to Boston immediately. Alden ran away from Hull House yesterday without telling them where he was going. When I saw him he was looking for you so I sent him here. I offered to come and look for him but Miss Cabot insisted on coming herself. She wouldn't listen to reason, and there's the end on it."

Marco's dark eyes darted between Fitz and me. "Ah, Mr. Alden Cabot, I see. Thank you, Penelope, but perhaps we can continue the soup later. I am, as always, grateful for your tender care, but perhaps you and Deirdre, here, could leave us while I attempt to answer this lady's questions? Yes, yes." The woman who had been feeding him gathered up her tray and sashayed out, giving Fitz a knock with her hip on the way. He glanced at me frowning. It was a guilty reaction.

The other woman had to climb over Marco and she took her time donning a Japanese silk robe and tying the sash into a special little bow. Meanwhile Fitz attempted to put himself between me and the woman as if to shield me from the sight of her almost naked body. I who had spent the last month washing and dressing and laying out bodies of victims of the disease. I was not sure why he thought the sight would shock me. She perched on the edge of the mattress to angle her feet into slippers.

"Come on then," Fitz told her.

It was the wrong thing to say. I could see the young woman's features form into a sulk that reminded me of my sister Rosemary when she did not get her way. Marco rubbed her arm. "Please, my dear, if you would be so kind."

She shrugged and stood up, jutting her breasts out. "Coming back tonight, Fitz?" she asked. "We had a full house last night." She stepped up to where she was face to face with him. "Better get here early." She began to sally by me to the door.

I put out my hand. "I am Emily Cabot. I am trying to find my brother Alden. Our mother is very ill and if we don't return to Boston as soon as possible, I am afraid she may die before we get there."

Her face contracted in a frown of concentration and she looked me up and down warily. Finally she took my hand with a boneless grip. Looking over her shoulder she said, "Marco knows. He'll tell you, honey." Then she sauntered out the door.

Fitz shook his head angrily.

Marco coughed. "Ah, I apologize for the condition in which you find me, Miss Cabot, but upon my release from the pest house Mrs. Jackson, who owns this establishment, was kind enough to offer me lodgings. Being in an impecunious state, I could only gratefully accept. I apologize for any inconvenience it may cause you."

"Mr. Marco, I must find Alden. Have you seen him? Do you know where he is?"

"I am afraid I do not know where he is now, my dear young lady. But he did come to see me yesterday, having ascertained my present abode from Fitz here."

"Did he say where he was going? We had an argument and he left Hull House."

"I conjectured something of the sort. He told me the man wanted in the death of your father had been arrested." Marco struggled to sit up straighter.

"Yes, but that man, Flaherty, claims he didn't do it and there is some reason to believe he might be telling the truth."

"I see. And it seems the man claimed that Weaver had done it instead?"

"Weaver?" Fitz interjected.

"No. He didn't say that. He claimed my father was alive when he left that night and he said he saw someone outside. He said some of the witnesses at the trial were really company men and that my father had a plan to expose their lies. He believed someone from the company did the killing."

"Your brother told me the police believe this man…" Marco faltered.

"Michael Flaherty," I prompted.

"That Michael Flaherty also killed Hanrahan, who was found dead in Hull House on Christmas Day."

"Yes. Alden convinced them that Flaherty killed him because he was recognized by the dead man. Hanrahan also worked for that horse trolley company in Boston."

"But you believe this man Flaherty?"

"I don't know, but if he did not kill my father—if he's telling the truth—then someone else killed them both. Or there were two separate killers." I could not give up the idea that the Franklins were somehow involved.

Marco exchanged a glance with Fitz who was becoming agitated. "It's all conjecture. Find your brother, Miss Cabot, and take him back to Boston with you. You don't belong here, either of you. They'll be safe there," he told Marco.

"Safe?" I asked. I turned to Marco.

"Your brother came to ask me about something I heard mentioned. It was something I heard but I was not present. It was about Hanrahan."

"What? Why did he want to know?"

"Apparently the good people of Hull House had planned to distribute turkeys Christmas Eve, is that right?"

"Yes."

"It was something that Mr. Fitzgibbons's man Powers does. I heard the shipment of turkeys for Hull House was destroyed."

"Yes. They attacked Mr. Simms and shot his horse."

"Mr. Weaver is supposed to have instigated the act. I was told that when Mr. Hanrahan heard of it he had an argument with Mr. Weaver. He was heard to tell him that he had gone too far, that he would be stopped. It is not wise to threaten a man like Weaver, Miss Cabot. But that is all I know. How Hanrahan planned to stop Weaver, I have no notion. What hold he thought he had over the man I also do not know. The one thing I do know—and Mr. Fitzgibbons here will back me up—is that Weaver is not the sort of man to be threatened with impunity. I told your brother that, after I told him the story."

"You think Hanrahan had a hold over Weaver and Weaver killed him?"

Marco and Fitz exchanged a glance and I saw the Irish ward boss roll his eyes.

"I said nothing of the sort, Miss Cabot. I truly do not know what their quarrel was about. And I cautioned your brother not to try to confront Weaver with this. There are some men who live instinctively and Mr. Weaver is one of these. They are not bad men, on the contrary they can be quite courageous. They are most at home on the frontier where so many ordinary men shrink and fade and are defeated by the fierceness of nature or the other lawless men who run free there. It is not that I like Mr. Weaver, but I have to admit I admire him. He will not back down, you see. No matter what obstacle is set against him and despite the odds, he is incapable of backing down.

"I told your brother he had no reason to believe he is guilty of your father's murder except the pleas of a weak, frightened man when he was finally cornered. But if you accuse a man like Weaver of such a crime to his face, he will not take you to court and sue you. He will shoot you then and there. He has nothing except his reputation for fearlessness. It is the only shield he carries. He could not let such an attack on him go. It would wound him fatally. I told your brother this when he came to me. He had the very foolish notion that he should confront Weaver to hear his side of the story. I tried to explain to him that the man he was seeking would not answer with words, he would answer with bullets. You cannot accuse him and expect anything else. I confess, I do not know what your brother intended when he left here late last night. I cannot say. But I just advise you, as I am sure Mr. Fitzgibbons has done, to go to your mother in Boston. By all means find your brother and carry him off with you. But even if you do not find him you must leave it to Fitz and your friend Detective Whitbread to find him for you."

"Without finding out if Weaver killed my father you mean? And you think if Alden confronts him he will kill Alden, too? But you want me to just leave?"

"Have ya not been listening to what he's been saying then?" Fitz grabbed my arm. "Weaver's a dangerous man. It's not a question of whether or not he shot your da some years ago. It doesn't matter. If you walk up to the man and suggest it, what do you think he would do? Ask you to sit down over a drink to discuss it, maybe? Are ye daft, then?

"I don't love the man but you have to respect him. What he does he does for others, you know, not himself alone. He's just making his way, same as everybody else. If ye don't like what he does, talk to the men who hire him. It's not him what decides, no more than those girls in them sweatshops decide the cut of the dresses they're sewing. He's a hard man but he's fair and he's only trying to make his way like the other souls down here. He's a lot more respectable than your swells on Prairie Avenue who won't get their lily-white hands dirty. He does what he has to do is all."

The two men exchanged a glance again as if to gauge how they were doing in convincing me. I remembered Florence Kelley challenging me after the scene of Mr. Bierly's humiliation by Weaver. These men admired Weaver even if they didn't like him. The tall black figure hiding his scarred face under the broad hat with a silver chain was striding through the city impressing these men because he defied those in power when they wouldn't, or couldn't. They made their compromises or knuckled under to forces beyond their power but he wouldn't and it seemed that they admired, perhaps even envied, his defiance.

Looking grim, still white and weak from his illness, Mr. Marco tried again. "It's a man's world, Miss Cabot. Like it or not, men like Weaver have a special place in it. I tried to make your brother understand that. If he goes against Weaver there's no one can help him."

Fitz straightened up. "You've nothing but the word of one scared fugitive when he was caught."

"But you don't even want to consider it, just because it might be Weaver?"

"Flaherty is lying. He's a weak little man who ran away. Why would you believe him?" The Irishman shook his head angrily. "I'll look for your brother and if I find him I'll stop him from facing Weaver if I have to tie him to a chair. Will that do it for you? But you must go back to Boston. Leave this place, Miss Cabot, before it leads to heartbreak or worse for you. You've friends and family back in Boston. Go home to them. Go to the university or to your friends in Prairie Avenue. You can do no more here, I'm telling ya. You're in a brothel in the Levee, for God's sake. You know you don't belong here."

"Fitz is right, Miss Cabot," Marco said. "There is nothing you can do. If anyone can find your brother, Fitz can. And he will. I am most sorry to hear of your mother's illness. She was kind to me when Teddy died. Surely where you belong is by her side now." He looked around him. "I hate to think what she would say about your finding me in such surroundings. It's a fine way of repaying her to cause her daughter to be subjected to this, and I regret it deeply."

I looked around. It was a poor room, and the downstairs projected some nightmare male fantasy in which these women lived. Yet I couldn't say it was more squalid than the sweatshops where I had seen so many women bending in cramped positions for hours and hours while the sands slid down the hourglass of their lives. This was the ruin Dr. Chapman feared for Maria turned out on the streets alone. It was a horror that terrified the men the most, that horror of having to inhabit their shoddiest dreams. I recalled then that it was meeting the prostitutes of Whitehall that had inspired Jane Addams to make a settlement house in the first place.

"I will return to Boston," I told them, and they exchanged a look of relief. "But as for Mr. Weaver, I do not share your admiration for the man. If it was he and not Mr. Flaherty who killed my father, I promise you I will not let the wrong man hang." I turned and left the room anxious to get out of this sad place haunted by so many distorted male dreams.

THIRTY

I left Mr. Fitzgibbons when the carriage dropped us off at the ward office, hurrying back to Hull House. But when I reached the door of the house Milton Bierly came running up. "Miss Cabot, Miss Cabot, I have news."

"You have found Alden?"

"No, but Mr. Simms has seen Miss Maglioni."

The cart driver walked up slowly behind Milton Bierly. "I saw her go into one of the tenements over on Taylor, miss. It's a sweatshop they say."

I stood for a moment, undecided. But I would have to wait for word from Mr. Fitzgibbons in any case and I must tell Maria that Mr. Langlois had taken the children. The news of my mother's illness had distracted me from everything else, but I still sorely regretted losing Maria. If there was anything I could do to get her to come out of hiding, I needed to do it before I left Chicago.

"Show me. I must speak to her."

They led me through crowded streets and down two alleys until we came to a narrow side street with several wooden tenements facing each other. They were in such poor repair as to seem deserted. The street was in terrible shape, sunken below the doorways and there were even planks balanced between the doors of two of the houses so that you could go from one to the other without climbing down into the street. Mr. Simms pointed to an upstairs window and I caught sight of

Weaver's tall figure. As I watched, he moved away and I saw Alden. A gunshot rang out.

"Oh, no. Go and get help. Quickly."

The older man hobbled away but Milton Bierly attached himself to my arm.

"You can't go up there."

"I must. You must go and get help. Please, Mr. Bierly. Hurry." Still he hesitated. What was wrong with all of these men? Like Alden, he wanted to face Weaver even if he knew he wouldn't have a chance. And he wouldn't. The man would shoot him without a thought. For me, he might at least hesitate. Or he might not think a woman worth the trouble. It was something, that, in dealing with the Weavers of the world. In any case, Alden was up there, perhaps bleeding to death. I had to do something and I would not have Mr. Bierly's blood on my hands if I could help it. "Please, Mr. Bierly. I cannot run in these skirts and Mr. Simms is having a hard time of it. Please, go."

He glanced after Mr. Simms, who was having difficulty maneuvering through the broken and icy pavement stones. Then he ran. I hoped he would not slip and kill himself but I turned my attention to gathering my skirts so I could climb up to the stairs that led to the second floor. I could hear women's voices raised in wails. The bottom floor appeared to be empty as I carefully climbed the broken slats. I had wanted to blame Sidney Franklin for Hanrahan's death, and I had tried to believe Hanrahan had shot my father. But it was Weaver who had killed my father; suddenly I was sure of it. I had to get to Alden, or I would lose him, too. When I reached the door, I took a breath and knocked. There was nothing else to do. Weaver must have a gun. I was afraid if I burst open the door he would shoot.

"Who is it?"

"Emily Cabot. I am looking for Maria Maglioni."

My thought was only to distract the man until help could arrive. I thought I should pretend I hadn't seen my brother or heard the shot.

The door creaked open wide and I saw a huddle of women opposite.

"Come in and close it."

I did as I was told, my eyes sweeping the room searching for my brother. There was a mound of clothes on the floor and I noticed a pool of wetness seeping out from under it. I held my breath and faced the gun in the hand of Mr. Weaver. He was leaning against the wall, his other hand hidden in the pocket of his long coat. He looked at me from under the brim of his black hat.

"Get over there with them."

I obeyed, forcing myself not to look at the mound of clothes. Maria was with the women.

"Maria. Mr. Langlois has taken the children. They are safe."

"Shut up," Weaver snapped. I jumped at the sound and Maria grabbed my hands.

Weaver was carefully peering out the window. "Who's with you?"

"No one. Someone saw Maria come here. I merely followed directions."

"You're lying. You haven't asked about the gun."

"I never ask a man with a gun pointed at me what he is doing, Mr. Weaver. It seems superfluous."

He laughed shortly.

"You killed Hanrahan, didn't you?" The gun pointed at me had a hole in the end of the barrel that was a bottomless pit.

"He was coming to tell me something, wasn't he? He was disgusted with your actions. He knew you were the one who shot my father and he was going to tell me, wasn't he? Why? Why did you kill my father?" The question ripped out of me without thought. I never thought he would answer it, except with a bullet that was going to tear right through me, killing me like the ones that had killed my father and brother. The thought of my mother lying unconscious in her bed in Boston passed through my mind. She'd never know and we would all be gone, all except Rosie.

"He had no call to be helping them. He was the judge. He had no call to take their side."

I swallowed. "You must have followed Flaherty and heard what my father told him that night. You were one of the ones who framed the men on trial. You made it look like they had thrown the bricks and stones then you swore you saw them do it. But they could prove you worked for the company and my father told them to ask. So you killed him and made sure somebody else was blamed for it. You always make sure somebody else is blamed for it, don't you? You killed Hanrahan because if he told Franklin what you had done, he would no longer employ you. You killed Hanrahan so you wouldn't lose your job. You killed him and tried to make it look like someone in Hull House had done it. You, sir, are a coward."

His eyes were in shadow from the hat but the only thing I could see was the hole at the end of that gun, pointing at me. I heard a click and stiffened. "I am alive, woman, which is more than you are going to be able to say tomorrow."

Several of the women were whimpering with fright. I was so angered by him I had an awful urge to rush at him and tear his eyes out. Maria squeezed my hands tightly to hold me back. Suddenly he took three steps toward me. She pulled me back, away from him and suddenly he was behind me with his back to the door.

"Shut up, y'all. I'm leaving. You make a noise after I'm gone I'll come back and shoot the lot of you. Understand?" He waved the gun. "Translate," he told Maria. She spoke to them in Italian, shushing them.

He smiled a tight smile and stepped out the door, closing it behind him. We stood frozen for a minute as we listened to him fumbling with the latch. He must have been wedging something to keep it shut. When we heard his boots on the stair planks one of the women started to wail but another clapped her hand on the woman's mouth.

"Shut up, I told you," he called up to us and the women shivered.

I moved quietly to the pile of clothes and started scattering them to find Alden. Maria silently helped me as we heard Weaver moving around below us. Alden moaned.

"Hush, Alden. Be quiet. He's downstairs."

He was shot in the right shoulder. Maria quickly wadded some cloth and held it to the wound. Alden's head lolled from side to side. I tried to comfort him, but then I smelled it and heard a crackle from below.

"Smoke. He's setting the building on fire," I whispered in horror.

One of the women screamed and ran to the door but it was blocked. There was a crack and a bullet tore through the wood of the door. He must have fired from where he was setting the fire below us. The woman retreated to a far corner whimpering, afraid to cry out. Maria and I dragged Alden as far back as we could get, then I crept to a dirty front window.

The smoke was coming up between the floorboards and we began to cough. I could hear the fire crackle and sizzle below us. When I peeked out I could see Weaver standing, arms folded, watching his handiwork. He retreated to somewhere out of my sight as someone yelled, "Fire!" People would come from further down the alley but it would be too late. Already flames began to lick up the walls.

Maria had run to the only other window that looked out on the side. There was a drop of thirty feet or more to the icy ground. Everyone was coughing now.

"Emily." It was Alden straining to move. "Put a plank across…the next house." He was pulling at a loose floorboard in the back of the room where the flames had not yet reached. The women were yelling now and two shots came through the front window. We froze.

"Never mind that," Alden said. "Come here, help me."

Maria and I understood him. The fire was moving so fast. We prized up a board, smashed the window and, balancing it between us, we managed to shove the board into the window of the next house. I could hear shouts in the street but, whoever it was, they weren't aware that we were up here. The women were panicking and choking with the smoke. There was no time to explain. Maria went out on to the plank on hands and knees, rocking precariously, but there were only a few feet between the buildings and she reached the other house safely.

We got the women across with Maria holding one end and me the other to steady the plank. But I had my wounded brother to deal with. I dragged him to the window unsure how I would be able to get him across but he stuck his head out coughing and took a breath of fresh air.

"Help me up."

"But you can't. Not by yourself."

Ignoring my protests he managed to climb over me. With his wound he never could have crawled, but he teetered for a moment on the sill then just danced across on his feet and fell into the arms of the waiting women. Blinded and choked by the smoke and deafened by the roar of the blaze now, I crawled across the board. I tried to keep my eyes on the plank so as not to become giddy with the view down to the ground below. When almost there, I tipped precariously but suddenly I felt hands as I was grabbed by the others.

As they pulled me in, the board tipped again and fell to the street below. Looking down I saw Weaver aim his gun at me. People had come but they were gathered at the front of the house unaware yet that anyone had been above. Before I could duck the shot rang out, shattering wood in the window frame beside me, but the figure below staggered. He had been tackled by a bear of a man.

"Marco."

Alden had fainted but Maria and the others gathered round as we watched the figures below locked in a deadly struggle. They were under the decrepit staircase that was licked with flames now. As they struggled the entire framework of the house seethed with flames. I watched helplessly. It was obvious that Marco's strength was still sapped by his sickness but he fought like a maniac. I cried out when I saw Weaver retrieve the gun that had fallen but as he fired it, Marco charged pushing the tall man into the side of the house, which shook with the impact. It hung for a moment, outlined in flame, then collapsed, crumbling down with crashes and tongues of flame, one piece after another like a card house. Suddenly the whole thing was on the ground smoldering, Weaver and Marco buried beneath it. I leaned back against the wall and felt tears of relief streaming down my cheeks.

THIRTY-ONE

"I was afraid you had left for good and would never return. We have missed you here." Dr. Chapman sat beside me in the dining room of Hull House some eight weeks later. Anna Farnsworth had arranged one of the famous luncheon parties and this time it was in my honor.

My mother had died. After the fire at the sweatshop, I rushed to Boston as soon as I could tell her Alden would recover. The doctor warned us not to count on her revival from the swoon she was in, and I spent two weary nights sitting up with my sister, Rose, awaiting the end. It was as I sat there in the darkness that I realized whatever happened to our mother I could never return to the life I had before going to Chicago. Like a kaleidoscope that had been turned a notch, all the pieces of our lives had shifted and it would never be possible for them to return to the earlier pattern. For better or worse the old shapes were gone and replaced by new ones.

Mother's doctor had not recognized her resilience, however, and when the fever broke, she recovered a little. She took the news of Alden's wound with fortitude and she hung on until he arrived in Boston, tended by Clara Shea. Seeing Clara with my brother had required an adjustment of my view of them as I realized the strength of their feelings for each other. It was less of a surprise to my mother whose greatest regret seemed to be the thought that she had ruined my hopes for a return to the university. I reassured her but she would not be comforted and at her insistence I started to correspond with Dean Talbot.

"How did she take the news about the man who shot your father?" Dr. Chapman asked.

"She wept for poor Marco and insisted we press the case to have Mr. Flaherty released."

She died before that could happen, completely worn out by the illness. It was with confidence of her support for my actions that I stayed on in Boston after the funeral. I knew she would have wanted me to contact my father's old friends and to press them and others until justice prevailed and Michael Flaherty was released. In that, at least, I was finally successful.

Flaherty and his children were also invited to the lunch at Hull House. We watched them at the other end of the table as the toddler, Liam, played with a toy flute Mr. Langlois had given him. Lucia Flaherty died in the pest house but when Michael Flaherty was finally released Mr. Langlois had taken him in.

"I think, despite everything, Maria is a happy bride," I told the doctor. She sat beside Michel Langlois who had an arm across the back of her chair. She and two of the other women were found to be infected by smallpox and were sent to the pest house after we were rescued from the fire. Unlike her sister she survived but she would bear the scars for the rest of her life. I saw a pained look on the doctor's face as he watched her and I knew he still regretted that he had failed to prevent that misfortune. Inevitably, I was reminded that I, too, had failed. I had promised to find her. In the end I had done so but it was almost too late. Her life was saved but at a heavy cost. Her beauty was certainly ruined forever.

"Mr. Langlois lost no time when he decided to marry," I commented.

The doctor sighed. "He had no choice. He found her in the pest house and took her away when she recovered. The French are so practical. He could not take her in and stay on good terms with his respectable landlady, so he merely stopped at a church on the way to his rooms and demanded the priest marry them."

"It is true then? I had heard something of it but I could hardly believe it."

"I had it from his own lips. He is a happy man to find a woman who can put up with his obsessions. Look, already he instructs the little boy on how to play the flute correctly."

"We are all happy for Maria and greatly relieved." The Hull House residents had flocked to tell me the news on my return.

"At least now she can go to as many concerts as she wishes. I will always remember the ecstatic look on her face the first time she heard the orchestra at Auditorium Theater."

"Will you? It is hard for me to recall that night without remembering all the disastrous events that followed." I looked at him with concern. He was eating with his left hand, his right arm still pinned to his side. He noticed my glance.

"It is useless. It will not get better."

"I am so sorry."

"But I am not, Emily. I was a surgeon, it is true, but I did not wish to continue in any case, you know that. It is not a loss I feel deeply. Truly, I would not lie to you."

I looked down to where Marguerite Larrimer sat chatting with Milton Bierly. I noticed the socialist had discarded his workingman's clothes for a wool suit this day. Dr. Chapman followed my gaze.

"You have not heard about Marguerite's latest enterprise?"

"I have not," I said levelly. He always used the woman's first name and it made me sure the intimacy between them had only increased during my absence. But I had expected that.

Mary Kenney, the printer who ran the Jane Club with her mother, was listening. "Mrs. Larrimer has purchased a clothing store from a family named Franklin," she told us. "She will run it as a union shop under union rules."

"When she heard of the terrible conditions in the sweatshops she wanted to use her dead husband's money to help. She consulted Miss Addams and together they developed this scheme," the doctor told me. I understood now why Marguerite had the place of honor next to our hostess. She was a recent convert.

"Mrs. Larrimer will become a business woman, then?" I asked. I found it difficult to imagine her in that role.

"Not herself, actually," Mary Kenney explained. "I don't think her interests lie in that direction. As a matter of fact she has hired Mr. Bierly to manage the concern." She turned to the doctor. "We have all had to listen to a great deal of nonsense from Mr. Bierly concerning social theory. We are looking forward to watching his efforts to put them into practice."

"Does he address Mrs. Larrimer as comrade?" I asked with quite honest curiosity. The doctor laughed.

"If he does, I'm sure Marguerite takes it as a kindly salute. She is not at all versed in social thought. Her ambitions run more to the arts. She will leave for Europe soon on an art buying trip." I saw him exchange a smile with her. She had heard her name spoken.

"Europe? And do you plan to travel also, doctor?"

"Me? Oh, no. Like most of the world that Marguerite inhabits, the world of art is beyond my comprehension. I have no appreciation of it. I expect it is like being tone deaf."

I looked again to where the elegant woman and the solemn Mr. Bierly were in earnest conversation. On my return I had been sure I would find Marguerite prepared to use her money to fund a clinic or research laboratory for Stephen Chapman.

"But you, if anyone, know how I am, Emily, how selfish in my single-minded pursuits, how lacking in patience or polish for the world of Marguerite and the Glessners and the Potter Palmers. I am too stubborn and churlish to be lured from my microscope."

"I should hope so," a small elderly woman on his other side spoke up. "He has work to do."

I searched my memory and recalled she was Helen Culver, the landlord of Hull House. For many years she had worked as assistant to the philanthropic millionaire Henry Hull and after his death she had continued to run both his businesses and his philanthropies according to his expressed wishes. This luncheon was the first time I had met her.

"Emily, I don't know if you are aware of it but Miss Culver has given the university the money to build the Hull Laboratories."

"And I expect you to do good work there, young man," she told the doctor, stabbing him with a bony finger for emphasis.

"As you see, Miss Cabot, my time is spoken for. No toddling off to Europe or anywhere else for me. Professor Jamieson and I are in the middle of some research that is very promising. I cannot be spared."

"Of course not," Miss Culver told him. "It is true that Mrs. Larrimer is contributing to the building fund but there will be no gadding off to Europe for this scientist. I should hope not. And what about you, young woman? What will you do with yourself?"

Dean Talbot smiled at me from across the table. "Professor Small was very sorry when Emily was unable to accept the fellowship that he offered her."

"It is gone, given to another," I explained. "I could not and did not wish to take it up and it had to be granted last month."

"I am so sorry," Stephen Chapman told me. "Does it mean you will return to Boston?"

"Oh, no, Doctor, I am delighted to announce that Emily will rejoin us next fall to help me establish a new school of Household Technology," Dean Talbot told him. "She will be a lecturer in household economy. I have persuaded President Harper to begin to establish this course of study."

I saw Florence Kelley shake her head.

"It will not be pure science, Mrs. Kelley, anything but," I told her. "I plan to continue to study law, not in the abstract but with a view towards helping to formulate and enforce laws that will work."

"We shall see, Miss Cabot," Mrs. Kelley told me. "I was afraid you meant to become one of these objective social scientists who use their skills only to defend the rights of the moneyed classes. Like your Mr. Lukas."

"I believe he has left the university to run the association," I told her.

"Oh, he intended to. Unfortunately in a stroke of pure irony he came down with the very illness he and the owners were trying to ignore. He contracted smallpox and I'm afraid he died of it."

Suddenly I remembered standing in the Franklin shop while Sidney Franklin smoothed the collar of a coat he said was intended for Mr. Lukas. Irony indeed.

A general conversation about the university was proceeding. The doctor turned to me and said quietly, "My dear Emily, I cannot tell you how happy it makes me to know that you will return. Until this moment I had not dared to hope after so many tragic events you could find the will to do so." He reached out to take my hand. "I had almost given up hope."

I looked at him, startled by the warmth of his statement and I felt a pang of regret. I had been sure there was a stirring of feeling in him that I thought had been for me. But that was before the little tailor had blasted our world apart with his shotgun. It seemed so long ago.

I turned away from him, gently removing my hand from his grasp. Looking down the table I was aware how much I had missed the constant bother and the daily struggles of Hull House during my sojourn in Boston. They were discussing the election that had been lost during my absence.

"It's a mixed blessing for Fitz that they won again," Mary Kenney was saying. "Mrs. Kelley has found a great ally in Detective Whitbread and they are making war on graft in the district."

"The detective is writing a book of memoirs," Florence Kelley told us. "He has a chapter describing the ills of graft in government officials. Fitzgibbons and Powers are afraid they will find themselves portrayed there if they do not reform."

"Poor Fitz." Mary Kenney shook her head.

"It is no more than he deserves," the doctor commented.

Like Mrs. Kelley, Stephen Chapman would always dismiss Fitz as a cog in the political machine. Yet he had helped us, however unwillingly, both to free the doctor from jail and to defeat Weaver.

I saw a figure pass by the door. "Was that Mr. Wall? He is still here?"

Stephen smiled. "Yes. Finally he is satisfied that the epidemic is over and he is returning to his family."

"Excuse me, I must say goodbye." I slipped from the room and down the stairs to where the little man was directing a driver to load his trunks into the cab.

"Miss Cabot. I heard there was a party for you. I hope you are well."

"Yes, Mr. Wall. We are all very well. I just wanted to thank you for your efforts."

"It is my job, Miss Cabot. Thankfully it is not often that such acute situations arise but when they do, we must all do our best."

"Your best is much appreciated, Mr. Wall, even if it is not shown by all of us."

"Not to worry, Miss Cabot. As I once mentioned, these painful days are all soon forgotten." He glanced down the street where children were playing a round game. "And we can all return to normal. I confess, I'm looking forward to it. Goodbye, Miss Cabot. Good luck with your studies."

I watched as he climbed into the cab and the horse moved through the pack of children, momentarily suspending their game. But they closed ranks and continued as soon as it was gone.

"Emily." It was Stephen at the bottom of the stairs looking at me. "Emily, I have been looking for an opportunity to speak with you. Will you come into the library with me?"

I closed the door and followed him into the familiar room. He cleared his throat. "I know you are alone now. I know that you and your brother have little to live on. I am not a wealthy man, you know that. I would never be able to give you a life of riches but if you would consent to be my wife, I promise you will never lack the necessities of life."

I looked into his kind brown eyes shocked to the core. I had not anticipated this. I thought I understood and it made me sad. He had seen so much of poverty and want that he was afraid for me. That was what I saw in his eyes and I was disappointed. I suppressed a sigh. It was not for the love of me that he made the offer but only from kindness. My heart was racing and I sensed a metallic taste in my mouth. Once again he saw me only as a foolish young girl in need of a protector. I longed for his love but only wholeheartedly, not on these terms. I felt myself stiffen. To rebuff him now would forever end any hopes in that direction but I was already committed. He did not seem to understand that I was no longer a child and I had work to do, things to accomplish.

"I thank you, Doctor, for a very generous offer. But I beg you not to concern yourself with my welfare. It is true that my brother and I inherit very little."

"I did not mean to say that…"

"It is all right, Doctor, you are correct in your assumptions. I have very little money to live on. Despite that fact, however, I am able to afford to live at Hull House and my appointment at the university will take effect in the fall. Dean Talbot assures me between the salary and an assistantship I will be able to live." I turned away from him to look out at the sunshine. "Like you, I have things to do, Doctor." I couldn't look at him as I made the final argument I knew he must accept. "You see, I *may* not marry if I want to accept the teaching position that is offered. It is not permitted at the university. So, I cannot accept your offer although I am deeply grateful to you for making it." It was the unfortunate truth of the matter. I had to choose. I could do one or the other, marry or continue my studies. I could not do both. I had already made my decision.

And thus I spun the top of my future, hoping it would keep its balance and spin on to better things. In any case, having lived at Hull House I would never be able to retreat to the university completely. I could sojourn there but I could not leave the work of the house. It was my home now.

AFTERWORD

As in the first book of this series, *Death at the Fair*, this book has a mixture of real and fictional characters. Many of the incidents are based on the accounts of Hull House told by Jane Addams herself in *Twenty Years at Hull House*, and Florence Kelley in her autobiography. During the winter following the World's Columbian Exposition, Chicago suffered from a severe recession and a smallpox epidemic that traced its origins to the Midway.

In the third chapter I have used some actual quotes and paraphrases from the writings of Jane Addams in order to provide a fairly accurate idea of her thoughts. There are a few paragraphs of Florence Kelley's dialogue in the meeting about the smallpox epidemic that are quoted from her autobiography as she gave such a vivid picture of the problems involved in getting the community and politicians involved to take the measures needed to contain the epidemic.

The chapter on St. Liberata is based on a statue that exists in The Shrine of Our Lady of Pompeii in Chicago and the stories that go with it. Florence Kelley's involvement with women who venerated this saint is purely fictional and used to forward the plot. Her activities as the first factory inspector, on the other hand, are very real and based on her accounts in her autobiography.

The Christmas Day murder is purely fictional as are Emily Cabot, her brother and the other characters. There was a strike at the South Boston Horse Car Company and it was later revealed that company agitators had done some of the damage, but there was no murder of a judge as in this story.

As in the first book of this series, Emily is loosely based on the progressive women reformers who came to Chicago both to work at Hull House and to study at the University of Chicago. Many of them, such as Edith Abbott and Sophonisba Breckinridge, actually came to Chicago a few years later. Their efforts to combine the collection of statistics on social problems with actual changes in laws and policies eventually led to the establishment of the School of Social Service Administration at the University of Chicago. Like my fictional character, many of these women alternated between life at the settlement house and life at the university.

Detective Whitbread is also loosely based on Clifton Wooldridge, a real Chicago police detective who published several books of memoirs.

Alderman Johnny Powers was a real political force of the time, but Fitzgibbons is a completely fictional character.

CPSIA information can be obtained
at www.ICGtesting.com
Printed in the USA
LVHW092302150219
607775LV00001B/9/P